Violet Ugly

J. Lynn Bailey

Copyright © 2018 by J. Lynn Bailey
All rights reserved.

Visit my website at www.jlynnbaileybooks.com
Editor and Interior Designer: Jovana Shirley, Unforeseen Editing,
www.unforeseenediting.com
Cover Designer: Hang Le, By Hang Le, www.byhangle.com
Proofreader: Julie Deaton, Deaton Author Services,
www.facebook.com/jdproofs
Proofreader: Kaitlyn Moodie,
www.facebook.com/KaitlynMoodieEditing

No part of this book may be reproduced or transmitted in any
form or by any means, electronic or mechanical, including
photocopying, recording, or by any information storage and
retrieval system without the written permission of the author,
except for the use of brief quotations in a book review.

This book is a work of fiction. Names, characters, places, and
incidents either are products of the author's imagination or are
used fictitiously. Any resemblance to actual persons, living or dead,
events, or locales is entirely coincidental.

ISBN-13: 978-1-7324855-1-8

Prologue

Merit
Granite Harbor, Maine
Summer 1995
Age Eleven

It's always easier, staring at Ryan Taylor from afar. His stormy, dark eyes give a warning to strangers: stay away. Tall at ten years old, Ryan pretends that his alcoholic father doesn't bother him. But he does. I see it in his navy-blue eyes when his dad returns from sea.

It's summer. The heat from the sun on my face makes me feel warm, almost happy. I watch as Ryan stalks toward me, quietly, as I lie in the middle of the mustard field. The scent of sea in my nose. I pray this pain goes away—the pain in my heart from the riptide that has torn through the Young family this morning. We knew it was coming. I should maybe feel relief that my mother is no longer in pain, but I want to retreat back to before she had cancer. When there wasn't a cluster of pills on the counter. When it didn't smell like a hospital on 4578 Opal Street at the top of the hill with the view of the ocean.

"Hey," he says, breathless.

"You been running?" I peer up at him through squinty eyes.

"Yeah. From my house. When I heard the news." Ryan sits down next to me and then lies down, placing his hands behind his head, peering up at the same summer sky.

"You okay?" I hear him whisper.

I don't know.

I feel sick, and numb, too, I guess.

"What are you supposed to feel when your parent dies, Ryan?"

The birds chirp.

Crickets sing.

I wait. Praying that his answer will deliver some peace.

Life is going on at a pace I wasn't prepared for. Moving forward. It has picked up and left my mother in the past. And I'm paralyzed.

"I don't know." He's quiet for a moment. "I guess it's supposed to feel like how ugly looks maybe."

I laugh because I picture Ryan as ugly, and I just can't with his skin that looks like the color of caramel, eyes the color of the Atlantic, short dark brown hair, and a long, lean body that is always ready, willing, and able.

I want to tell him I'm sorry his mother left. Before Ryan could walk, his father had just come home from a two-week sea trip, and his mother bent down, kissed him good-bye, and never came back. According to Ryan.

I suppose he knows what ugly feels like. I suppose he knows what it's like to have his life turned upside down, twisted, knotted, nasty.

"People are shitty," I say.

"Yeah. People are shitty."

We both stare up at the bright blue sky and look for our mothers. We see the sadness, life's imperfections as the clouds float by. We take heed in the fact that life would just be easier if we didn't get so attached, if we didn't become loved, if we didn't give love. Because, in the end, this ache in our hearts wouldn't hurt so bad.

I feel Ryan's eyes on me, but I continue to stare at the deformed elephant that drifts past me.

"One day, this all won't hurt so much, Violet," he whispers.

And, when he calls me this, the stinging of my eyes begins.

Swallow it. Crying won't bring her back, Mer, so you just stop it right now.

I don't feel like I'll be okay. I feel as though my skin has been turned inside out.

He doesn't offer any other words, but he pulls his hand from his head and reaches through the grass to hold mine.

"Thanks." I smile through my pain.

With barely a sound, Eli appears and takes his spot next to Ryan, placing his hands behind his head, staring up at the sky that extends from here to California, where things might be easier. Maybe, in California, the sun makes everything better. I wonder if the sun shines brighter there and if maybe, because of that, death doesn't feel so heavy, like overweight baggage that you can't manage to put down or walk away from. I wonder if people in California feel death the way people in Maine do.

"Funeral's Friday." Eli's voice is tired. "Pop put you down as pallbearer. To help carry Mom's casket, Ryan."

Ryan doesn't have to say yes. Eli knows he'd do anything for Mom.

"Mrs. Ida's bringing over her famous chicken tonight, Mer," Eli says.

And this is where my role as sister, daughter, and mother begins. "We'll have that for dinner."

One

Merit
Monterey, California
July 2019
Present Day

"You're late."

Abbey's feet against the cement floor are at a quick pace. She throws her bag on the chair and runs to our clock-in machine. A machine that Eddie, our boss, still insists we need. A machine from circa 1960. A machine, he claims, that is still valid and relevant even though Abbey has somehow enabled it to work to her advantage, so every morning she runs in late, it inaccurately reflects her arrival as on time.

She pops her gum in her mouth, grinning from ear to ear. She clocks in at 9 a.m. even though it's clearly 9:37 a.m. The collar of Abbey's lab coat is coiled, twisted, as if her attire is an afterthought, pulled out of the bottom of her drawer, even though our lab coats are a requirement for the job, per Edith in Human Resources. Eddie doesn't give a shit.

Pencil in hand, writing up lab notes from yesterday's observations from Lucy's and Ethel's eating patterns—two of our resident river otters here at Monterey Bay Aquarium, I watch as Abbey pours herself a cup of coffee, grabs a doughnut, and sits in the chair next to mine.

"What?" she asks with a mouthful of doughnut after placing her gum behind her ear.

Abbey got me the job at the aquarium. Fresh out of graduate school with motivation to do well in this world, we both left our pasts behind. She's also been my roommate for the last eight years. And, if I were to give her a classification in the friend arena, I'd say she's a close second to Eli, my younger brother by a year and a half. But Abbey and me, we couldn't be more opposite.

She's late.

I'm always fifteen minutes early.

She's messy.

I'm neat.

She's a night owl.

I'm an early bird.

Raised Mormon with a secret penchant for one-night stands, Abbey is uniquely her own character.

Raised without religion, I haven't had sex in … well, I'd rather not go there. Let's just say, I'm a thirty-something single woman still weighing my options.

"So, did you call him back?" She licks her fingers.

"Who?"

Abbey pulls her chair forward, so she can see the face of my phone that sits on my desk. "Ryan Taylor. See where it says Missed Call?"

Abbey O'Brien is a smart ass.

"No." I flip the phone over, so I can't see the missed call.

"Come on, Young, you never talk about this guy. You never have. But I see he calls you every now and then. I've read through the texts he's sent you."

I look back to face Abbey. "You have not."

She shrugs. "No. No, I haven't. That would be an invasion of your privacy, and I would never do that."

"Liar."

"It was only twice, Mer. He seems like a nice guy. He seems like he's really into you."

I laugh. "You don't know Ryan Taylor, Abbs."

Abbey's phone starts to ring. She leans back in her chair, grabs her bag, and pulls out her phone. "Oh, for Pete's sake. It's Andrew. From four nights ago." She rolls her eyes.

"Toe fetish guy?"

"That's the one." She hits Ignore.

"You never give out your number."

"Hey, if you'd had three Long Islands and he whispered the lyrics of Color Me Badd's 'I Wanna Sex You Up,' you'd have given him your number, too."

"I highly doubt that. Wait, can we just go back to that for a second?"

"Morning, ladies." Eddie's lifestyle, an old surfer from Santa Barbara, slowly drags the sentence out. His smooth steps make it look as though he's floating around the aquarium, like the fish we keep. The swoosh of his board shorts is the only indicator that he's actually walking. "Glad to see you're on time, O'Brien." His tan, a collection of years spent waiting for the perfect wave, is resilient, waterproof even. His silvery-white hair is still thick and full.

Abbey looks at me as Eddie saunters to the copier. She leans in and whispers, "So, does he know I'm always late and that I've fixed our clock-in machine?"

"No idea. But I think I know how to fix the situation," I whisper back.

"How?"

"Get here on time."

Abbey rolls her eyes. Her phone sounds again. "Fuck," she whispers. "It's my mom."

"When's the last time you talked to your mom?" Eddie asks from the copier.

"Whatever, Eddie." Abbey picks up her phone. "Hey, Mom." She rolls her eyes.

Eddie walks to my desk as we both stare at Abbey. "She realizes, I know she's late every morning, right?"

"I'd hope so."

He looks at me. "Doing okay, kid?"

Define okay.

"Never better."

Eddie's thick white eyebrows pull together. "You know what my dad used to say?" His words are drawn out—and not because he smoked too many joints when he lived on the beach, but

7

because that's his pace. No rush to do anything. Methodical. He's brilliant actually. "If you don't let the turtles in close, you'll die alone."

Eddie is notorious for ocean metaphors. He's like a wise owl that quietly whispers the answers to life, hoping you'll come to your conclusions. And, God forbid, you ask him to explain. He'll give you a smug look, draw up his shoulders, and say, "Dunno. What do you think?"

"Mom. Mom. My phone's going to die. I've gotta go. I'm at work." Abbey pretends her voice is cutting out. "M—ca—hea—me? M—" And, just like that, Abbey hangs up and shoves the phone in her bag. Her phone probably is dying. It's always dying. But also, she and her mother don't have the best relationship.

"All right, ladies, see you out on the floor today." Eddie turns, his flip-flops squeaking with each step as he leaves our main office.

Abbey goes into work mode. I think work is a welcome distraction from her family issues.

Her dad left her mom about five years ago. Left the Mormon Church. Just upped and left everything. I think it really took its toll on Abbey. An only child, she was really close with her dad. He's tried to call her. Make it right. But Abbey refuses to talk to him. I think that's what has attributed to her infatuation with the male body.

I left Granite Harbor, Maine, at eighteen to attend college at the University of San Diego for their marine biology program. I needed as much space from Ryan Taylor as I could get.

"Drinks after work?" I hear Abbey calling me from my thoughts.

"Yes," comes from my lips before I can protest.

"Mingo's?" she suggests. "Oh, no. No, wait. Can't go there."

"Why not?"

Abbey searches her desk with overly eager eyes, trying to escape our conversation.

"Abbey." My eyes narrow.

She briefly looks at me, and then her eyes fall back to her desk. "I thought I put that paper clip—"

"Abbey O'Brien, did you sleep with Brad the bartender? Come on. He was off-limits. Mingo's was our neutral spot."

She nervously bites her lip. "Merit, in my defense, he came on to me."

I roll my eyes. "Abbey, he comes on to everyone. That is not an excuse."

"There's a new place down on Pacific Street. We could try there?"

My phone illuminates. It's Alex. I debate on picking up. Our normal mode of conversation is text. She doesn't call me often, and the last time she did, it was to tell me that Pop was really sick.

I hit Talk. "Hey." My voice changes to something softer.

"Thank you, Mer. They're beautiful," Alex says.

She's received the bouquet of red peonies I sent her.

"Hey, it's not every day your sister-in-law releases a book."

"How are you?" she asks.

"Good," I lie. "The otter count out here on the West Coast is thriving. Ethel is about to give birth any day now." Biting my lower lip, I wait to see if she buys this.

There's a short silence on the other end. She could have bought my excuse, my feeble attempt at a life lived to its fullest, or she isn't buying it but doesn't feel comfortable with calling me out.

Instead, I change the subject. "How are Pop and Meredith?" Meredith is Alex's mom who moved out to Granite Harbor from Belle's Hollow.

"She's like a watchdog with your dad, making sure he eats right. They seem really happy."

I mull this over for a moment, relishing in the satisfaction this gives me. That Eli and I don't have to worry about Pop so much anymore. He's finally happy. I just wish he hadn't waited so long. But, then again, Meredith wasn't available then.

"How's Emily?"

"Sweeter than ever. Your brother is changing her diaper at the moment. She managed to get poop all the way up her back. It's amazing what can come out of such a small child."

I feel every inch of the three thousand miles that separates us. Something's up. Off.

"You're stalling, Alex."

"Well, it's just …" she sighs. "Ryan would kill me if he knew I was telling you this. He got into an accident last night."

Tiny, microscopic needles make the surface of my skin tingle. "What?"

"Tore up his left shoulder. Broken ribs." She stalls again. "But you know Ryan. He won't allow anyone to take care of him. Says he'll be fine. Mer, he can feed himself but it isn't pretty."

"His dad is worthless," I say. *An asshole, to be exact.*

"So, I was thinking, maybe you could, um … well, it's a funny thing …you know your brother, Eli. He thinks the only person Ryan will listen to is you."

"Did my brother put you up to this, Alex?" My stomach grows into a messy ball of knots, tangled in past love, old hurts, and a lot of baggage. "Put him on the phone, Alex."

I'm fuming.

There's a whispered exchange and muffled voices, as if someone has covered the receiver.

"Well, hey, Bug."

"Don't you *Bug* me, and don't bullshit me either, little brother. How bad is it?"

Bug is my brother's nickname for me. He's called me this since we were kids because of my fascination with bugs.

"Well, let's just say that Ryan is finally out of the hospital, but it was a good three days before they released him."

"For Christ's sake, Eli."

He lets out a long, exasperated sigh. "Mer, he needs help. I'm covering at work for him. Alex has Emily. And there's no way in hell he'd ever let Pop or Meredith come over and help. So … well, that leaves you."

"The problem with that is, I'm on the West Coast! Eli, I live here. I can't just up and leave my job."

Abbey is in the background, nodding. She whispers, "All you do is work. You have enough comp time on the books for a six-month sabbatical, Steve Jobs." She takes a sip of coffee.

I roll my eyes and rub my forehead. "I can't."

Eli sighs. "Look, Mer, I wouldn't have called you if I didn't need you."

"*You* didn't call me. You had your wife call me." Sarcasm and truth bleed through my tone. "Eli, you're asking me to leave my job to come help take care of Ryan."

"Look, I don't know what happened to you two at eighteen, but, Mer, it's Ryan. He was there when Mom died. He was there when Dad took a fall at work, and he helped around the house. He's always been there. So, as much as you want to hate him, you don't." He sighs heavily into the phone. "You and I both know you don't hate him. So, please, it'll just be for a few weeks. At least until he can get back to work and sit at his desk."

"I can't." My tone wavers.

"For me, Mer?"

"I just can't, Eli." I won't. For several reasons. "I can't." And I hang up the phone.

Two

Merit
Granite Harbor, Maine
Fall 1994
Age Ten

Ryan chokes his red flannel hash down, but in his last bite, I swear on my life, his eyeballs turn green. Eli has eaten his, too, but not without gagging.

"Merit Young, you'd better finish your supper, or there's no dessert," my mother calls from the sink, her back to us, like she has eyes in the back of her head.

Mothers have superpowers.

Mind readers.

X-ray vision.

Arms that can stretch into the back seat of a minivan and flick your cheek.

Bionic hearing for the late-night cookie jar runs.

Built-in lie detector.

I'd rather die than eat red flannel hash—corned beef and cabbage mushed with beets. I'd rather swim with sharks in the deep

Atlantic or shovel snow every day in winter than eat red flannel hash. I'd rather have the flu even.

"Mom, I don't feel well." I'm not lying. Just thinking about taking a bite of this makes my stomach hurt.

"Mom, can I be excused, please?" Eli asks.

She doesn't have to turn to look at Eli's bowl to know he's finished because, with her X-ray vision, she already knows he's done. "Yes. Rinse your bowl."

Eli gets up and walks to the sink.

I roll my eyes and look at Ryan, still across the table, his face the color of a Venus flytrap. He attempts a smile.

The phone rings, and when Mom goes to answer it in the living room, Ryan whispers, "Trade me bowls."

"What?" I whisper back, quickly glancing into the living room, checking on the authority.

"Trade me bowls, Mer."

"You want mine?" I start to push it across the table while taking Ryan's empty one.

"No, I don't *want* yours. But chocolate cake is your favorite."

My tummy starts to twist and turn, and I wonder what this feeling is. Ryan slides my bowl to him and shovels seven big bites into his mouth. He gags. Twice.

I look back into the living room, but Mom doesn't know any better.

"Are you all right?" I ask.

Ryan wipes his mouth with the back of his hand and nods. But he's not. His shade of green is even darker than it was after the first bowl.

"Thank you."

Eli comes back to the table after rinsing his bowl, and Mom enters the kitchen again, stopping behind me. She stares at my bowl, and I give her a smug look—a look that says, *So, there. I ate it.*

"See, Mer? It wasn't so bad, was it?" Mom bends and kisses me on the cheek.

I don't dare answer her for two reasons. First, if I agree it wasn't that bad, she'll expect me to eat it again, and two, I'm a terrible liar.

"I've gotta go home. Thanks for dinner, Mrs. Young."

Ryan stands and attempts to take his bowl to the sink, but I stop him.

"I've got your bowl tonight."

"You can't stay for chocolate cake, Ryan?" my mother asks.

"Nah. Early morning fishing trip with my dad."

He's lying. I can tell he's lying because his eye is twitching. I'm not sure that everyone notices this, but I do.

Like the time he said his mom just went on vacation for a second time—eye twitch. Eli and I found the note in the garbage. Not that we were looking through the garbage, but we were helping Ryan take it out, and the note somehow floated to the ground with a puff of air. We never asked Ryan about it. We knew it'd hurt too much, so we pretended to believe the lie he'd told us.

Or the time he said he was sick and couldn't go to school—eye twitch. We saw the bruises his dad had left behind, periodically making an appearance out from underneath his shirt.

Eli and I walk Ryan out.

"Going fishing with your dad tomorrow?" Eli asks, surprised.

"No, I don't feel good. Just didn't have the heart to tell your mom. Didn't want her to think it was her red flannel hash."

"Why not? It's disgusting," I say.

Ryan shrugs and wipes his nose with the back of his hand.

"Want us to ride with you home?" Eli asks.

"Nah." Ryan gets on his bike. "See you tomorrow."

"Hey, Ryan?" I call out. "Thanks."

Ryan smiles, nods, turns, pedals down our lane, and disappears into the quickly fading sun.

Eli and I turn and walk back inside.

"He ate your hash for you?"

"Yeah."

"Where the heck was I?"

"Doing your dishes."

"Ryan's got a crush on you."

"Shut up. Does not. He's like my brother. Ew."

But I remember the way my tummy felt when he said I liked chocolate cake. It didn't feel like all the times my mom or Pop had said something nice. It didn't feel like the times Eli had shared his toys with me. It felt nothing like that.

"Why else would he eat your hash? That stuff is disgusting."

We hear Pop's work truck pull up behind us.

"Pop!" we both yell.

He rolls down the window, and we hop up on the side step of his truck. Bessie, Dad's K9, whines in the back.

"Hey, Besser-Boo!" I put my hand in her kennel behind the driver's side, and she gives me kisses.

"What's for dinner?" Pop asks.

Eli and I both laugh. Pop hates it, too.

"Steak and potatoes!" I call out, laughing.

"Red flannel hash." Eli's voice droops.

"Oh." Pop puffs up his cheeks and pretends to throw up.

Eli and I laugh harder.

"We ate already. Mom wasn't sure what time you'd be home," Eli says.

"Hold on!" Pop calls as he slowly accelerates, creeping toward the house as Eli and I hang on to the side of the truck.

That night, as I lie in bed, I think about Ryan. What he went home to. Eli and I've never told anyone what we've seen on Ryan's body or how his dad treats him. It eats me up inside.

I grab my walkie-talkie and press the Talk button. "Eli. You awake?"

"No. Go to sleep, Mer." His voice is full of static.

"I want to tell Mom about Ryan and his dad." My stomach turns into nerves.

Eli sighs into the device. "Shit, Mer, I told you, Ryan made us swear. We can't. Told us, if we ever said anything, his dad said he would kill him."

I know. I know what he said.

Releasing the Talk button on the walkie-talkie, I set it down at my side.

I remember that day clearly, the day another bruise showed up on his abdomen. The one Eli and I saw when we finished our final roll down the hill. The one where his shirt came up, and I gasped. Ryan tried to cover it up. Tried to make excuses.

"Ryan, why do you protect your dad? He's a jerk." I pulled myself up to my feet and followed Ryan's lead.

16

Eli said, "Ryan, we've gotta tell someone."

"I ran into my bed." He pushed our words, our concern, away.

"You're lying, Ryan." Eli stepped up, faced him, eye-to-eye. Eli was mad.

Ryan stared back. His fists in balls at his sides. "I ran into my bed." His jaw was clenched.

What about your arm two weeks ago? And your thigh just last week, *I wanted to say, but I was too scared to say it. I wanted to believe that he was telling us the truth. I wanted to believe that his dad didn't hit him. Hurt him. It was simpler that way. Soft. Not messy. Easier on my heart.*

"Come on. We've gotta get home. It's getting dark," I told the boys and took the lead.

"Stop," Ryan said.

We did and turned back to face him.

"If you guys tell anyone, he'll kill me." He tried to cover up the fear in his voice, but I heard it.

It settled in my veins, and then I grew angry, but Eli didn't.

That night, in bed, after Ryan went home, I prayed for him. I prayed that God would take care of Ryan.

How could you let this happen? *I asked him.*

But he didn't answer.

The next day, Ryan didn't show up for school at Granite Harbor Elementary.

Or the next day or the next day.

Eli and I decided to go to his house after school. Ryan's house was just up from Main Street in Granite Harbor. A fishing boat sat, perched in the yard at an angle, set up on stilts, while patches of tall yellow weeds grew up the sides of the boat, attempting to make their attack. The once-white house with green shutters was now a sanctuary for dirt, and old, cheap paint had been begun to curl and twist up the old house. There should be a sign in the yard that said, Keep Out. No Trespassing. Unsafe. But we pushed back the white picket gate and made our way around the old ice chests, fishing poles, and tackle boxes that lay in the walk path.

"Mom would have a fit," I whispered to my brother, who was almost to the front door.

Pop had told us this place was off-limits to us. And I thought, if Pop could get custody of Ryan, he'd have been at our house a long time ago.

We knocked on the door, but Ryan never answered.

I sneak downstairs to see if Mom and Pop are still awake, but I don't want to talk with them. I just want another piece of cake. I hear them whispering at the kitchen table instead, so I stop in the hallway just before the kitchen and peek in.

"Ruthie walked by last week on her way downtown and said Dubbs was screaming at Ryan. Screaming nonsense. So, Ruthie marched up to the door, but no one answered. The screaming stopped. Didn't stop her from calling the state police," Pop says.

Mom takes a sip of her tea. "And they couldn't do anything?"

Pop shrugs. "Ryan said it didn't happen."

"You know good and well it happened if Ruthie Murdock heard it." Her lips were in a firm line.

Pop nods.

The stupid floor creaks as I take another step closer. My parents look to the doorway to the kitchen.

"Mer, what are you doing up so late?" My dad, still in his uniform, beckons me to him.

I crawl up into his lap. So badly, I want to tell Mom and Pop what I know. What I've seen.

My dad pulls my hair back and kisses my forehead as I put my head to his chest.

"Were you guys talking about Ryan?" I ask.

Mom looks at Pop and takes my hand. "Yeah. We're worried about him."

I don't say anything, but if my stomach could talk, I'd scream out my anger and my hatred for Dubbs Taylor and what he does to his son when no one's looking.

Ryan does a really good job of covering up the bruises, so no one sees them. Except for Eli and me. We lie to protect his safety. Our safety.

A web grows in my throat, and my heart stops the truth from coming out. I don't want Ryan to die, and I know every ounce of what Ryan said about his dad killing him would happen.

"Do you know anything about what's happening at his home, Mer?" Pop asks in his slow, calm game warden voice. The leader of our family. "Has Ryan said anything to you and Eli?"

I can't tell.

I won't lose his trust.

I can't lose Ryan.

So, I tell the best lie I know. Not out of spite for Dubbs, not out of hurt for Ryan, but out of fear. "No." I look down the hallway, too scared to look my parents in the eye, and I see Eli standing in the darkness. A tear streaming down his nine-year-old cheek, he eases back into the darkness.

Sometimes, there are secrets we keep so deep that our minds forget, not wanting to remember what the quiet chaos feels like against our hearts. But I'll keep this secret. I will hang on to it if it's going to keep Ryan safe.

Safe from his own secrets.

Three

Merit
San Francisco International Airport
Present Day

"All right, Mer, remember, no talking to strangers, and call me when you get there." Abbey slaps me on the shoulder and then winces. "I'm sorry. I'm no good at this." She pulls me in for an awkward and stiff hug. She whispers, "This is the right decision. It might not feel like it, but whatever you and Ryan need to work out, I think you're getting a sign that it's time to get in the weeds."

I curl my lip. "Get in the weeds?"

"You know, like get to work."

Eddie pulls me in for a side hug. He drove me to the airport since Abbey doesn't drive. "We'll be fine. Just go. Jesus H. Christ, family is family."

"This isn't a vacation," I clarify. "This is an act of guilt, Eddie."

I can't believe I let my brother talk me into this. I haven't spoken to Ryan, if I could help it, since the day I left Granite Harbor when I was eighteen. When he shattered my heart. So, maybe this isn't an act of bravery. Maybe it's stupidity.

Eddie's silvery hair glimmers in the open light the airport provides. "Give 'em hell, Mer. Give 'em hell, sweetheart. And don't let the octopus get you." His eyebrows rise.

"The octopus?" I ask quizzically.

Eddie shrugs. "Means, don't get wrapped up in it. Just ride it out. Those tentacles will let go eventually. You just need to slow down, ride it out."

Of course, he uses an analogy like this.

Eddie doesn't know the story. Neither does Abbey. Nobody does. Nobody needs to know. But, somehow, Eddie's words slow my heart down a little bit, which allows me to breathe, expand my lungs.

"Remember to text me when you get there, Merit." Abbey bites her thumbnail. "You're flying all the way across the United States."

"Abbs, I've taken the trip plenty of times."

Her eyes grow shifty. "I know. I'm just nervous this time. I-I'm not sure why."

"I'll be fine." I reach for her and whisper, "I'll text you. Don't worry."

Though I'm not so sure I'm ready for all this.

What happened between Ryan and me changed us. It changed me. The only reason I'm doing this is for Eli's and Alex's sakes. To ease the burden for them. And Ryan, he's so damn hardheaded. Nothing has changed since I left and yet everything has. Seventeen years. I'm thirty-five now. He's thirty-four. Years and time have changed us. We aren't the same people anymore.

I walk down the terminal and turn back to wave at my friends. Eddie in his board shorts and his white tank top with rough, leather brown skin, flip-flops, and a casual wave. Abbey in a sweatshirt and jeans, her flip-flops a hot pink, blonde hair in two braids down her back, chewing on her nail, and waving with her other hand.

I turn away and make my way to the 747 to Chicago, Illinois, and then on to Portland, Maine.

"Granite Harbor, be gentle," I whisper as my stomach does a flip. Here's to facing my past, my present, and my heart. "Please be gentle."

Violet Ugly

It's just after eight in the evening in Maine.

"I'm glad you came." Eli rests his hand on the wheel.

"Sure glad one of us is." I give him a sideways smile. "I'm looking forward to seeing my niece and sister-in-law."

"Funny. You might want to think about kissing my ass because who's going to take care of you when you're old? Like feed you? As your brother, I'd assume this responsibility, so if you want to eat ..." His voice trails off as he looks out the window.

I allow this to get under my skin. I know Eli means nothing by it. He doesn't know why his words cut through me.

I'm in my thirties, and I don't have children.

"Hey! I found a shortcut." Eli hangs a left somewhere between Portland and Granite Harbor. A road I'm unfamiliar with.

I roll my eyes. "You know, game wardens always think they know a shortcut. And then it ends up being twice as long. So, really, you mean, detour."

"No, really, it's a shortcut."

"Yep. We'll see."

"There's something else." Eli scratches the back of his head, and his eyebrows rise. He stares out the window.

"Oh, God. That's not a good start, E. What?" I sigh.

"Well, Ryan doesn't know you're coming."

I freeze. "What? Are you kidding me, E? You brought me home to babysit him, and you didn't tell him I was coming?" *You've gotta be fucking kidding me.*

"Come on, Mer. You know Ryan. He'll shut down like a brick wall. First, he'll be pissed at me for asking you. Then, he'll be pissed at the world. Embarrassed. I figured, if you just showed up at his doorstep, he wouldn't be able to shut the door in your face. He needs help, Merit."

"I get that. You've made that quite clear." *Cannot believe I'm in this spot right now.* I shake my head. "Where's he live now?"

Eli coughs into his fist. "Just outside of Hallowell."

My eyes grow big. "Are you kidding me, Eli? That's an hour commute to Granite Harbor—one way!" I grit my teeth. "Oh my God! I'm expected to stay there with him?"

"He's got a big enough house. He sleeps downstairs anyway. Besides, Pop or I can come get you when you need a break."

"Oh, yeah, like I'm going to make you do that with a new baby and a new wife at home."

I'm so pissed right now that I close my eyes and let my head fall back to the headrest. Eli has no idea what happened to us, Ryan and me. I'd like to keep it that way. He has no idea what Ryan said to me that night. What he asked me to do. So, to Eli, this is no big deal. He also knows Ryan and I haven't been the same since I left for college that night, but he doesn't know my heart broke.

"Just take me to Ryan's. I'll figure it out from there." And, as his name slides between my lips, I push any feelings that come up to my throat down. Bury them. I grow sick to my stomach, and my face turns to fire. I roll down the window and welcome the warm summer night air on my face.

"Mer, I'm just not sure how to help him."

I know what Eli is feeling. It's the same way we felt when we were kids. We couldn't help Ryan. But could we have? We could have told someone. We should have. And we didn't.

We drive and curve with the road as if we were an extension. As if we were part of it.

Down a dirt road that will most likely be a mud pit in the spring, we pull up to Ryan's house. It's two stories from what I can see from the headlights. I've always known Ryan would do better for himself despite his upbringing. I think, deep down, he knew what he didn't have and it wasn't right. What he had to go without.

Eli and I get out of the truck, and Eli grabs my suitcase. The one he'll take into Ryan's house. The one that is supposed to stay in a room where I'll sleep. In a bed that is not mine. In a place I'm unfamiliar with.

I have no business being here. Panic sets in my chest. Panic and unrequited love. Love I had for a boy who isn't the same boy. Love I had for a boy who seemed unaffected by the words that I spoke that night so many years ago. A man who changed. A man who changed me.

There are twelve steps leading up to the porch.

Twelve steps in which I have the ability to turn around. Tell my brother no. Tell him and Alex that they're on their own.

But I can't. My heart won't allow it.

Not this time.

Eli opens the door.

I hold my breath.

My heart beats against my chest.

Eli pushes the door open. "Yo, Ryan, where are you?" He sets my suitcase down in the entryway. A dining room sits just off to the left.

"Living room," he calls as the television grows quiet.

Shit.

Ryan probably thinks my brother is on duty and just stopping by to check on him.

SportsCenter blares on the television as Eli takes the lead.

My heart still hammering against my chest, I try to draw in some big, deep breaths.

It's been seventeen years.

Not since I've seen him. I last saw him in May when Emily, my niece and Eli's daughter, was born. But I didn't have to interact with him. Always a group of people around us. Never alone. Although he's made several attempts to reach out, I just couldn't go there.

So, when I come around the corner, his eyes are on the television.

"Did you hear Richards got traded?" Ryan says to Eli as his head slowly turns.

But, instead of my brother's eyes, he meets mine.

A lot of time passes. I'm not sure how much, but it seems like the sun rises and sets, all in a matter of minutes. The same man as when he was eighteen stares back. The same boy as when he was sixteen stares back. Fifteen. Thirteen. Twelve. Eleven. Ten. Nine. And six. His stormy, dark eyes.

Eli coughs to break up the silence. "Merit came to help you. Knew you wouldn't take any help from us. But Mer came."

Still, silence.

And the only light in the room is from the television.

"Okay." My brother looks to me. "Call me?"

"Yeah," I whisper.

"Ryan, let her help," Eli says to his best friend.

Ryan doesn't answer.

When Eli leaves, there's nothing but loud static between us.

"You can sit," he says.

I walk over to the dark brown leather couch that sits against the far wall of the living room. Ryan's eyes break away from mine, so he's watching television again, and I sit.

Though I don't think he's really watching.

I take him in. All six foot four of him. Same broad, muscly chest that reflects a lot of gym activity. Protruding long jaw that's flexed right now. His neck, thick like his thighs. His clean-shaven head that matches his face. Big arms and hands. The unchanged hands that touched my breasts, the same mouth that touched mine. The same body that took my virginity all those years ago and left me like a puddle on the floor. The same body that has cursed mine for years. Ruined me for all other men.

One of his arms is in a sling that's stuck to his middle. I assume it's for his shoulder. He tries to move but grimaces.

"Sore?" I whisper, my voice hoarse.

His head snaps to me. "I'm fine."

"When's the last time you took your pain medication?" I know he probably hasn't. Knowing where he comes from. Knowing what the little white pills of death did to his father.

"Why are you here, Merit?"

Stay the course, Mer. Stay the course.

"Because you need me." My voice reflects an unrecognized confidence.

Ryan stares at me for a long time, mulling over his thoughts, wanting to spit some out.

I stare back.

In this moment, unspoken words are exchanged. Ones of love. Ones of anger. Hurt. Sadness.

"I don't need your charity," he finally says. "I'll be just fine." He adjusts himself in his recliner, wincing once more.

"I don't need your attitude. Besides, I get it. You're a grown man. You don't need a woman to take care of you. But, for the record, I'm not here for you; I'm here for my brother and Alex."

A tinge of a smile starts to form in the corners of his mouth, and he almost laughs, but it fades quickly as he groans and puts his face down, so I can't see his pain. Something he's been doing since childhood.

Ryan Taylor wears many masks, I remind myself.

I stand and walk past his chair. "You threw the pain medication away, didn't you?"

Ryan face is still in his lap.

"Goddamn it, Ryan. You don't have to play tough guy all the time. Where's your trash?"

When the pain subsides, he speaks again, "Under the sink. Kitchen."

I walk into the kitchen and flip on the light. Then, I grab the trash can from underneath the sink.

Eli was right.

"This is exactly why Eli called me, Ryan. You're so damn stubborn," I call back into the living room.

Sifting through the trash, I find the bright orange bottle of pain pills. I find another one for stool softeners and chuckle to myself.

This will keep him humble, I think.

I put the trash can back underneath the sink and wash my hands. I get a glass of water, grab the bottle of pain pills, and head back into the living room. I sit down on the couch and read the instructions.

Take one to two pills every four hours.

"I take it, you haven't taken any of these?"

He shakes his head.

I give him two pain pills and hand him the water.

"Mer—"

"Ryan," I say in a cool voice, "I just need you to shut up and take the damn pills."

He hesitates for a few seconds. Then, he throws them in his mouth and takes the water down. "Happy now?"

"This isn't my problem, Ryan. This is yours. I'm just the warden to enforce it."

He clicks off the television, so the moon lights up the living room.

The tree frogs and crickets are louder now. They converse, and I welcome the darkness to my eyes as I lean back on Ryan Taylor's couch.

"Can we talk about that night, Violet?" he asks.

I flinch. *Don't use that name, Ryan. You know what it means,* I want to say. But I don't. "Not if you want me to stay."

Four

Merit
Granite Harbor, Maine
Summer 1995
Age Eleven

Ryan, Milton Murdock, and Travis Jeffers—fellow game wardens—Ethan and Aaron Casey, Bill Casey—my dad's best friend and dad to the twins—carry my mom's coffin out from First Christian Church in downtown Granite Harbor, just off Main Street.

Mom made us attend First Christian every Sunday. I remember asking my mother if church ever closed on Sunday. Took a holiday. A break.

She laughed and replied, "God never takes a break, and neither does the praise."

Although Eli, Ryan, and the Casey twins are just ten at the time, that day, they look like men. Faces stoic. Ryan's and Eli's eyes are hidden behind sunglasses to hide the hurt.

I don't cry. I don't have tears left. I just sit, numb, and watch the parade pass by. Part of me pretends it isn't her body in the coffin. Part of me pretends it is a stranger and that I am just a watcher. I am just there for moral support to console the man in uniform who sits next to me, cold and sad.

Please, God, let this all be a bad dream, I tell myself.

But I open my eyes and see the same sad scene with my mother's picture up onstage, smiling, full of life. Anger starts to stir in my gut.

Why do men like Dubbs, who treats his child bad, get to live while my mother, who loved Ryan more than his own father and mother, goes to heaven? It isn't fair, God. Nothing about this is fair.

My fists tighten at my sides, and my body grows hot.

Don't you dare cry, Merit Albaleen Young. Don't you dare cry.

I push my tongue to the roof of my mouth hard, just to be sure the tears don't come. All I can do is face forward and stare at a picture of a woman who did good in this world. Loved her kids. Loved her husband. Helped others.

My dad's arm comes around me.

It is the first time in my life that I feel empty and angry.

I remember the last conversation I had with my mom, alone, in the bed she spent weeks in before she died. She told me that it was my job now to take care of Pop and Eli. That, without a woman's touch—someone to make meals, remember deadlines, run errands—they might not survive. She laughed and then coughed after she said it. But I didn't. I was terrified.

I miss her terribly.

She took my hands in hers. Told me to take care of Ryan. That he'd need it, too. He'd need love. Someone to help him through the rough patches that life would bring him. I told her that I couldn't be that girl. Couldn't do what she did. Take care of so many people. She smiled and pulled me close to her chest, and I lay and listened to her heart thump in my ear.

"Don't worry, Mer; you have life all figured out. All you have to do is show up and do the next right thing."

A touch on my shoulder brings me out of my thoughts. It's Ryan.

"Hey, you ready?"

"Yeah." I stand, and we walk out of the church in silence.

The sunlight outside pains my eyes. What should feel good against my face feels more like a throbbing toothache. As if the sun and what I'm feeling on the inside don't match, and it hurts.

Living in a small town, it's no surprise that most of Granite Harbor is shut down for two hours with signs on local businesses that read, *Closed from 10 a.m. to noon. Young funeral.*

I'm sure my dad will be preoccupied with many of the community members passing on their condolences at the Firemen's Hall.

"Hey, Ryan?" I guard my eyes from the sun with my hand and look at him.

He's staring at the ground, still wearing his sunglasses.

"I don't want to go to Firemen's Hall."

He shrugs and shoves his hands in his pockets. The black suit he's wearing fits him perfectly. "Okay, where do you want to go?"

"Come on, I'll show you."

Summer in Granite Harbor brings the tourists from not only the neighboring states, but also from all over the country. We watch as a group of tourists unload next to the statue of Andre the Seal. Totally unaffected by Rebecca Young's untimely death. Their world is wrapped around photographs and angles and where to go next.

But, hidden from the tourists, there's a tree with my name on it. A place buried under the softwoods and evergreens, a place I don't have to hide my heart. A place she used to take Eli and me to since we were little. The best time to be there is right before the sun rises. When the seagulls are starting their morning calls. When the seals make their first barks of the day though quiet, as if not to wake anyone. As if the animals know the human protocol of time and sleep.

We find a spot right on the water's edge, and I slip off my open-toed sandals and let the Atlantic swim between my toes. I breathe deep as I feel the soft breeze blowing off the ocean, our faces protected from the mean old sun by the trees above.

There's a long silence between Ryan and me, but it isn't awkward. It never is. Even with the commotion from the harbor—the boats coming and going, the seals calling out, and the seagulls fighting for their next meal—this is my safe place. A place where I can disappear and just watch life go by.

"The obituary was nice," I say to Ryan as I draw in the rocky sand with a stick. But that's not what I want to say. I pause. Take a big, long breath. "You'll still come over, right, Ryan? Nothing will change? You'll still be there, right?"

"Your dad rented this suit for me. I don't want to ruin it," he says as he sits down next to me. "Nothing's going to change, Mer. Nothing."

"I wish you'd leave Dubbs and come live with us." I know it isn't the right thing to say, but I don't care. Most of my life, I've tiptoed around others' feelings, too scared to tell them what I think, for fear of hurting them.

"It's not that easy, Mer."

"Why not? He's an awful man, Ryan. I lied to Mom and Pop."

Ryan's head snaps back to me. "What happened?"

I stare out at the ocean, plastering my tongue against the roof of my mouth, not allowing any tears. "They asked if I knew of anything that was going on at your home. Asked if it was unsafe and stuff."

He picks up a small rock and throws it in the ocean. He doesn't say anything. He just sits with his thoughts, and I welcome it. I welcome the silence of my mind, to just be. To exist in nature and not have the expectations of others weighing on my shoulders.

He tosses another rock in the ocean, this time softer. "Sometimes, people do really shitty stuff, Mer. But it's not because they're bad people. It's because that's what they know."

I try not to react. I know I'm real sad right now, and the last thing I want to do is chase away one of my oldest friends. Ryan has made excuse after excuse, trying to justify why his dad treats him the way he does.

What I want to say is, *Pop has seen some real bad stuff in his career as a game warden, real bad stuff. And never has he ever treated me or Eli shitty because of it. You can't justify a jerk.*

But I don't answer Ryan. I allow his words to seep into my mind, and I question every last thing I've been taught.

"You going to school on Monday?" He tosses another rock into the ocean after a long silence.

I dread it, knowing that over half of my school was at my mother's funeral today. Knowing people will look at me funny, not knowing what to say. What to do or how to act. I wish we could fast-forward through time and ask God to give others some grace. And me some peace and space.

"Probably. Why?"

He shrugs. "Just easier to face life that way."

"What do you mean?"

"Seems like school lets me forget about what's going on at home. Gives my mind a break, I guess. Gives me something normal."

"Yeah, I need that."

"Me, too." Ryan tosses one last rock in the ocean.

"Should we head back?"

"Yeah. Probably. Eli needs us."

We stand, and I dust off the back of my dress, slip my shoes back on, and head back to my new normal.

"What's with all the rock tossing?" I ask him on our way back to Firemen's Hall.

A grin starts on the right side of his face and then disappears.

"What?" I hit his arm.

Ryan slips his hands in his pockets. "Wishes."

And, as the sun fades behind the tree line, I see this imperfect human being who has spent the last hour with me, trying to console my heart. I can't help but notice how the suit fits him. And, if I'm being honest with myself, when I first saw him walking up the road to our house to ride with us to the funeral, his silhouette made my stomach and heart do things that I'd never felt before.

"What'd you wish for?"

"For this not to hurt so bad for you and Eli." He looks up the road and then back at me.

A knot forms in my throat as I stare back at him because I know how he feels. I pray for the same thing for him every night.

That night, I go to bed on my own while Pop falls asleep in his chair and Eli on the couch. I wait for my mother to kiss me good night. Even though, the last weeks before her death, she couldn't get out of bed, still, I wait. And, every hour that passes, I cry. I cry for myself and Eli and Pop and Ryan.

"Please, God," I whisper, "no more death."

Ryan
Hallowell, Maine
Present Day

O*h, this fucking hurts so bad.* I roll over onto my side and try to find a position that's comfortable. The pain pills sit at the bottom of my trash.

I should go get them.

No. No, you shouldn't. You want to turn out like Dubbs? Then, go ahead and go get them.

Hitting a moose, going fifty miles an hour, could have killed me, yes, but I might take death over this pain I'm feeling right now.

My phone chimes again.

Fucking Eli.

Very slowly, I turn to my side and grab my phone with my right hand because my shoulder is tied to my side with a sling that I fucking hate.

> *Eli: I'll be over tonight to give you shit.*

I glance at the clock. It's just after five at night. I don't text him back, but instead, I scoot my ass to the edge of the bed and push myself up, trying like hell not to use my stomach muscles and touch the wall.

"Oh, fuck." My breath has been taken away by the pain searing through my ribs and my shoulder.

My phone chimes again.

"Motherfucker." Still in my hand, I look down, and it's a text from Sadie. I roll my eyes.

Since Merit came back into town last October, I haven't been able to get her out of my head. For that matter, I also haven't touched Sadie or any other woman since then.

I don't even read the text.

I use the wall as my guide from my bedroom to the living room. I'm careful not to stray too far from these two locations.

I don't know why Eli is making such a big fucking deal about me taking care of myself. I don't need anyone. I reach my chair and pray real quick because this always hurts so bad, trying to sit in my chair.

"Goddamn it." I take five short breaths and try to breathe through the pain eating away at my nerves as I sit. "Oh my God."

I'm not sure how I'm going to survive the next month with the television, my chair, and my broken bones. I'd rather stick needles in my eyes. I'm bored out of my mind.

Maybe, if you'd take some of those painkillers, you might heal faster, dumb shit.

No, those aren't going to help. They'll just make me loopy and tired.

That might be what you need to get better quicker.

Carefully, I reach for the remote on the table next to my chair and click the television on.

And there are so many more hours of daylight left. I'm screwed.

My phone rings, calling me from an infomercial.

"Yeah?" I answer.

Why the hell is Dubbs calling?

Someone gets hurt, and all of a sudden, everyone wants to talk on the goddamn phone.

"You feelin' all right?"

"Fine." I reach down and try like hell not to make a sound to grab the pillow sitting on the floor next to the recliner. *Fuck, this hurts.* My face grows hot and then cold. I hold my breath and pull the pillow up to me. I hold it to my middle, praying the pain goes away.

"Heard they made moose stew down at some mission in Augusta." The voice on the other end of the line chuckles, followed by a raspy laugh.

When wild game is hit and killed, the game wardens can call local charities, so they can harvest the meat.

"You need help at your place?"

"No." I question why he called me. When he calls, it's usually because he wants something.

And why does everyone think I need so much goddamn help?

"All right then."

"All right then. Bye, Dubbs." I hit End.

I stopped calling him Dad when I turned sixteen, the last time I had to defend myself against his fist. The last time I had to hit a man to protect myself.

I'd spent years taking it, scared to death, if I said anything, he'd go after Merit and Eli. He'd told me that much. That, if I opened up my trap, he'd kill them. That wasn't what I told them. Because I knew, if I played it that way, they'd have talked. They'd have told Brand and Rebecca. But, if I played my cards right, said it was me, they'd keep quiet.

Then, I just got fed up. I'd grown eight painful inches that summer. Eight. It almost hurt as much as cracked ribs and a torn-up shoulder. I'd grown into my body and matched it hour for hour at the school gym in the morning before and after football practice. I towered over the fisherman who had once terrorized my dreams.

The pillow placed firmly against my middle gives me some relief, and the pain has somewhat subsided, but I dare not move. Now, I'm tired again. Finally. I lean my head back and close my eyes.

My front door opens, and I jump, sending another shot of pain through my middle.

Motherfucker, I want to scream, but instead, I just shake through it.

"Yo, Ryan, where are you?" It's Eli.

"Living room," I say, pushing through the pain, not allowing my tone to be affected.

Eli comes around the corner.

"Did you hear Richards got traded?" I try to act casual.

But behind Eli is my past, my mistakes, staring back at me. The only person I've ever loved, looking at me with her big green eyes.

37

My heart starts to hammer against my chest as I attempt to figure out why and how she's here, standing in my living room in Hallowell. I don't say anything as they fully emerge from behind the wall that separates the entryway from the living room.

Eli coughs. "Merit came to help you. Knew you wouldn't take any help from us. But Mer came."

Is he looking for an answer? Because, right now, I'm in shock. Shock that she came. After all I'd put her through.

"Okay. Call me?" Eli says to Merit.

I can't look away from her.

"Yeah," she whispers.

Her eyes grow shifty, which means she nervous. I've seen that look before. Too many times.

"Ryan, let her help," Eli says.

I don't answer because I can't answer. I don't have a voice. It's lost somewhere between the seams of my heart that have grown rigid and callous over the years. Years since we last made love. Years since I felt her milky-white skin beneath mine. Measured her breaths and promised that I'd take care of her.

Eli leaves, but now, there's nothing but loud silence that sits between us.

Christ. Speak, Ryan.

"You can sit."

She walks over to the brown leather couch where I've taken countless women from behind, and immediately, I get frustrated with myself.

You should have waited for her, Ryan.

I'm pissed she's even anywhere near that fucking couch.

"Sore?" I hear her angelic voice come from her mouth.

My head snaps to her. "Fine." And it comes out fifty ways of fucked up. I'm not mad at her, and now, I'm coming off like a dick.

"When's the last time you took your pain medication?" she asks because she knows me so well.

"Why are you here, Merit?"

I want her to say, *Because I love you. Because I choose you. Because I forgive you.*

"Because you need me."

And she's fucking right. I need her. I needed her when she left at eighteen, but I sure as hell wasn't going to be the one to hold her back. She had her sights set on California. But I don't want her here out of pity. I want her here because she wants to be here.

"I don't need your charity. I'll be fine." Maybe it's the lie I just told or the fact that I've just adjusted my body in the recliner a bit, but another shot of pain meets my rib cage.

"I don't need your attitude. Besides, I get it. You're a grown man. You don't need a woman to take care of you. But, for the record, I'm not here for you; I'm here for my brother and Alex."

There's the Merit I know. I try not to smile, knowing she's come back. Knowing it took a lot for her to come all the way back from California.

"You threw the pain medication away, didn't you?" she asks.

I try my hardest not to make a face, not to show the remnants of my body fighting back, calling out for mercy.

"Goddamn it, Ryan. You don't have to play tough guy all the time. Where's your trash?"

When I catch my breath again, I say, "Under the sink. Kitchen."

Merit walks into the kitchen and grabs the trash can. "This is exactly why Eli called me, Ryan. You're so damn stubborn."

Is she seriously going through my trash? I cringe in pain, trying not to move too much.

"I take it, you haven't taken any of these?" Merit's standing at my chair.

I shake my head. She knows. She doesn't have to ask, but she knows my past, and she knows what I came from. My upbringing.

This time, I welcome the relief. Maybe part of it is knowing that she's here, to hold me accountable. Maybe part of it is just knowing, if I take these, someone else knows, so I don't have to hide.

"Mer—"

She says, "Ryan, I just need you to shut up and take the damn pills."

I want to say, *Thank you*, and, *I'm sorry*, but I know it will fall on deaf ears until she's ready to hear it, so instead, I throw the pills to the back of my throat. "Happy now?"

"This isn't my problem, Ryan. This is yours. I'm just the warden to enforce it."

I turn off the television, wanting to be in a quiet place with Merit. Meet her where she is, in the darkness and with nothing but the sound of my loud heart, waiting for her to hear the beat.

"Can we talk about that night, Violet?" I whisper.

"Not if you want me to stay."

We sit in silence, and the pain medication slowly starts to make its way through my system. Finally, after a few days, I feel relief from my body and my head.

Some time passes.

"How do you feel now?" she asks.

"Really good," I say as I look over at Merit.

Her long blonde hair is pulled back off her slender neck—a place where my lips have been, searched, touched. My mouth around each of her perfect full breasts. Her long, lean hips that rocked against mine in the middle of many nights that summer.

The Young green eyes are a family trait passed down from Brand. Hers can lure any man off a barstool, and right now, they're staring back at me. She's taller than most women but not as tall as me. She's most comfortable in her home or in the Maine outdoors. Too many people aren't her thing, and she's been that way since her mother's service.

Her heart is tucked back behind the armor in her chest, and I know a lot of this was caused by her mother's death. I know it was partly me who caused this, too. I don't know if that's all changed in the last seventeen years, but it hasn't seemed so. Merit is the type of woman who doesn't ask for approval from anyone. If there's work to be done, she grabs a shovel. If there's someone in need, she's first to volunteer. If there's justice to be stood for, she's the willing participant. That hasn't changed a bit. I think she gets that from both Rebecca and Brand. And she never backs down from a challenge.

She pulls her eyes from mine and looks out the window at the moon. "Do you need help with getting into bed?"

Yes. I want you to be in my bed because I need to feel your skin against mine again. Feel all of you. Be inside you.

But I know I can't rush this. I know I have to move patiently. Because I can't live the next seventeen years without Merit. I knew, when we were kids and when she left, that I had to survive without her. So, I did everything in my power to forget her. And, now, she's back. In my home. Sleeping in my sheets. I'll just have to convince her that she needs to stay forever. But I'll bide my time. I'll take it slow. I just hope she can forgive me.

"No, I'll manage."

Six

Merit
Hallowell, Maine
Present Day

It's the grunting I hear that wakes me. The door to the spare room I'm sleeping in, next to Ryan's, is open. I quickly sit up. More grunting. My head gains clarity, and I know I'm not at my place in California. I'm not at Pop's, but I'm at Ryan's, and Ryan is injured.

Quickly, I untangle myself from the sheets and walk to his bedroom. I push the door open. He's sitting on the side of the bed. His back muscles flex and fill his T-shirt. He's thick and solid in all the places a man can be. A lot has changed about Ryan when it comes to outwardly appearances, but I can't think about that now.

"Ryan? Are you all right?" I call from the door.

He doesn't speak.

So, I walk to his bedside. His left arm is still strapped tight to his side.

I get down on my knees in front of him. His eyes are closed.

"Ryan, look at me. Are you in pain?"

He doesn't nod at first, but he knows I'll stay in this position and wait for an answer for as long as it takes.

Slowly, he nods.

I go to the kitchen and grab two pain pills, a stool softener, and a glass of water.

Better to get these in his system now, I think to myself.

When I walk back into his bedroom, he's standing. I roll my eyes. I don't tell him he could have waited until I came back to help him for two reasons. One, he's in pain, and he doesn't want to hear it, and two, he wouldn't listen anyway. He's too damn stubborn.

I walk to him and stand in front of him as he towers over me. His chest fills the front of his T-shirt as he takes a big breath in.

"Here. Take these right now."

Ryan's eyes melt into mine. He holds his middle. He reluctantly puts his hand out, and I drop the pills.

"What's this one?"

"Stool softener." My lip curls in delight. "You'll thank me later."

He throws the pills in his mouth. I hand him the water, and he swallows them down.

"Where do you want to go? Living room or back to bed?" I cross my arms over my chest, realizing my nipples are hard—and not because of the man standing in front of me, but because I'm cold. "Or shower?"

"Shower," he says without hesitation.

"All right. Well, we'll need to get your shirt off. What'd the doctor say about the brace?"

"Don't get it wet." His eyes are still on me.

"Can we take it off?"

"Yeah. But I think I can take it from here, Mer," he says.

"Trust me, if I wanted to help, you'd know." I try to push off any heat that's reached my voice, my body.

Deflect, Mer. Deflect.

The curiosity of what he looks like under his shirt does affect the part of my brain that influences all other female parts of my body.

I blow a big breath out. "Yell if you need me."

44

Sitting in the living room, I pick at my nails, really not focused on my cuticles, but what the beads of water look like while sliding down his body. The same body I've touched in intimate ways. Though we were much younger, I wonder if his muscles move the same, if his climax creeps the same way, and if he loves me differently.

"Hey." I see him in the hallway.

"Hey. With the cracked ribs, I'm having a hell of a time with pulling off the brace," he sighs. "Can you help me?"

I nod and walk to him as if it's just between friends. As if he'd asked me to mail letters. Buy postage. Make soup. But, really, this is more. More personal than I've been with a man in a long time.

You're assisting with a brace, Merit, not asking to give him a blowjob.

Ryan turns his back to me. "See the piece of Velcro? Just pull that back, and I can get the rest."

One thing about Ryan is that he always smells good. Even after football practice in high school, yes, he smelled like sweat, but he always seemed to smell fresh, too. Like a bar of soap and expensive cologne.

With his back to me, I take him in. I wander around in his scent, taking in our memories, both good and bad, pushing back on the want that I've spent years fighting. I pull back the Velcro with one quick movement, proving to myself and him that I can push the need for him back further, not allow myself, my heart, to get wrapped up in him again.

The brace loosens, and he groans, his back still to me.

"Are you all right?" slips from my lips and out into the space that surrounds us.

"Fine," he says through clenched teeth.

"Is the pain medication kicking in yet?"

"Gettin' there." He turns to me. "I lied."

I stand, staring up at him, waiting for his response. One thing Ryan is not is a liar.

"I need help with my shirt."

Oh. Keep your shit together, Merit. You're here to help, not be his latest fuck. You'll never be his latest fuck either. Remember that. As bad as it gets, you'll never give in to his ways. The ones he uses with Sadie or the other women he's been taking home since you left. He's a different person now. Hang on to that.

Ryan keeps his arm in the same position and attempts to slide the brace off. "Ahh," he calls out, an uncontrollable sound.

Carefully, I reach up and help him slide it off his shoulder and his middle, and it drops to the floor.

"Let's slide my shirt up and over my right side, pull it over my head, and down my left side."

I nod, taking my fingertips and sliding the hem of his shirt up his stomach, not allowing myself to look at his body. He winces again as he slowly pulls his arm out of the armhole and very gently slides his left shoulder and bicep through the armhole of the left side.

I try not to stare at the broken man in front of me. The one who has owned my heart since we were kids. The one with cigarette burns just below his left pectoral muscle and two more on his chest and several that cover his back. It doesn't help that Ryan's body has changed from the gangly teenager into a man whose beautiful body would be better left untouched, untainted by a woman who should know better. By a man who sleeps with women to bury his trauma. Even with his abs that protrude and broad shoulders that make my hips shake, I yearn more for his heart. The one I couldn't quite capture. I want to reach out and run my hand over the scars, both emotional and physical, but a loud voice inside me screams for me to stop.

I look up and meet his eyes as a strand of my hair falls to my face, and I hear his breath hitch. He knows what I'm staring at. He knows that I'd have done just about anything to get him to leave Dubbs's place when he was eight, ten, twelve, thirteen, and sixteen. Those were the years when it was real bad.

Ryan reaches out and slowly pushes the fallen strand of hair back behind my ear. "The scars are just remnants of my childhood, Mer. They don't hurt anymore."

But, sometimes, we don't recognize how we've been hurt and heal the way we should. Sometimes, we turn to anything to help heal the hurt we can't see. But I don't say this out loud for Ryan or for me. I think both of us are just trying to get by in the best way we know how. I also don't respond with *I know* because I don't think that's the truth; it isn't a lie Ryan's telling. I think it's what he believes.

"You'd better go shower while the pain medication is still working."

He lingers in the space that separates us, looking down at me, searching my eyes, but I turn away and make it easy for him. I walk to the couch, my back to Ryan.

I pretend to look out the window, but really, I'm holding my breath, praying to hear his footsteps back down the hallway. Finally, I do.

This isn't a good idea. I'm setting myself up for failure, I say to myself as Ryan comes down the hallway, clean-shaven head and face. I'm sure it took a lot of pain to get there.

"Feel better?" I stand in front of eggs and bacon at the stove, glancing back at him as his scent drifts toward me, making my thoughts go haywire.

He nods and pours some coffee into a mug. He walks to the fridge where he attempts to bend down and winces.

"Hey, He-Man. I've got it." I walk to the fridge and bend at the waist, not thinking that my ass is hanging out for him to see.

I snap up with the half-and-half, set it on the counter, and realize I need to shower. "Eggs and bacon are on the stove. I'm going to shower."

When I come out, the kitchen is clean, and I find Ryan staring out the window, his back to me.

"I have a doctor's appointment today at twelve thirty."

"I'll drive you," I say, looking down at my black tank and green shorts, pushing my hands against my outfit, making sure everything is in place.

He nods.

Ryan slowly turns around, and I look at the clock. He last took his pain medication at seven in the morning.

"How's your pain?"

"Fine."

"One thing you're not, Ryan, is a liar. What's your pain at?"

"Four."

I roll my eyes.

"Six."

My head tilts.

"Eight. It's at an eight."

I walk to the windowsill where I've been keeping the medication. I want to be a smart-ass and ask him how the stool softener is working, but I don't. I want to make jokes and be light, but we're not there yet.

"I'm going to wait, Mer."

"Wait for what? For your pain to be at a ten, so you can live in excruciating pain until the meds finally kick in? Then, you'll silently wish you'd have taken them before you were at a ten, but you won't say anything because that's how you are. You keep everything in," I huff. "Right?"

Ryan doesn't say anything. He stands there, stiff as a board, unable to move—probably because of the pain. Because it is really at a ten already.

"Take the fucking pills, Ryan." I grab his large hand and drop the pills in it. I barely manage a smile after I turn around and wash the only glass that's in the sink.

I pretend to be bothered, but really, a small part of me misses taking care of people. Albeit a very small, small piece, but I do; I miss it. I cared for Pop and Eli for years before I left home. It's what Mom had asked me to do before she died. I cared. I cleaned. I cooked. I made lunches. Made beds. Washed dishes. Did laundry. Pop was too busy, in his work and with his grief, to look up and notice. And that was okay.

"You go to Dr. Stein in Granite Harbor still, or do you see someone in Hallowell?" I dry my hands on a dish towel and turn around to find Ryan staring at me.

"Stein in Granite Harbor."

"Well"—I lean against the counter—"we'd better get going."

Seven

Merit
Granite Harbor, Maine
Present Day

After the doctor's appointment in Granite Harbor, we drive down Main Street. Granite Harbor is a small town tucked against the East Coast. Even though Granite Harbor could make more money from its tourist season with more inns, more restaurants, and more specialty shops, we won't build more. We love our small town, and adding more won't give it the same quaint feel when you get here. I see that nothing has really changed in the time I've been gone. And I can't decide if it's suffocating or reminiscent.

"You miss it?" Ryan is looking out the window.

Yes.

I left because I couldn't bear seeing Ryan with another woman. I would have stayed or come back after college if he'd only asked.

"Sometimes."

Harbor Theater, Merryman's Restaurant, The Angler's Tavern, Ring's Pharmacy, and The Harbor Inn are five staples that have been here since my childhood. The history of the town is what we want to preserve. We get the tourists who commute in and those who plan ahead to stay. Lampposts line Main Street and give the small town the magical flair during our winters. Just like a Norman Rockwell painting. It used to be that locals would steer clear of Main Street during peak hours between ten a.m. and two p.m. during the summertime. Our population didn't quite double, but traffic seemed to increase with both walkers and drivers.

I look at the clock. Locals know where to go when the town fills with guests. From Lobster Tom's, just north of town, to the quiet beach just south of the harbor, which was my spot, where Ryan first kissed me.

"That was dumb, coming downtown at noon with all the tourists." I laugh at myself as we follow a Buick LeSabre that seems to be running on vacation time.

While tourists stop, look, take photos, laugh, eat, or walk, they pass us and the LeSabre ahead of us.

"We have some time to kill. We can go see Eli and Alex." Ryan looks at me.

"Hey, guys!" Alex is standing on the porch, waving with one hand and holding Emily with the other.

We exchange hugs, and then I grab for Emily. "Let me see my girl." I carefully take Emily from Alex while she's asleep on her mother's shoulder. "Is she ever awake?" I cradle her head in the crook of my arm.

Ryan kisses Alex on the cheek. "Eli working?"

"Oh, no, he's in the shop in the back."

"Ryan Taylor, you hurt yourself, and you'll feel my wrath."

I stare him down, but he's not looking at me. He's looking at Emily in my arms, transfixed. I catch his eye.

"What?" he asks.

Don't do this, Ryan, not here.

I shake off the cold feeling his stare gives me.

"Don't hurt yourself," I say.

"Yeah, there's not much I can do." He turns and walks to the back of the house and out the back door to the shop behind the house.

Alex eyes me, though her words don't come.

"What?" I drop my shoulders, looking to Alex and then back to Emily, who's asleep in my arms.

I use my other hand and comb her soft hair. She smiles intermittently, and knowing what I know about babies, which is minimal, she's not smiling because of what she's dreaming about; it's probably gas.

I sigh, bending down, gently kissing her forehead and taking in her scent. "Babies always smell so good."

"Come on. I'll get you some iced tea," Alex says. She stops. "Or a cocktail?"

"I'd better stick to tea. I've got to drive home." When I say *home*, I mean, Ryan's. A feeling enters me that is uncomfortable. I try to brush it off, but it sticks with me like jealousy to a black heart.

You remember how this ended the first time, Merit. Don't let him fool you again.

"How's he doing?" Alex asks as I sit down at the dining room table, Emily still fast asleep in my arms while Alex pours the tea.

"He's so damn hardheaded. I'd forgotten. Thanks," I say as she hands me a glass.

Alex sits down across the table, staring adoringly at her child. Her eyes meet mine.

"You know, since the accident, he wasn't taking any pain medication until I came along?"

Her mouth falls open. "What?"

I shake my head. "Nothing. He was in so much pain. Little asshole. I told him he didn't have a choice."

"Eli told me about Dubbs and his issues."

I lean down and give Emily another kiss. "Yeah, he's a real piece of work. I can't understand how a sweet, innocent child can be left to the devices of a completely narcissistic asshole. Sorry, Em," I whisper in her ear. *Em … I love the way that sounds.*

"It's amazing how Ryan turned out." She takes a sip of her tea.

"I know," comes out of my mouth quicker than I'd like.

What I notice, too, is what Alex doesn't say. She doesn't mention the fact that he's slept with half the state of Maine. I'm almost certain she's seen that side of him.

"How's the writing?" I ask.

"It's good. For now. I can get stuff done while she naps. But I'm not so sure how it will work once she's mobile. I have a feeling, she's going to be hell on wheels."

"You'll make it work." I stare at Emily's outline. Her forehead, her button nose, perfect lips, and little chin.

You didn't get the chance to make it work, Merit. Accept that.

"You guys want to stay for dinner? Nothing fancy, just pizza from Granite Harbor Pizza Company. We can see if Pop and my mom want to come, too?"

Shit. I haven't seen Pop yet. "Have you talked to Pop?"

"Eli ran the idea of you helping with Ryan by him, so I think he knew you were coming."

Pop has a soft spot for Ryan. He's always had a lot of respect for Ryan for sticking it out with Dubbs. Never complaining. Even though we tried for years to get Ryan to come live with us. I think it was when Pop started taking notice to the way Ryan looked at me that Pop knew Ryan felt differently toward me than he did most people. Pop was a colonel in the Warden Service when he finally retired. Took Ryan under his wing. Secretly, I think Pop was pulling for Ryan and me. Though my brother never noticed us. Probably because he was so caught up with Grace, Eli's now ex-wife. And also because I didn't want him to know.

The boys come through the back door.

"God, it's hot out there." Eli comes in first, kisses Alex on the mouth and me on the cheek. "You still mad at me?"

"Shut up. It's good you have a great wife and a super-cute kid."

Ryan leans against the counter, and I see him flinch.

"You guys want to stay for dinner?" Eli leans in the fridge and grabs two beers. He hands one to Ryan.

"Better ask the warden about the beer," Ryan says as his eyes fall to mine.

I shrug. "You're a big boy. You can make big-boy choices. But"—I stand and hand my niece to Alex—"I have to pee."

I come out of the bathroom and freeze in my tracks when I see Ryan holding Emily with his good arm. His biceps are as big as Emily. He's got his cheek resting on the top of her head. A violent surge of tears gets stuck in my throat—thankfully.

I cough. "Going to run out to the car real quick."

Ryan catches my eye, and he knows. He knows I'm stuck, caught, somewhere between anger and sadness.

"I'll go with you," he says.

"No, you won't." I open the front door because I can't breathe.

We say our good-byes to Meredith, Pop, Eli, and Alex as we make our way down to the truck.

Silence can be loud. It can crawl into the dark corners of a lit room and worsen, sitting where quiet secrets fester, spreading like weeds across issues in our own heads.

"Can we tal—" he starts.

"No."

A pin drops. A cymbal sounds. A burning in my ear begins from the quiet that hurt created.

The road is dark as we follow the yellow line to Hallowell.

I don't have to look over to see that his jaw is flexed. That his lips are in a thin line. That he's deep in thought. I don't have to look because I know him like I know my own heart. I know him better than he knows himself. And the hard, cold truth is, he knows me better than I know myself. I don't dare breathe a word, for fear that fire will light the dashboard, and I'll say something that I'll regret.

Bide your time. Do your good deed, Merit. Then, let go. For good.

We get out of his truck when we get to his house, and I don't offer to help him out. I don't offer to help him up the steps of his house. I quickly walk to the front door, unlock it, and leave it open for him. Setting my purse down, I stop. My back to the door.

He's breathing hard, and he's behind me too quick. "Merit, don't you dare walk away from me. Look, we don't have to talk about it, but, fuck, please don't walk away."

"I'm going to bed," I whisper. "Your pain medication"—I pull it from my purse and set it down—"take it before you go to bed."

"Merit."

"Stop, Ryan. Just stop." I hold up my hand. "I can't."

After washing my face in the bathroom down the hall, I tiptoe back to my bedroom, careful not to run into Ryan, and shut the door, attempting to push out the world, including Ryan. I shut off the light and roll to my side, lying in darkness.

And the tears silently start to fall.

I hear a quiet knock on the door and feel his tone through his broken words. "Merit, please, talk to me."

But I don't answer him. I just let the tears fall against the pillow. I cry for him. For me. And for the world and its totally fucked up timing.

My phone vibrates on the nightstand. It's a text from Abbey.

> *Abbey: Hey. Just wanted to tell you that someone was thinking about you right now at this very moment. And I miss you. Ethel had her baby. You'd be proud.*

And the tears start to fall as I shake in my own silence.

"What's on the agenda for today?" I ask as Ryan slowly makes his way to the kitchen the next morning.

"Was thinking we could hike Tolman Pond. Count eels. Run a few miles in the afternoon, and then eat red flannel hash for dinner," Ryan says.

I can't help but smile and gag at the same time. "Too bad we don't have leftovers." Sarcasm is loud and clear, and Ryan hears it.

He laughs.

I laugh.

I'm thankful what happened last night doesn't make its way into today. My hope is that we can leave it where it belongs. I know we'll eventually need to talk about it but not right now.

The morning sun pours through the kitchen window as I stand at the counter. I welcome it.

"We could head to headquarters. I have a few things I need to do there." His tone is light.

I feel him only inches behind me. His proximity gives me the chills, just as it always has.

"I'll grab some stuff for dinner while we're in town." *Make up for last night,* I want to say.

When are you going to forgive him, Merit? At the very least. You don't have to date him. Have sex with him. Or marry him. But, at least, after all these years, finally forgive him.

"I have some moose meat in the freezer. Can you still make those kabobs that you used to? Wrapped in bacon?"

"I think I can do that. You sure are a pain in the ass though, Mr. Taylor."

"When you're absolutely sure about something, like the kabobs, everything else comes second. It always will."

Meaning, he's not talking about the kabobs, he's talking about us. He gives me a side-eye and doesn't smile; it's a serious look. One he doesn't give the neighbor. Or a person he's arresting. This look is only for me. Whether he knows he's doing it or not, I feel it in my bones. In my stomach. In my stupid heart that is really betraying me right now.

"One more thing, Dubbs is stopping by. We have business to take care of."

Just the mention of his name makes the hair at the back of my neck stand at attention. My lip curls.

His life, not your life, Merit. Anger pools in my stomach. *You're here to help Ryan. Not make things worse. A new day.*

Eight

Ryan
Hallowell, Maine
Present Day

"Hello?" I grumble into my phone.

"Ryan? You sleepin'?" It's Dubbs.

I glance at the clock. It's ten thirty p.m.

"What do you want, Dubbs?"

"Well, got myself into some trouble."

I can tell just by the tone of his voice that he's been drinking. Gambling and drinking and fishing became his lifelong companions a long time ago.

One thing my father has never done is ask me for help—whether it be financial or otherwise.

"What kind of trouble?" I run my hand over my face to quicken the waking-up process.

"Well, I sorta borrowed some money from a guy in Augusta, and he wants it back. Problem is, I need some more time to get all of it back."

"You borrowed money from a money shark?"

"Well, when you put it like that—"

"Fuck." I struggle to sit up, my ribs giving me every reason to stay in the lying-down position. "How much?"

"Five."

"Hundred?"

"Thousand."

Fucking A.

"You've got to be kidding me."

"If you give me the money, I'll get it back to you next week. I promise. Look, it's been a rough fishing season."

I don't ask why he owes the money. I know. It's the gambling. He gets drunk and makes bets that end up as bad debts that he thinks he can pay back or maybe talk his way out of. I've seen this happen over and over again; he's just never asked me to help.

Do I have the money? Yes.

Will I see it again? I'm not sure.

Has my father ever asked for my help? No.

"Come by in the morning."

"Thank you, s—"

I hang up and throw my phone next to me on the bed. I don't want to hear it. Whatever excuse he has. Whatever shit he has going on.

What'll I tell Merit when Dubbs shows up?

I can't drive and meet him somewhere while I'm on pain medication. I'm sure as hell not going to ask her to drive me somewhere and lie to her about it. Not ever again. I'll never put her safety in jeopardy. It's my business with Dubbs, and the answer I give her is the answer she'll have to accept. But it's Merit. She'll push because she can't stand Dubbs. Doesn't trust him.

So, I lie here, in the dark, and listen for her. She shut the door to her bedroom, like she's done before. On life. On Granite Harbor. On me. I'll wait patiently though and slowly work back toward us. Because one thing I won't accept is another seventeen years without her.

To fall asleep, I imagine Merit in the meadow next to the Youngs' house. She's wearing the blue dress she put on the day of Rebecca's funeral. She's smiling, and we're young. She's reaching for my fingertips as the daisies dance around her. She controls the clouds and the sun and the grass below our feet. When she moves, they move. And, if they had faces, they'd smile, too. They'd give in to her lean jaw, her defined cheekbones, her purposeful walk, and the love she gives the world.

Holding tight to this image, my eyes feel heavy once again. And I don't think about tomorrow. All I think about is her smile and the way she pushes her blonde hair behind her ear. The grass. The clouds. And the daisies.

"One more thing, Dubbs is stopping by. We have business to take care of." One thing I'll never do again is not tell her something because I love her too much, too much to give her the truth or how I feel.

But I see her lip curl up, as if it's an involuntary movement.

But Merit surprises me when she asks, "Worst-case scenario?"

It's a game we haven't played since we were kids. A game we played as kids and teenagers to put off the fears of what the future might really hold or not.

Carefully, I cross my arms, coffee in hand, staring at Merit in my home, smiling. Something I've dreamed about for years. Years when I used other women to try to satisfy a need that only Merit could fill. This I know now. Calling on last loves and situations to break up the heartache I still feel toward Merit.

"That Dubbs owes one hundred thousand dollars in back taxes, and he wants you to hide him from the IRS."

Merit nods, picking up her coffee, taking a slow sip. She smiles. "Dubbs apologizes and wants a father-son relationship now."

I tilt my head. "You've stepped up your game."

"I taught the game to Abbey, my colleague on the West Coast. She's pretty damn good."

"That Dubbs owes one hundred thousand dollars in back taxes to the government, and he wants me to shoot him so he can fake his own death."

She grins.

And, with this single act, I tell her what's going on, "Dubbs needs to borrow five grand. He's stopping by to pick it up this morning."

Her jaw drops. "Five thousand dollars?"

I nod, taking a sip of my coffee and setting it down on the counter. "Merit, I'll never *not* tell you the truth ever again."

This comment makes her grow nervous, and I know this because she pulls at the tips of her hair in search of split ends.

Gently and carefully, I reach for her hand. She's hesitant at first, but she lets me touch her skin, and I feel it in every dark place in my body. "He owes a guy in Augusta," I continue.

Our hands stay where they are. The warmth of her slender fingers between mine makes me want to stay put.

"This is a worst-case scenario. You know that, right, Ryan?" she whispers, staring down at our hands.

I nod.

I didn't ask Dubbs who because I don't want to know.

There's a knock at the door.

"Stay here."

"I didn't want to come back here, Ryan," she says before I turn to answer the door.

"I know."

"No, I didn't want to come back here because I'm terrified of you."

I don't rush out the words that come to my mind. I want them to be heard. I know how she feels. I know how she feels because I saw her heart break into a million pieces seventeen years ago.

Instead of saying something reassuring, which I planned initially, all I say is, "I know, Violet. You have to let go of my hand because I can't let go of yours." I stare at her. "Not this time."

Merit's eyes leave our intertwined fingers, and she meets my gaze. She starts to say something, but the knock at the door interrupts her. She releases my hand and walks to her bedroom, so I can deal with Dubbs.

I grab the cash I keep in my gun safe and put it in a bag as I walk to the front door. I see a man standing there, who looks much less scary than he did when I was just a boy. A man who looks tired. Weak. The alcohol and the cigarettes have taken their toll. His thinning gray hair is combed back. His gaunt and yellowing face tells me there's some sort of liver damage, but I don't ask. I haven't seen Dubbs in more than six months. Living in Hallowell, I don't have the need or the want to stop and visit him in Granite Harbor. We've never had a stop-and-visit sort of relationship.

"Hey." His hands shoved in his pockets, he waits, unsure of what to do.

"Money's all there." I toss him the bag full of bills. "You can count it if you'd like."

Dubbs looks down at the bag. "Nah, I don't have to." His lonely, dark eyes first search the bag and then the ground for conversation starters. "How's the shoulder?"

"Getting by."

"Ribs?"

"I'll live."

Dubbs stopped by the hospital when he heard about the accident.

Dubbs never laid a hand on me after that day I stood up to him at sixteen. Never touched me again. He also never gave me a second look. Thought I should be a man. But the thing is, he didn't teach me about the basic fundamentals of life. Love. Family. Responsibility. I learned all that from the Young family. And, even then, I've failed. Just look at the woman who came back to care for me, take care of me, after all these years.

"Just take the money and go, Dubbs. I don't need your small talk." Though, as a small boy, I would have died for a hug from my dad. But I don't need it now.

He slowly nods, still staring down at the slats of wood in the porch, mulling over my words and his regret. There's a long pause. "Thanks. Thanks for this." He meets my eyes but only momentarily.

I give a slight nod and shut the door, leaving Dubbs standing there.

"You all right?"

"Jesus Christ!" I jump and wince and moan with pain, all at the same time, and grab my rib cage.

Merit is standing in the entryway behind me.

"How long have you been there?"

"Long enough."

I hold my ribs as I wait for the pain to subside. Take a few short breaths. After a few seconds, I say, "Want to head to headquarters?"

She nods reluctantly and grabs my arm before I walk past her. We're only inches apart, close enough for me to touch her face and put my lips to hers.

"Why do you continue to help him?" She isn't asking out of spite or protectiveness; she's asking to understand because she's watched me do this time after time after time. Not so much the money part, but the part where I keep the metaphorical door open for Dubbs.

"Because no one else will."

Her grip on my arm loosens, as if allowing me space, but I don't want any.

"What about you, Ryan? Who is going to help you?"

I want to tell her she's already doing it. She's here. But I don't say it out loud because my heart stands in the way, too afraid. But, at the same time, I need to prove she's all I want. She's all I've ever wanted.

So, instead, with my good arm, I reach up and slowly take the space between her cheek and neck. I take my thumb and rub it against her jaw, staring at her, willing her to see my regret.

Her breath hitches when I do this. Her eyes become slits, and my chest becomes heavy with ache. I want to kiss her mouth the way I used to. I can't rush this. This can't be on my terms. It has to be hers.

I think, too, she knows the answer to her question, but I can't keep allowing her to pick up the pieces. Merit always seemed to be the one to fix my hurts, both emotionally and physically, when we were kids. At a young age, the mother to two boys and her father. I think she felt, maybe still feels, that it's her responsibility to take on that role. Or it's harder for her to separate between mother and woman.

The sexiest woman I've ever seen, both inside and out. I remember the small of her back after the first time we made love when I was seventeen. It wasn't awkward. It wasn't clumsy. It was as if our bodies had been made to do this just to each other. Forever.

"What?" she says. Her hand slides from my arm.

I want to tell her what I'm thinking about. About the way her body looked, open for only me. The way each of her breasts fit perfectly in my mouth and only my mouth. The way she felt the first time I pushed into her. The only person who'd done that.

I lean in close to her ear, pulling her to me, wanting her to know that nobody stands a chance against her, and that it's always been her. I whisper, "Nothing." Because I can't tell her all this yet. It will only put her in a place she isn't ready for.

Nine

Merit
Hallowell, Maine
Present Day

I stand in the entryway, behind Ryan.

I want to remind Dubbs about each time Ryan came to our house with a new bruise that two kids had to keep a secret to protect him. That, every time Ryan had a new cigarette burn, he'd make an excuse to hide the way you didn't love him. Every time you broke his heart. The time you killed his dog. You broke your son, and he defends you to this day. Not because he has to, but because he thinks it's the right thing to do. That nothing can be done about it.

I want to say, *I hate you, Dubbs, for taking a perfect human being and creating scars that sit in his subconscious, the ones I see come alive in his nightmares. And, when he's trying to move on with his life, you seem to make appearances that set him back a few paces. You always do this; you might not know it, but you do. I see that because Eli and I have been there. The Young family has been there for Ryan, even at times when he didn't want us to be. I don't hate you, Dubbs Taylor, but Ryan should.*

"You all right?"

"Jesus Christ!" Ryan jumps and grabs his ribs, all at the same time, and after a minute, he says, "How long have you been there?"

"Long enough."

Ryan's looking at me with the same eyes he did when we were kids, and he was scared to death of his father. Though it's changed over time and the fear isn't so loud, I see the residual effects of the abuse in his adulthood. Him wanting to help his dad, no matter the cost. Ryan Taylor, Granite Harbor's ladies' man. But I still see the nine-year-old boy staring back at me. Eyes that have changed with time. A guarded look. More protection, more armor since our last encounter. Our past lives it seems.

"Want to head to headquarters?"

He tries to walk past me, tries to run away from this, but I gently grab his arm as he passes.

"Why do you continue to help him?"

I feel the tension surging through his body.

"Because no one else will."

My grip loosens, but he moves closer.

"What about you, Ryan? Who is going to help you?"

I have flashbacks of when we were kids. When the grief for my mom got so heavy some days that I couldn't get out of bed, Ryan would come to my bedside and bring me breakfast and lunch while Pop or Eli would take over at dinner. And, when Dad had to work overtime, Ryan would be back. He would stand me up on my own two feet when I couldn't walk. I'd trudge forward. I had a family to take care of.

His words permeate and twist in my mind. *"Because no one else will."*

Please don't touch me, I pray.

He reaches up with his good arm, and his large hand slowly takes me at my cheek where he rubs my jaw with his thumb.

Breathe, Merit. Just breathe.

His deep, dark navy-blue eyes fold into mine, and I remember all the times he helped me from the floor when I didn't think I could help myself. So badly, I want to take his hurt and his loss, just as much I know he wanted to take mine away after my mom died. This is the Ryan I fell in love with.

"What?" I ask, trying to remember where we were in all this. My hand slides from his arm because my entire body is on fire right now.

"Nothing," he says, his lips inches from mine.

I remember how well our mouths moved together. How good he felt against my body. His hardness ached for more in moments when we couldn't go any further. The way his mouth felt against my insides. The way we moved like sand and water. He sank into me, and we lost sight of who we were as separate people. I wonder, too, if that was our age. Our youthfulness. Wanting nothing more than to be united as one.

The drive to headquarters is only six minutes from Hallowell. It's quiet and quick. Knowing I'll see people Ryan and I have both known since we were kids, people I haven't seen in quite some time, I'll have to put on a face that doesn't reflect what my insides feel. Many will be my dad's colleagues. I'm sure it will bring up reminders of my mother. Though the good reminders, not the bad.

"You can pull in here," Ryan directs.

I pull into the spot next to a Maine Department of Inland Fisheries and Wildlife van.

We walk into the department, and the familiar scent of a well-kept, dated building wafts through my nose, bringing a piece of my childhood back. A safe, secure feeling reminds me of where I am. A distinct smell. The office is bustling with wildlife biologists, secretaries, leaders. Printers sound. Phones ring. Nothing has changed since I left, and yet everything has.

"Well, if I didn't know better, I'd say this is the clone of the long-lost Merit Young coming through the doors of the department. This time, you decided to pay us a visit," Linda says with open arms from behind the counter.

"Hey, Linda." I drift into her arms.

Her scent of vanilla is familiar, warm.

She whispers as her arms close in around me, "Heard you were in town." She pulls back and looks me over. "Girl, you need some food. Meat on your bones. You feedin' her, Warden Taylor?"

Ryan smiles. "You try to give this woman direction, Linda."

"Yeah, you're right. Well, there are doughnuts in the staff lounge." She rubs my shoulder before she goes back to her desk. "Good to see you, Mer." She winks.

"We have to go see the benefits manager. She's in the back," Ryan whispers to me.

I follow him to an office in the back.

My mouth twitches when I see the leggy brunette stand from behind her desk. Her hair is pulled back into a tight, sleek ponytail. Her glasses give her a sophisticated look. And her facial features are blaring reminders that bone structure is key to beauty.

She's beautiful and smart. Wonderful.

"Warden Taylor," she drawls, coming around her desk. But then she sees me and stops in her tracks. "Oh, hello."

"Faynette Dowd, this is Merit Young." Ryan stands between us.

Faynette. What kind of name is Faynette?

I assume she's Southern by her accent. The best of me is robbed by jealousy, and grace seems to be unreachable today.

I shove my hand out to take hers. "Hello. You must be new here." I establish my time in the department with my tone. Time of not employment, but time spent growing up in this building with its people. Hours spent on the floor, Eli and me, with coloring crayons while Dad pulled long nights sometimes.

Faynette takes my hand. "I am. Just started about six months ago."

"Well, welcome. It's a great place to work." I look to Ryan.

"That paperwork you called for?" Ryan scratches the back of his head for no reason at all but maybe to break the tension in the office.

"Oh, right, yes." She walks back around her desk and pulls his file. She takes a packet and gives it to Ryan. "Get this signed by your doctor."

"Will do," Ryan says.

"Warden Taylor? Can I have a word with you?" Faynette asks as we turn to leave.

Ryan looks to me as if to ask my permission. This is Faynette's way of getting me out of her office. I'm a woman. I know her tricks.

"I'll be out front with Linda." I try to act as if I don't care in the slightest. But, really, my heart is pounding in my chest.

Why? Ryan and I aren't together. She's gorgeous. Who cares?

But a little voice inside me says, *You do.*

I walk to where I'm out of earshot of Faynette and Ryan.

Look.

Don't look.

Look.

Stop.

I look.

Ryan's settled back on the heels of his feet, his good arm at his side, a look on his face that is unapologetic.

She's talking to him, rubbing her forehead with her hand, staring at him. I can't hear anything they're saying, but I can tell Ryan is trying to keep it professional.

She moves a little closer to Ryan, but he doesn't budge. The same unapologetic face is worn well. She reaches in for a hug, but his body stays as is until he touches her waist. Carefully shakes his head. Gently pushes her away.

And I walk to the front.

"How's your dad?" Linda asks as I come around front. "Blood clot fine now?"

I lean against her desk, pushing the feeling to throw up back down. "Yeah, he seems to be doing really well." I'm only half in the conversation.

"Has a new girlfriend I see."

I'm not sure how I would classify Meredith Fisher. We all adore her, but Pop hasn't come right out and said that he and Meredith are dating. Maybe it might be awkward since she's Alex's mom, and Eli and Alex are married. But they have fun together, and they both love Emily. I think there comes an age where companionship becomes more important than sex ever will be.

"You ready?" I hear Ryan's voice behind me.

I try not to look at him, so I don't make assumptions based on his facial gestures.

Don't read into it, Merit. He's not yours. Anymore.

I try to pretend that seeing him and Faynette together in her office didn't affect me, but it did. It shouldn't have, but it did.

"Yes." I walk around to Linda and give her neck a squeeze. "Good to see you," I say into her thinning, dark hair.

"You, too, sweetheart. You're not a girl anymore. You're a beautiful young woman. You should have seen the eyes in the department move when you walked in."

Ryan's eyes dart around, as if trying to see who's looking and who's not.

We leave headquarters. The air smells fresh, untouched, as the morning sun welcomes us to the outside. It's warm but not uncomfortably warm, just as I remember the summers in Maine.

What I want to ask is what I shouldn't. *Who's Faynette? Have you fucked her, too?*

I unlock the truck, and we get in. There's a silence among us that wafts like smoke.

Ryan's staring at me.

"What?" I ask, putting the truck in reverse.

"You're so goddamn beautiful."

His look smolders across the center console, and when he reaches my face, all my words leave me.

I turn my eyes to the road, pull away from the parking space, and don't say a word. My heart hits the floorboard, and I feel every inch of his words even though I don't want to.

Sometimes, questions are better left unasked. Sometimes, the seconds between the question and answer can be debilitating. This makes me realize that my feelings for Ryan haven't faded. They're still sitting in the dark corners of my heart, waiting for him and only him. Feelings that I've been pushing away for years. Feelings that I could never give another man, which explains the lack of love in my life. It explains why the handful of relationships I've had in the past haven't worked. I have an excuse. An explanation for each one.

Leif wore the wrong pants, which down the rabbit hole my mind went, eventually led to the issue I had with his cats. His murderous cats, Penelope and Cruz, that plotted my death while I slept. And I'm an animal lover.

Travis snored.

Blaine rushed into things too early, and I wasn't willing to wear his ring.

Steven was too perfect, and … well, there's no such thing.

This is also why I'll never be able to love Ryan forever. The brokenness he left in his wake when he walked out that day, I'm still recovering from it. He ruined me. Set the bar too high.

"Do you want to know who Faynette is?" Ryan asks.

Ten

Merit
Granite Harbor, Maine
December 1998
Age Fourteen

"Dinner's ready!" I call out to the quiet house.

I hear Pop's work truck pull up just in time.

I called him earlier to tell him he hadn't made it to dinner in a week. Told him it was time to sit down at home and not at his desk. I think working after Mom died partly gave him something else to think about. A way to hide his emotions. Lose them. Bury them.

Cooking somehow made me feel closer to her. And, sometimes, when I cooked alone, I could smell her perfume, wafting in and out of my airways, and I'd pray she would stay the night.

Pop comes through the back door, and Eli's behind him, done mowing the lawn. Pop hangs his coat on the coat rack next to Mom's knitted sweater, which hasn't left the peg in three years. Her tissue still in her pocket. I push my nose into the sweater when I want to cry, careful not to touch it too much, for fear that my scent will overcome hers and there will be nothing left but woven knots.

"Smells good, Mer." Pop kisses my head.

I take the kabobs from the oven, keeping them warm, and set them on the dinner table on top of a pot holder. Eli's washing his hands at the sink. Pop sits on the sofa in the living room to take off his work boots and his duty belt.

"Arrest any bad guys today, Pop?" Eli walks to the cabinet and grabs three plates, three cups, three napkins, and three forks.

It took a long time for him to stop grabbing four of everything. Eli has never talked about Mom after she passed. I guess boys carry their emotions differently. I know, when Pop's at work, Eli feels like the man of the house, and I think he doesn't want to show what he thinks is weakness. Every time he set the table, I reminded him that we needed place settings for three instead of four, but he continued to do it, so I stopped saying anything. I let him be. Maybe it was his way of grieving.

"Not today. Recovery operation today."

Pop carries his emotions differently, too.

He doesn't say anything about what we've read in the *Granite Harbor Times* about the body recovery of Aidan Laramy today. The reporter from the newspaper interviewed Pop. Eli and I read it.

He never talks about work with us—only the good stuff. And I guess, we need the good stuff, especially after losing Mom. Like the time the Warden Service helped a struggling moose cow have her baby. Or the time they found Penny Lane, who'd walked away from her parents' camp to chase a duck. Penny Lane had gotten lost, and the fall temperatures had dipped down into the twenties that night. She was found safe and alive. I think he told us that story more to give us a healthy fear of our surroundings and to encourage us to make good decisions.

As I crawled into bed that night, I thought of Penny before they found her. I prayed for her. Just like I pray for Aidan.

Eli, Pop, and I sit in our kitchen, huddled around our four-person table, eating the kabobs, rice pilaf, and broccoli I prepared. The fire in the fireplace crackles and sparks, and the flames twist and turn.

"You get that project turned in, Mer?" Pop takes a drink of milk.

I nod, finishing up my bite of rice before I speak, "Today."

"What about you, Eli? How was school?"

A whip of wind howls around the house as the fire cracks.

"School was good." He takes a small bite of his kabob, eyeing me, wondering if I'll say something about Grace and the fact that I caught them kissing at school today.

I take another bite of my kabob, looking out into our living room window into darkness, listening to the wind howl, making our one-hundred-year-old house readjust to its foundation.

We finish dinner, and I clean up the kitchen and make lunches for the next day while Pop retreats to the shower, and Eli finishes homework. It's the job Mom told me to do when she died.

"Take care of the boys."

Over the past three years she's been gone, Pop and Eli have to offered to make lunches, but I give the same answer every single time. *"No, I've got it."*

Pop:

Leftover kabobs

Two apples, sliced

A handful of carrots

A bag of chips

Two granola bars

Eli:

A muffin for the morning

Two peanut butter and jelly sandwiches

An apple, sliced

A bag of chips

A granola bar

Chances are, Pop will come home, only having eaten the kabobs. He'll say he got busy at work. He'll say time is a luxury not afforded to everyone. This will make me think of Mom. And the people who complain about gray hair. Mom didn't have any when she died. Not a single one.

Eli will most likely come home with all his lunch eaten and then say he's starving after school. This will make me add more apple slices and more granola bars for the next few weeks.

I make my lunch, too, which consists of a peanut butter and jelly sandwich, two oranges, a banana, and a Pop-Tart. I keep the Pop-Tarts hidden behind the Crock-Pot that never gets used in the cabinet below the microwave. Why do I hide them? They're bad for you. Full of sugar. But they're my guilty pleasure, so I hide them, and I tell myself I'm hiding them, so Pop and Eli don't put the poison in their bodies. But, really, I think I hide them, so I can have them all to myself. But, tonight, I'll eat one.

The house is quiet when I finish the dishes and lunches. I grab my guilty pleasure and tiptoe to the living room where I sit by the warm fire.

A knock at the door makes me wonder who'd show up at our house in the evening when the wind is angry, and the winter temperatures keep dropping.

I push my Pop-Tart between the couch cushions and look through the peephole.

Quickly, I open the door. "Ryan, what are you doing out there? Come in right now." I use my mom's tone, and it surprises me as I pull him by the arm.

Ryan removes his hood, and from underneath his coat, he pulls out a box of Pop-Tarts.

My first reaction is to deny my sweet temptation. My second reaction is to grab the box from his hands, look around to see if anyone's noticed, and carefully place them in my hiding spot. My third reaction catches me off guard. "How did you know?"

Ryan smirks, staring down at his feet and then up to my eyes, shaking his head. "Merit, you don't fool anyone. Especially me. I checked yesterday before I left. So, I grabbed some at Granite Harbor Grocery. It's no big deal."

I take the box from his hand. My stomach does flip-flops, my heart picking up speed. It isn't the Pop-Tarts that make my body have this reaction. "It is a big deal, Ryan. There's a storm out there, and you're on a bike." I look at the box of Pop-Tarts. "Thank you."

"Where's Eli? And Brand?" Ryan sits down on the couch.

"Shower and homework." I walk into the kitchen, pull out the Crock-Pot, and set the box of goodness there. I walk back into the living room and sit at the end of the couch, marveling in the fact that he traveled this way for me.

The wind howls.

My heart pounds.

And the rain begins.

"Pop can give you a ride home, or you can sleep on the couch," I say, trying to convince my heart it's better to slow down than to kill me.

"Yeah," he says.

The snapping fire grows louder as another log has burned to ash.

Heart, please, slow down.

The heart palpitations started about six months ago. I don't have heart disease. It's Ryan. And the gesture of the Pop-Tarts, the thoughtfulness behind it, has just about sent me over the edge.

"How about Eli and Grace dating?" Ryan says, pushing himself back against the couch, attempting to break the silence.

"Weird," I say, but I don't say I don't care for her. That her motives are wrong. And that I think she's dating my brother because her girlfriends say he's hot. Not because she thinks he's hot. Puke. My brother and the word *hot* should never go in the same sentence.

I lean my head against the back of the couch. I just want to be. Exist with Ryan.

Out of the side of my eye, I notice his shoulders drop. Mine are easing their way down, too.

"He's probably in his bedroom, on the phone with her." I laugh nervously, pushing my hands against my jeans, attempting to wipe the sweat.

"You should have seen him after he asked her out." He drops his head, smiling.

I love Ryan Taylor's smile. I love the cowlick that sits up front in his dark brown hair. Sometimes, I find myself thinking about asking him if he wants to go to a movie. Hold my hand. Calm my heart. I want to tell him that, every time he's been around recently, my knees knock and my hands sweat. But I don't.

I reach under the couch cushion and grab the two Pop-Tarts. I hand one to Ryan.

"Thanks," he says.

It makes me wonder when he had his last meal.

"Did you eat dinner?" I ask, my motherly ways shining or being annoying.

He doesn't answer but takes a bite of the Pop-Tart instead.

I set mine back in the package and shove it back under the couch cushion to hide the evidence. I walk to the refrigerator and take out a container from Pop's lunch. I pull out two kabobs and warm them up in the microwave with some rice.

I bring the plate of food out to the living room and hand it to Ryan. "Here."

Hesitantly, he sets down the dessert treat/breakfast food and gently takes the plate of food. "Thanks," he whispers.

So, we sit on opposite sides of the couch. He eats dinner, and I finish off my Pop-Tart, existing.

"Sleep here," I say after we've been sitting awhile.

Ryan and I have always been able to talk, but recently, there's been some sort of shift. I'm not sure if it's age, our bodies, or fear. Maybe it's the promise that he asked Eli and me to make—to keep the secret from our parents, the one that makes us different, Eli, me, and Ryan. That his dad hurts him on purpose.

"That sounds good." Ryan stands. He takes his plate and fork to the kitchen, washes it, and puts it away, so no one will know he's been here.

I wonder if Ryan has spent his entire life hiding his tracks. Running—and not out of fear, but maybe out of escape. So, people won't ask questions. So, people will stop asking if he's okay or if he needs something. I stopped asking these questions a long time ago. Because I know the answer.

No, he doesn't need anything.

And he'll be all right—eventually.

Eleven

Ryan
Augusta, Maine
Present Day

You know what you're stepping into, Ryan. A fucking tiger's cage. You've seen Faynette in the bedroom. You know what she's capable of with her clothes off. You'd better be good and well prepared for what she'll do if you bring Merit to her office.

But I can't hide from Merit. She's the one person I've never been able to hide anything from.

Except once.

"Warden Taylor? Can I have a word with you?" Faynette asks.

I look to Merit. I don't want this to get uncomfortable, and I want to be completely honest with Merit.

"I'll be out front with Linda," she says and walks away.

"Is that your girlfriend?" Faynette rubs her forehead, staring at me.

"Was." I look at Merit as she casually makes her way to the front, seemingly unbothered by Faynette.

"Does she know we've slept together? Had mind-altering sex?" Her voice changes. It's lower. Slower.

She tries to move in for a hug, but I put my hands on her waist and keep her from moving any closer.

"That won't be happening anymore."

"Why not? You said yourself that she wasn't your girlfriend. Besides, don't you remember what you did to me in the shower? Three times." Her laugh is sultry as she reflects on the memory. She steps back.

I don't feed into it. "I want to be clear, Faynette. I don't mean to hurt you, and I apologize for the way this will come out, as, most likely, these words will sting." I pause. "The only mind-altering sex I've had is with that beautiful woman walking down the hallway right now. What I did to you wasn't love. It was just sex. An act of two people feeding into their desires. That's it. What I have with that woman you just met is so much more. And I can't afford to lose it this time." My eyes are clear. My head is right. "Now, if there isn't anything work-related that I need to do, I'll see you later."

I turn and walk down the hallway.

"You ready?" I say from behind Merit, probably a little too close, wanting to smell her hair. Take in her scent.

"Yes." Merit hugs Linda. "Good to see you."

"You, too, sweetheart. You're not a girl anymore. You're a beautiful young woman. You should have seen the eyes in the department move when you walked in."

Ice shoots through my veins as I eye every moving uniform in my line of sight. Every man. Every woman. Letting them know that Merit belongs to me.

We walk out the front doors of headquarters like we've done a million times as kids and teenagers and now adults. But this time is different. This time is so different. I feel the sun on my face. I see the vibrant shades of summer. I know what love feels like, but I'm older now, far more experienced, and tainted, too.

My heart throbs against my chest. When my eyes meet hers, I can't control my words or what she does to my body.

"What?" she asks, putting the truck in reverse.

"You're so goddamn beautiful."

I don't want her to answer. I want her to take my words and shove them in her pocket for the trying times that we'll have in the future and pull them out when she needs them. She doesn't answer, not that I expected her to.

I also feel the need to discuss Faynette. I want Merit to know all my secrets, so we can move forward. But I won't if she's not ready to hear them. I put myself in her shoes. I wouldn't want to know about another man and Merit. The curiosity though would kill me, and I feel like Merit would want the opportunity to know, so she knows I'm not keeping anything from her.

"Do you want to know who Faynette is?"

Merit's eyes are on the road. She swallows. "No. It's not my business, Ryan. We aren't a couple. You don't belong to me."

"But I want to."

A small breath of air escapes Merit's mouth, but I catch it. I see the air leave her lungs.

"Worst-case scenario," I say. Then, I cough to give myself time, because I don't want to know what she'll say next, too afraid of how her words will feel.

You know this can't work, Ryan.

We've been here before.

You don't belong to me.

You and I are impossible.

So, I start instead, "You leave when I'm better and fly back to California. You marry Theo. Or Levi. Or Brad. Or whatever their names were. You have two children. A dog named Trigger. And a white picket fence that wraps around your house. And you have a smile that tells me it's a genuine kind of love." I know how selfish this sounds. I do. But I need to show her what and who I am, so she'll start to fight for us.

Merit's eyes are still on the road. The low hum of the tires against the pavement and the buzz of insects that summer brings breaks up the silence.

"Worst-case scenario," she starts. "I stay. You break my heart. Again. I leave and spend the next twenty years picking up the pieces, unable to fall in love with Theo, Levi, or Brad, and I don't have two children with a white picket fence because of the damage that I allowed to happen to my heart. Then, I become unlovable, so I foster cats in my retirement years. Cats because they're easy. Low maintenance. Harder to get attached to. They have basic needs, and I'll be able to provide that. But anything more, and they'll have to find somewhere else to go." She takes a left toward Granite Harbor. "We need to get stuff for supper."

I don't push her even though I have an itch that wants to force her to talk about it. I don't. Even though she makes me want to take back what I said to her, what I did, all those years ago. Some things are unforgivable. This was one. But I can't *not* fight for what I love, for what I know is right. I also understand where she's coming from.

We park in Granite Harbor Grocery and keep a two-feet distance as we walk into the store, the black asphalt drawing in the summer heat.

"Shit. What time is it?" I glance at my watch. It's eleven thirty a.m. "We'd better not drive through town on the way back to Hallowell. There's a back road we can take."

"Oh, God. You and Eli and the rest of the Maine Warden Service." She shakes her head, smiling.

I can stare at her smile for the next thirty years and never get bored. I've missed it.

"What?" I stop walking.

"*Oh, it's a shortcut. Just a back road,*" she starts in her best warden voice, which is strong, manly. Merit continues, "Then, you find a dead deer that was poached, and you decide to investigate it. And then you call the warden whose district it's in. Then, you find casings. And it ends up taking twice as long to get home. But, by God, you'll get another poacher off the road."

"You don't do a good warden voice, just so you know." I smile as the air-conditioning greets the top of my clean-shaven head as we enter the store.

"And you know I'm right. I'll find a quicker way home, Taylor. Thanks." She gives me a wink. "Let's see. We need bacon, canned potatoes, bell peppers, red onions, rice pilaf, and broccoli for dinner. But I added much more stuff to the list because you have zero in your house to eat." She stops. "Wait, you still like broccoli, right?"

She remembers. It was the only vegetable I ate as a kid. With a shitload of mayonnaise. Though, as I've gotten older, the mayonnaise isn't needed as much. But canned potatoes, not so much anymore. I won't tell her that. I'll choke them down.

We walk to the meat case in the back of the store for the bacon.

"Well, I'll be. Is that Merit and Ryan?"

We turn to see Ruthie and Milton Murdock, who are in the butter section, and her mother, Ida, comes around the corner.

"Hot dog!" Ida slaps her hands together.

Ida is eighty-seven years young. She was my favorite librarian, growing up.

"Are you two making the whoopee now?"

"Mother!" Ruthie's eyes roll. "Her filter done left when she turned another year older. I'm so sorry, you two."

Ida walks to Merit and gives her a hug. "Such a beautiful girl."

"Ms. Ida, I've missed you," Merit says.

"Nothing stopping you from coming by Granite Harbor Springs Retirement Village for a visit. Unless, you know, Albert and I are having relations." Ida shrugs.

"Dear God, Mother." Ruthie shakes her head.

"And look at my sweet Ryan Taylor. You're so handsome." Ida takes my face in her hands. "When are you going to marry this girl? The whole town knows you've been sidestepping the issue for years."

I laugh.

Merit turns to the bacon, red-faced.

"Don't play it off like you two don't look at each other with stars in your eyes. Don't waste any more time. Get married. Have sex. And make babies. Okay?"

"Mom, let's go." Ruthie takes Ida by the arm. "You two have a nice day." Ruthie and Ida make their way down toward the milk, Ruthie whispering in her mother's ear.

Milton stands. Staring. There's a long pause. "If Ida is any indication of what Ruthie will be like at her age, I hope I'm dead by then." And he walks past. "Good to see you." He waves.

Merit and I stand here, looking at the bacon and start to laugh hysterically.

Once we regain control, Merit says, "I don't remember Ms. Ida having such a vulgar tongue."

"Yeah, in the past year, she's really opened up, I guess."

Our eyes awkwardly search the bacon.

"This'll do." Merit grabs a package of bacon.

We walk to the canned potatoes like we're a couple shopping for food. Like we do this every Sunday. Like we should be holding hands. I want to take her by the hand, but I follow behind, trying not to stare at her ass in the jeans that she's wearing. The ass that every warden who had a dick stole a glance from as we made our way through headquarters. The ass I've taken in my hands and held against me.

She stops and turns to look at the wall of canned food. It makes me want to hurl, thinking of canned potatoes. Not that I didn't like them before. It was a night tequila was involved.

Merit plucks two cans—not one, ugh—off the shelf. I swallow the tequila taste that has somehow made it to my throat.

We grab the rest of the items and check out but not before running into the Prescotts and the Bravermans.

"About time you got it right, Warden Taylor," Bob, our elected sheriff, says. He looks at Merit. "How's Brand, Merit? See he's got a new lady friend."

Merit nods. I can tell she's unsure of how to answer the sheriff's question about Brand, but nevertheless, she's happy Pop isn't alone anymore.

"See you guys," I say, removing Merit from the situation.

"Thank you," she whispers, her elbow in my hand.

I don't let go until we're outside and close to my truck. We load the groceries into the back of the truck. I know Merit isn't a you'd-better-get-the-door-for-me woman. She never has been, so I don't even try to open the door for her.

As we pull out of the parking lot of Granite Harbor Grocery, Merit bites her lip. "We'll have to drive by Dubbs's place to take the road I'm thinking of."

I nod. "It's just a house, Mer. That's it. A house. The memories stay with the house." Saying that took a few visits of mandatory therapy. But I'll never admit to that.

"No, I'll drive through town," she says.

"No, Mer. It's all right."

Her eyes grow big as she turns on her blinker. On the corner sits the house I spent most of my adolescence in. A house that doesn't mean shit to me. I won't allow Dubbs to have that over me. The memories can stay, too.

You can keep them, Dubbs.

But on the porch of the house is a tall man, and his profile looks familiar. And the familiarity isn't a good one.

Dubbs hands the man the bag of money that I'd given him.

Dubbs sees my truck that Merit is driving.

"Who's he talking to?" Merit tries not to look obvious.

"I'm not sure." As we drive past, I make sure the man on the porch sees me. Takes in my profile.

A protective side to me flares up for Dubbs, the father and son thing, I guess that side will never fade no matter what happens.

Twelve

Ryan
Granite Harbor, Maine
Spring 2001
Age Sixteen

"Get the fuck out of here. I don't want to see your face here for a week while I'm home!" Dubbs yells across the couch-less living room. A living room that doesn't look like a living room at all. It looks more like a dying room. A coffee table with four full ashtrays where a heavy layer of smoke sits, smolders, waits.

I tower over the aging man now. The washed-up fisherman who uses fear to rear children. The marks on my body prove it.

His cigarette hangs from his mouth like a loosely worn garment. His eyes slit, he stares at me, trying to intimidate me. With a four-day-old beard, he stinks like whiskey and smoke. A combination that proves detrimental to children. His button-up red plaid shirt smells of old musk, and sweat stains sit at the armpits. Although tall like me, one of the only attributes I hope I'll ever get from Dubbs, he's bloated and red-faced due to his inability to stop drinking.

I stare him down, adrenaline coursing through my veins.

"Think you're tough now that you're bigger than me? Idiot." His cigarette bounces fluidly, dangling like an added appendage. "Think you can kick my ass?"

For the first time in all my life, I know I can do damage to this man. Really hurt him. I'm tired of running in fear. I wait for him to jump at me because that's what he always does. Scare tactic.

I allow his words in, soak them up, and the anger to flow through my veins like a drug.

Come at me.

As I turn my back, planning my next move, I feel his hands slam into my back.

That's all it takes.

Flipping around, I take his head and shove it against my knee, and he staggers backward, falling against the wall. His cigarette still sits between his lips as he is stunned. He tries to get up, but I take my foot with my steel-toed boot and shove it against his chest.

"Touch me again, asshole, and I will really fuck you up. And don't ever call me a fucking idiot again—unless you want to be buried alive." I give his chest one last push with my shoe before I turn around.

I find Merit at her tree down at the harbor. The sun is setting behind the trees, and the peepers welcome the change in light.

"Hey," she says as I walk up.

I don't sit. I'm still fucking pissed.

"What's wrong?" She's the only one, other than Eli, who knows me better than I know myself.

Starting to laugh, allowing the fear behind the adrenaline to quietly come out, I pull her up by extending my hands. She smiles and allows me to do so. I rest my hands on her hips, and we slowly move behind an evergreen, her back against the tree.

I breathe in deep her scent of honeysuckle and touch my lips to hers, careful to keep my body from resting on hers. We haven't made it that far. She's never felt me the way I feel her in my dreams every single damn night, but today, I feel unstoppable.

This is the fourth time we've kissed.

Giving my lips more pressure, I feel them in areas I shouldn't. I let my lips dangle against hers, my tongue sliding into familiar territory, and she opens her mouth more. I gently pull away and drop my head to her neck and groan.

"This feels too good, Mer. You feel too good."

Her hands slide to the sides of my cheeks, and she forcefully pulls my mouth to hers. Merit's mouth crashes against mine, and I'm lost in her. In her kiss. In her scent. But I can't stop. Unsure of where to put my hands, I rest them on the tree trunk above her head and allow my body to brush against hers. She feels me, and this makes her kiss me harder. Wanting more. I explore her mouth with my tongue, and her fingers slide up my chest.

"We've gotta stop, Mer," I breathe, pulling away, resting my head on the side of her cheek, attempting to gain clarity and think with the right head.

I feel her heart pound against mine, and it makes me smile.

I do this to her.

My dick hurts so bad. She's wearing a cute sundress that's long enough, but all I want to do is touch what's underneath it.

Breathing deep, I use my face to push hers back up toward mine, and I put my tongue in her mouth again. I get lost in her. All I want to do is kiss Merit Young for the rest of my life. I feel her legs spread more, knowing she's turned on by me. Knowing she can't stop this as much as we should. With no one at the harbor because of dusk, I could easily pull her dress up, pull her panties aside, and feel her from the inside, but Merit is worth so much more than that. Even though my dick tells me otherwise, I need to slow down. Be patient.

"Come on," I say breathlessly. I pull away and grab her by the hand.

We started kissing about two months ago, a pattern that we haven't been able to stop. She doesn't want Eli to know, and I can't help but steal her lips when I can, even when Eli and I are hanging out. When at their house, I'll go to get water, only to find Merit in the kitchen, getting the dishes done after dinner. I'll steal a kiss against her neck. But, the last time that happened, we almost took it too far.

It's the dresses.

It's her body.

It's Merit.

We walk along the water's edge, her hand in mine. The way it should be. This way, life makes sense. I can make sense of why Dubbs used to hurt me. I can make sense of why I was brought up in Granite Harbor and why the Young family is part of my life.

"I stood up to Dubbs tonight, Mer."

Her grip tightens. Lost in her own thoughts, she stops. "You did?" I hear the courage I felt just a half hour ago in her voice.

"Yeah, it felt good." I grin. "Really good."

I know Dubbs is a touchy subject for Merit. She can't understand why I stay at home. Why I don't leave. I've tried to explain it. I don't know normal. I don't know a life without dysfunction. Sure, I see her family, but I've never lived it. I know how to act in my house. I know triggers. Warnings. Signs. I'm not sure I'd know what to do if I left. Living in the chaos is easy because I've done it for so long.

I look up in time to see Merit pick up a rock and skip it across the ocean's surface. It doesn't make it very far because it's a rough day on the ocean. The small waves curl in quick succession.

"I wish you'd leave and come live with us." Merit turns back to me, hands on her hips. She's said this before, and I've heard it before but never with the command or the love I hear in her voice. "We have an extra bedroom."

But I give her the line. The one I give her every time. "I can't."

I wish I could say yes. I wish I could ask her to marry me. But she wants college, and I want that for her. Some school out in California. I'll never hold her back from chasing her dreams even though I want to. Maybe it'd be easier if I try to forget Merit now. Slowly wean myself away from her to make it easier for her to leave next year.

I'm not sure that I can though.

We begin to walk again. I follow behind her a half-step to take her in. Not in a sexual way, but in a way that I can appreciate her curves, the way she carries herself. The way she loves. I can't remember the last time I looked at another girl. I can't remember the last time I felt this way about someone else. I know I'm a teenager. I know I have a dick. I know puberty can be a bitch. I wasn't taught to love. Love isn't in the Taylor home. Merit, her family, taught me about love.

"You coming?" She looks over her shoulder. As much as I care about Merit, she's hesitant. Since her mom died, I think her faith has changed, too. She loves guarded, attempting to protect her heart.

Always, I want to say. But, instead, I say, "Right behind you."

We're at the entrance to the harbor, close to Main Street. This is where we stop touching. This is where Merit draws the line in the sand. For reasons I understand. Eli is my best friend, and Merit is his sister. Just someone the best friend is not supposed to fall in love with.

In my eyes though, she's not *just someone.* She's my forever.

Eli and I sit in the living room, mindlessly flipping through the television channels.

"Grace and I are going to dinner," Eli says.

We settle on *SportsCenter.*

"Where?" I ask.

"Merryman's."

I nod, thinking about Merit. What she's doing. Where she is. Somewhere in the house.

"Start calling you Daddy Warbucks." I punch his arm. "Well, I guess it took you long enough to go on a real date, which means you probably should have started saving when you were ten."

The home phone rings, and Eli gets up to go to the kitchen to answer it, but Merit beats him. She probably heard us talking. Merit doesn't much care for Grace—not that she's ever said anything, but I can just tell. Merit's lip curls when Grace is around. But she'd never sabotage the courage it took Eli to finally ask her out. He's been gunning for her since we were in third grade.

"Hello?" She pauses. "Oh, Eli? Uh, yeah. Just a second." Merit leans in the living room. "Duh, Eli, it's for you."

Merit wanders into the living room as Eli says, "Hello?" in a deeper voice than he had ten seconds ago.

She sits down on the edge of the couch, next to me. "He'll be on the phone for a while."

We both stare at the television, not listening to it or Eli's conversation, but listening to whatever is happening between us.

"Come to my room," she says. "I need to show you something."

I stand. Follow her upstairs. She quietly shuts the door behind me.

"Don't laugh," she says as she walks to her closet.

I shake my head. My stomach is raging.

You've been in this room before, Ryan. Door was closed. Don't let your dick do the talking.

Merit pulls out a strapless violet dress, and I lose all feeling in my legs. I take my hand and rub the back of my neck, trying to chase the feeling of want from my body.

Catch your breath, bro.

"Where are you going to wear that?"

"Prom."

My stomach falls to my feet. I want to throw up right here, all over her bedroom floor. Scared to death of asking the only question that needs asking. I try to hide behind the silence in the room, pretending to take notice of the curtains. On her nightstand, a picture of Rebecca sits in a frame, urging me on to ask her daughter a question in which I'm not prepared to hear the answer to, but I ask it anyway.

"Who are you going with?"

Thirteen

Merit
Granite Harbor, Maine
Present Day

"Who was that guy?"

"Don't know." Ryan looks behind his shoulder as we drive past Dubbs's place.

I look in the rearview mirror, and the man on the porch with Dubbs is still staring back at us.

"Dubbs elaborate on who he owed money to?"

The anger is beginning to build in my stomach—and not for Ryan, but for Dubbs. How could he have asked his son to give him five thousand dollars? I guess for the same reason he can push a lit cigarette to his own son's skin.

Ryan finally turns to face forward. "He looks somewhat familiar."

"Is the pain coming back?"

"I'm good," he says, carefully pulling out his phone from his pocket. He sucks in another deep breath.

I roll my eyes. "Ryan, stop playing tough guy with me. It's me, Merit. Remember? I saw your penis when you were five while you peed behind a tree, right in front of me."

Ryan freezes. Turns his head to look at me. And then starts laughing. "That's right. I forgot about that."

"Yeah, you thought I was just one of the guys until you realized that I didn't have a penis. That was a sad day."

It wasn't really sad. But it was a milestone in our relationship. Having a brother, I knew the difference between boys and girls. Ryan didn't at that age—or at least the anatomy part of it anyway. I know, too, that Dubbs didn't explain sex to Ryan and that he probably learned about sex from school and his dad's porn collection. Maybe.

We pull into Ryan's driveway in Hallowell an hour later, and I decide I'm not going to ask him if he needs help to the house because I know he's sore for waiting too long to take the pain medication. He needs to know what that feels like.

I grab the bag of groceries in the back, and it makes me think of Ryan's dog, Hero, and the night he came to my window in tears. Because Dubbs had killed Hero. He never mentioned it again after that night. I never did either. I'd never seen Ryan cry. I was seventeen, and he was sixteen. That was the night we kissed for the first time. I don't know if Ryan ever got permission to cry. So, I held him against my chest, and I told him it was all right to cry. It was when his lips touched my chest. At first, I thought it was his tears. But his lips slowly moved from my chest to my mouth. It was my first kiss. As if he'd been practicing, he was slow, patient, and he made my whole body tingle.

He explored my breasts that were full and waiting. My lips knew what to do, as if they'd been waiting for his mouth for a long, long time. When my nipples grew hard, he sighed and explained that we needed to stop. I should have stopped. But I was too selfish that night. I shouldn't have been, but I was.

"Earth to Merit." I hear Ryan say.

"What?"

"Where'd you go?"

He's at the front door, and I'm still standing at the side of the truck, groceries in hand.

I feel my face grow hot.

Never in my life since that night have I felt such a strong connection to someone.

"Nowhere." I walk up to the porch, trying to push the butterflies from my stomach.

I stare at his mouth and then his broad shoulders, his chest. The parts of him that grew bigger since that night when he was sixteen. New parts that I can't help but wonder about.

He takes his finger and gently moves my chin to meet his gaze. "What were you thinking about?" Now, he's asking me out of concern, and he shouldn't be concerned.

"Did you ever get a dog after Hero?"

His fingers stay put; he doesn't budge. "Just haven't felt the need." He's lying.

I know he's scared of heartbreak again. So, he knows how I feel.

Ryan moves his fingers from my chin to the side of my face and runs his thumb against my cheek. I try to keep my face stoic, unattached, and not emotionally vested. My head screams at me to pull away. Though my heart says otherwise.

I look away from him and out across the empty field in front of his house. "Time you get a dog, Taylor."

"I'll get a dog when you let me back in," he whispers.

My heart seizes. "I'm looking out for you." I whip my head back to him.

Ryan's phone rings, allowing us some space. I push through the door as he picks up his phone and follows me inside.

"Taylor." He's quiet, his big body standing in the doorway.

I steal a glance backward.

My phone vibrates, and I pull it from my purse. It's a text from Abbey.

> *Abbey: Okay, so I just need to be sure that you have haven't been kidnapped and that you're still alive. Haven't heard from you. Sarcasm intended.*

She ends with the eye-roll emoji.

I smile and text her back.

> *Me: Still alive. Sorry. How are you guys?*

Abbey: Good. Eddie is driving me crazy. Making me come to work on time. Says, since you're not here, I need to be more accountable. Like adult and shit.

Me: How is the old man?

Abbey: Ornery. More important stuff ... how's Ryan?

Me: Good.

Abbey: Um ... do I need to pick up the phone and call you? These one-worded answers aren't getting me anywhere.

I laugh to myself and look up, only to find Ryan staring at me. "What?" The hotness races to my face.

"Your cheeks will always give you away, Mer. Always. They're red."

I set my phone facedown and decide to text her later. "Who called?" I start to put the groceries away.

"Eli." He walks to the bag and grabs the bacon. He winces again because he moved in a way that he shouldn't have.

I reach for his pain medication.

"I'm good, Mer."

Taking one pill from the bottle, I also pour him a glass of water. "When's the last time we ate?"

"This morning." He slowly shuts the refrigerator.

"Sit down."

"Mer—"

"Ryan, I'm not here to debate this with you. I'm here to help and to keep your ass in line. You need to get better, and fighting this inner struggle you have, this tough guy image, doesn't fucking fly with me. Got it?"

I think Ryan appreciates that I'm the only one, aside from Eli, who can knock down the wall he tries to keep up. But, by the same token, I think he also gets irritated that I know him so well.

Ryan eases down to the barstool, and I hand him one pill and some water.

He stares me down.

I cross my arms and stare back.

He takes the pill after the awkward silence and washes it down with the water.

"Look, Ryan," I whisper, "I know you struggle with your demons. That, somehow, taking a pill or drinking more than two beers will allow you to slip into someone you're not. But you're not him. You're not Dubbs. Okay?"

He doesn't answer, and he doesn't look at me either.

"How come we get to talk about me and my fucked up childhood and the lasting effects, but we can't talk about the one thing that's keeping you from staying here?"

I wonder what he means by the word *here*. Here as in this house? Or here as in Maine? Or maybe he means him. I loved Granite Harbor. I loved Maine. But, that night, I wanted nothing more than to get as far away from this place as possible. The feelings I associated with the place where I had grown up turned cold, bitter. Angry. But Ryan's asked me a question. It needs answering. I can deflect. I can. I can push it off me and back to him. Why? Because I'm scared as hell.

"I'm not here for me, Ryan."

"Why do you deflect?"

Because it's easier.

"Why have you slept with so many women?" The hurt starts to pour in.

Push away, Merit, or this will get ugly.

I know why. *Did I ask it because I want him to acknowledge it? Did I ask it, so he'd know I knew? Who doesn't know?*

A big gust of air pushes past his lips. He rubs his bald head with his good hand. His broad shoulders and chest move in unison as he takes another breath and looks up at me, wanting to answer the question honestly.

"Hello?" my brother's voice calls out.

Ryan's stare is hard. His hand drops from his head to the counter.

"Hello, little brother," I say as Eli comes around the corner to the kitchen in uniform.

Ryan turns, too. "That was quick."

"In the area." Eli shrugs and walks to the refrigerator.

"You hungry?" I glance at the clock. It's just after four thirty.

"Starving."

I get out the fixings to make two sandwiches as Eli pulls up a chair next to Ryan.

Just like old times.

"So, you've seen the guy before?" Eli asks as I slide an ice water to him. "Thanks, Mer."

"He looks familiar, E. And it wasn't just a familiarity. His face was burned into my memory." Ryan scrolls through his phone. "Googled Maine booking photos."

"Did you ask your dad?" Eli sets down his water as I pass him and Ryan sandwiches.

"Thanks," they say in unison.

I don't do well with sitting still, so I grab the bell pepper, canned potatoes, and the onion and begin to chop as I listen.

"Yeah, texted him, and he hasn't texted me back yet."

"So, he saw you guys pass by his house?" Eli asks, his eyes darting from mine to Ryan's.

"Both of them saw us. Dubbs knew it was us."

"And you gave him five grand?" Eli clarifies.

Ryan shrugs. "When you say it like that, it sounds stupid. Like I just handed five thousand dollars to a stranger." He looks between Eli and me. "He's my dad."

We don't ask where Ryan got the money. We know. He's been a saver since we were kids. He got a job as a bagger at Granite Harbor Grocery when he was fourteen. He asked Eli to keep his paychecks for him. Said it wasn't safe to keep them at his house.

I'll never forget, one day, we walked into the grocery store in search of ice cream on a humid summer day, and the manager, Mr. Pete, pulled Ryan aside and asked about the uncashed paychecks.

Ryan shrugged. "I just don't need the money yet."

Ryan looks down at his phone after it vibrates, and his jaw clenches. "Says he's not sure of the guy's name."

I tilt my head and stop chopping. "Dubbs was just seen on his front porch, handing this dude five thousand dollars in a sack that you had given him, and he doesn't know his name?" I shake my head and continue chopping. "Liar."

Eli takes another sip of water and sets his glass back down. "What if Dubbs doesn't want you to know his name?"

"That's a given, Eli." Ryan laughs.

"No, I mean—and don't get me wrong; Dubbs is a fucking asshole. That doesn't change—what if he doesn't want you to know because, in a weird fucked up way, he's protecting you?"

I hold the knife out. "The guy who used to take cigarettes to his own son's body is protecting him?" I laugh. "I highly doubt that."

"What other reason would Dubbs not tell Ryan the guy's name, Mer?"

"Maybe he doesn't want Ryan to know because he's embarrassed, as he should be, that he had to ask his own son for money," I say.

Fourteen

Ryan
Hallowell, Maine
Present Day

"That was really good, Mer. I gotta say, just like your mom." I stand to clear the table.

"Sit your butt in that chair in the living room. You're not helping with dishes."

"You cook; I clean."

"Well, I'd take you up on that offer, but you have busted ribs and a shoulder injury, so the deal is off until the doctor releases you."

"It's dishes, Mer." I grab a plate.

"Ryan Taylor, you touch another plate, and I will eat your fingers." She stands and grabs a plate. "Go sit. I've got this."

But I won't go sit. I'll help her clear the table and watch her load the dishwasher. Partly because the manly side of me needs to see her ass as she bends to load it. But a bigger part wants her to know that nothing's changed since we were kids. When I had dinner at their house, which was often, Eli, Brand, and I would clean the kitchen after Merit cooked but only if she let us. Many times, she didn't want the help.

Merit walks away with our plates, and I follow behind her, close enough to make her notice I'm there.

I'm not going anywhere, Mer. Not right now and not ever. I'm here to stay.

A trail of honeysuckle follows her.

I see her chest heave in and out as she sets the plates in the sink.

I put my good arm down against the counter from behind her. We stare at our reflection in the window. I know she can feel my chest against her back. I never want her to feel like she's stuck. Safe but not stuck.

"What-what are you doing, Ryan?" I hear the break in her voice, and it makes me move an inch closer.

I drop my head to her ear. Maybe it's the pain medication that is breaking down my inhibitions, but I want—no, I need her to know how I feel. That the same feelings are still there. Only intensified. Only more.

I want to say, *I need you.* I want to say, *This is the end for me. You're all I need.* Things I've never said to her because I was too scared.

"Does this make you uncomfortable? Say the fucking word, and I'll stop, Mer." There's a tone in my voice that says, *Please don't tell me to back away.*

But, instead, she rests her hands on the sink in front of her, making sure not to brush up against me. As if bracing herself for impact. Bracing herself for hurt but wanting it, all at the same time.

"I'm not going to hurt you again," I whisper as my heart slams against my chest.

There's a long silence.

"Remember, that's what you said when we were kids," she whispers back.

And I close my eyes and absorb her words. Now, I brace for impact. I remember that night. The night I held her. Our naked bodies intertwined, tangled under her pink comforter.

This time, I can't make excuses. I can't say, *But not this time,* because that would be a broken record. Actions speak louder than words ever will.

I want her to fall back on me. To trust me. To know I'll catch her when she falls. But she doesn't. So, I don't say anything at all.

I will myself to move back. To move away. To gain clarity. Slowly, I ease back from her. But she doesn't move. Stays put. Leaning over the sink.

"Mer?"

She doesn't answer.

I reach out and touch her shoulder. "Merit?"

She falls into my touch, yet resists it.

"Hey." I gently pull her shoulder, so she's facing me. Merit's eyes tear right through me. "Talk to me."

"I can't do this with you, Ryan." Her voice is clearer. Stronger this time.

"Do what?"

"This. You. Me. Your hands. Your body. Your familiarity." She shakes her head. Laughs. "I can't believe I put myself back in this position after all these years. It's not you, Ryan. It's me. I shouldn't have allowed this."

I take a step closer. Take charge. *Fuck that.* "You're here for a reason, Mer. Why'd you come back?"

Her mouth falls open. "Because you were hurt. That's why. And because Eli asked me to."

"Why'd you come back?" I repeat.

Her face contorts, as if to say, *Didn't you hear me?* "I came back to help you."

"No. Fuck that. I'll ask you again. Why'd you come back?"

She laughs.

"You came back because you love me. You know that there's always been something fundamentally different with us. You came back because, while you can't admit it, you spent years trying to forget me. Forget us. And you can't. Did I hurt you? God, yes. And I spend every fucking day trying to forgive myself for that. Not for me, but for you. I can't love you the way you deserve to be loved until I can forgive myself.

Merit, I never, ever want to see the look you gave me when you left for college in California." I pause. "But, if you want to live in the past, I'll stay there with you. I'll wait. I'll do what it takes. You're going to have to talk about it sooner or later." I pause and wait for her to catch up or speak or do something other than just stand there. "Tell me something, Mer," I whisper. "Tell me you're angry. That you're hurt. Tell me the worst-case scenario."

Merit meets my eyes with a sharp stare. Her blonde hair is pulled back with a pencil. I want to feel the loose strands of hair fall against my face as she makes love to me. Feel the loose strands of her hair fall to my abdomen, against my thighs, as her head drops backward. I swallow.

She repeats the same story but with a twist, "Worst-case scenario: I go back to California. I marry Brad. I have two-point-five children with a white picket fence. A dog named Trigger. But the smile isn't genuine. It's one I hide behind to protect the truth."

My heart slams against my chest. "What's the truth?"

"That I married the wrong man. But, now, there are kids involved. And maybe the dog has emotional issues. Let's say Trigger is very picky about his routine. I can't leave Brad. I won't. Because I love my children more than I love anything in this world." Her eyes fill with tears. "Do you know what that feels like, Ryan?" she whispers.

I reach out and want to pull her to me. Take away this pain she's been carrying for years. Take away the hurt. The sadness.

Merit shakes her head and covers her mouth with her hand. "I just need time. Just give me space. Please."

"Okay."

I'll do anything to give her what she needs. Anything. But so badly, I want to take her in my arms. Hold her. Make her promises. But she's got to do this in her own time. Even if she decides she can't do this, us, I still want her heart to be mended. For her to go on. To live. To be happy. To remove the wall she puts up that separates her. I know, when Rebecca died, that was the beginning of the wall. And I know, when I did what I did before she left for college, that finished her.

"Let me finish the dishes. Then, I'm going to take a bath."

"Okay," is all I say.

She turns to the sink and begins loading the dishwasher, but I stand and stare at the back of her. Her shoulders that droop from the sadness she keeps.

I want to say, *I love you.* I want to take back that night. I want to take back every single time I kissed her. Made love to her. All my memories. Our memories if that means it will make it easier for her.

I turn and walk to the bathroom. I get some body wash for her bath. A clean washrag, two towels. One for her hair and one for her body. I don't run her water because I'm not sure the temperature of the water she wants. I remember the emergency kit that I have in the front closet with a candle. I grab it with some matches I find in the bathroom drawer and put them next to her towels.

I turn wrong when I stand, and the excruciating pain I get from it rips through my lungs and chest. "Fuck."

I suck in air as I make my way to my bedroom. Gently closing the door, I lean against it.

I hear the soft sound of her feet against the hardwood floor as she makes her way to the bathroom. Waiting several minutes, I hear the door to the bathroom shut, and then I walk the house to make sure the doors are locked, and the lights are turned off.

As I walk past the bathroom, I want to knock. To check to see if she needs anything. Water. Wine.

I stop at the door and listen from the outside. I hear muffled, faint cries, and my heart sinks. I did this. I hurt her. Now, it's time to see the consequences. But I let her cry. I allow her time. Although I want to rip through the door and pull her to me, apologize over and over and over again, that would be for me, not for her. So, I make my way to my bedroom, carefully sit down on the bed, push myself to a sitting position, and rest my head against the headboard.

A text message comes in.

> *Eli: Since you're not released to work yet, Granite Harbor Elementary has a summer science camp, and they called and asked for a game warden to meet with the kids. I let them know you'd be there at 8:30 a.m. on Thursday. Chalk it up to community service.*

Eli knows I don't do well when I don't have things to do. He also knows I have a soft spot for kids.

> *Me: On it.*

I scroll through my phone and look through work emails. Thank God, Faynette hasn't emailed me. Though I don't think she'd use the work server to do that if it wasn't work-related. She hasn't texted me either, which is also good. I think she got the clue pretty clearly when Mer and I were there today.

105

It's past eleven when I hear the door open, and her footsteps make their way to her bedroom. Although I'm barely able to keep my eyes open, I can't fall asleep without knowing she made it to bed. Giving her some time to get dressed and crawl in bed, I slowly get up, holding my middle with my good arm so that the movement won't pain me too deep. I check the house one more time.

When I get to her door, it's slightly open, and I peek in. She's on the bed in her pajamas, hair wet, asleep with the bedside light still turned on. I hunch down against the bedside table, and my ribs scream at me to stop.

I can endure the pain, I tell myself.

After Merit took what I did to her, this is the least I can do. After I get into a semi-comfortable position, I look over at her. Fast asleep. Like when she was twelve. Fourteen. Fifteen and seventeen.

Merit's never been one for scary movies, so when Eli and I rented them on occasion, Merit would sit with us at the beginning and quickly fall asleep because she hated the way they scared her for the following weeks.

Her long blonde lashes are pressed against her cheeks. Her expression, peaceful and saddened. As if she wears two hats. I want to take my finger and smooth them out, pushing the feelings away. But I don't. Her wet hair sits still behind her, falling against the blue sheets of the guest bed.

A jab of pain shoots through my chest because I take a bigger breath than normal, but I breathe through it.

She falls deeper and deeper asleep as I watch her. Slow, easy breaths, steady.

I turn off the lamp above me but not without my ribs letting me know that this position is the worst. Before I do, I take in a long look at Merit. Burn it to my memory. Tuck it back into my brain where I put all the dark things that I've experienced.

"Good night, Violet," I whisper.

Fifteen

Merit
Hallowell, Maine
Present Day

The sun peeks through the blinds, catching my eye.

I've always loved summer in Maine. Maybe it's the tourists. The ones who gather and flock to our piece of heaven. To experience our way of life. The beauty that comes from lighthouses, small towns, our rugged coastline. Through and through, no matter how far I travel, no matter how far I run, I'll always be a Mainer. Somewhere inside me, I find pride in that.

I stretch and twist and pop and turn. "Jesus!" But it's quiet enough so that Ryan doesn't wake.

He's in an awkward position up against the bedside table. He's going to be so sore today. His head is against his good arm, which is resting against his knees.

We left things at odds last night. Or rather, I left things at odds.

I see his five o'clock shadow make its way up his jawline. The Maine Warden Service looks down upon facial hair.

Has he been here all night?

Why would he do this to his body?

Did he get stuck here and maybe couldn't get back up?
Was he afraid to leave me alone?

His long, calculated breaths tell me he's sound asleep. I should wake him. Get him to his bed where it's more comfortable.

What did you do to yourself, Ryan?

I drop my feet to the side of the bed, and the strap of my nightgown slides off my shoulder. I push it up and get down on the floor next to him.

"Ryan? Come on, buddy. You need to get to your bed."

A groan escapes his mouth.

"Let's get you to bed."

Slowly, he stirs and then gasps as he becomes aware of his body. He meets my gaze with a pained expression.

"Hey." My voice is softer than last night. Easier. "What happened?"

His look grows as his body begins to talk to him.

"I'll help you up."

Slowly, we ease him up, but Ryan takes it in stride even though I can imagine he's probably dying inside from pain. He grimaces and contorts but doesn't say a word as I take his good arm and allow my fingers to wrap around his large arm.

We get him to his bedroom on his side of the bed, and I tell him to place his good arm around my waist so that he can brace himself to sit down on the edge of his bed.

The strap of my nightgown falls to my shoulder again. There's no way to pull it up without letting go of him, and I'm not about to do that, but as it slides lower, my breast becomes more visible.

Ryan's eyes stay fixated on me, and I feel the cool air against my newly exposed skin.

Once he's sitting upright on the bed, his eyes fall to my shoulder, my breast. But I don't push it up. I allow him to stare. I allow his eyes to undress my body as he takes me in with one deep breath. He doesn't tell me I'm beautiful. He doesn't tell me that my skin is the shade of milk as his eyes inspect every inch of me.

My middle begins to ache, and this isn't a safe place for me to be. At least, my heart anyway. I feel my nightgown dangling mid-thigh. The gentle rub from the lace makes me feel more alive, more attractive, than I've felt in an awfully long time. I'm well aware of my body. That my nipples are standing at attention, and if Ryan reached out right now and took me by my hips, I'd fall. I'd fall into his touch, his grip, and I'm not sure I'd be able to find my way out again.

My breath hitches as he reaches up and pushes the strap back up on my shoulder, his lips parted, his eyes intense. This is not what he wants to do. But it's what he needs to do.

My middle gives me another push of anticipation, and I feel the wetness against my panties.

I swallow as he stares back.

You need to stop, Merit.

His fingertips dance down my shoulder and barely graze my breast, my hip, my leg before his hand slowly falls to his side.

The only thing that separates us is a thin layer of cotton because I know, with the pajama pants he has on, there's a hole that is used for his penis. Easy access.

After I can breathe again, I say, "I'll get your pain pills."

"No," Ryan says and grabs at the hem of my nightgown.

My heart begins to slam against my chest so hard that I feel it in my ears. "You're sore, Ryan," I whisper, my lips barely moving, coming up with excuses, more for myself than for him.

"Not right now." His eyes rage against mine. My nightgown still in his hand.

The ache between my legs deepens.

My body wants to lean into his. To feel him. To touch his skin.

The last time he grabbed the backs of my thighs and pulled was when we were teenagers. The first time I felt his tongue rub against my sex, I thought I'd scream. I'm not sure if it was our age or our inexperience, but whatever it was, I quietly whimpered as he pushed me over the edge.

My sundress had been pushed over my waist, and we were down by the harbor in the cool green grass, late in the evening. I wasn't ready for sex yet. I thought Ryan was, but he never let me know. I could feel it when he kissed me, the way his hands moved, sometimes roughly, but he never asked. It was after prom when we reached our maximum capacity for everything but sex.

I know, the day he had seen my dress, he'd thought I was going with someone else. Why he'd thought that, I have no idea. But, when I'd asked him if he'd like to go, I'm not sure I got an answer because, when he'd stood, his kiss had come hard and fast.

My knees grow weak as he tugs at my hem once more, bringing me back to the present moment. I spread my legs—not by conscious thought, but by hope and want. I look down into his eyes, and they're shielded with the same desire. His lips are slightly parted, his jaw clenched, his hand still hanging on to my hem. I know what he needs, but I know what I want and what I need are two separate things.

Want is my desire for his body against mine. Inside me. Pushing me to the limit. And the slow quiver of recovery when the damage is done.

Need is my head protecting my heart. That this situation right here won't end well because I know I'll walk away from this, dragging my heart behind me, my regret in tow.

Thank God, Ryan's phone rings.

I suck in a deep breath of uncertainty and relief. Uncertainty of how this situation would have worked out had the phone not rung and relief that we didn't have to dig our way out of this. When a warden's work phone rings, they answer. No matter the circumstances because, if he doesn't, it could mean a real bad outcome.

Ryan drops his hand from the hem of my nightgown, and I don't step back when he carefully leans forward to retrieve his work phone from the nightstand. When he does this, his head almost brushes my thigh. I should move. I should step back, but I can't. I barely swallow. My heart still fluttering with no signs of slowing down, I know Ryan feels what I'm feeling right now.

If he had two good arms right now, I know he would have grabbed his work phone with one hand and the back of my thigh with the other and thrust me on top of him as I towered over him. But, instead, with his good arm, he grabs his work phone, pulls back, and winces, now his face a flurry of red, but I think it's from pain.

"Warden Taylor." His eyes burn into mine.

And, when there's a pause, I walk to the kitchen to grab his pain medication and some water.

I need to create some distance between us, I think.

I need to do things differently.

That can't happen again.

But why? my heart says.

My head chimes in, *Your past. Your heartache. Don't you remember?*

I do. All too well.

Create distance, my head says, trying to preserve what's been trying to heal for years.

Like with a scab, I just keep picking, hoping for a different outcome.

Things I tell myself:

Maybe you can give it one more chance. Maybe it won't hurt this time.

Maybe try it from this angle, and it won't feel so bad.

Try to leave it alone, ignore it, and stuff it down deep. Try to forget.

None of these have worked. The only one I haven't tried—giving myself to Ryan, isn't a price I'm willing to pay yet.

I take the two pain pills and the water to him.

"So, Eli asked me to go speak to the kids at Granite Harbor Elementary this morning," he says as I enter his bedroom again, pills and water in hand.

I look at the clock, trying to act normal as I hand him the pills. "What time?"

"Eight thirty a.m."

It's just after seven.

"Well, we'd better get moving if we want to make it on time."

"Are you all right with going?" he asks.

"Yes," I lie as I step back to create some distance between us. "Do you need help with your shoulder brace before you get in the shower?"

He takes both pills, not very willingly, and chases them with water.

He sees the look in my eyes.

Fear.

"No, I can handle it." He groans as he stands.

When our bodies are inches apart, my heart—my stupid, stupid heart—starts to pick up pace. Ryan pushes a strand of my hair from my face behind my ear and is careful about not touching my body before his good hand falls back to his side.

Step away, Merit.

"You ought to take a cold shower, Ryan." I take a few steps back, so I can breathe again. So that my heart stops annoying my chest.

Ryan smiles, drops his head, and laughs. "Yes, ma'am."

Ryan's work truck, because I've been driving his personal truck, isn't as hard to drive as I thought. He said the gears get stuck sometimes, but I haven't experienced it yet. I turn onto the highway toward Granite Harbor. I'm pretty sure non-wardens are not allowed to drive the warden trucks, but in this case, I don't care. It's for the kids.

I look over, and Ryan's black sunglasses are sitting on the bridge of his nose. I must say, he looks really good in his uniform. A uniform I'm all too familiar with. One that doesn't look quite as good on my brother or my father. This uniform looks particularly good on Ryan. It fits his chest, broad shoulders, and thick thighs in all the right places. My cheeks grow warm.

Get control of your thoughts, Merit. You're going to an elementary school, for God's sake.

"What are you going to say to the kids?" I ask, attempting to add conversation to the quiet truck.

"I'll wing it. Maybe I'll talk about some of the laws that wardens have to uphold. Maybe I'll let the little ones turn on the siren in the truck."

Ryan has always been good with kids. Exceptional.

"You could talk about water safety, too."

He nods, his good arm hanging from the handle above the door. "You're pretty good at driving the truck."

"Learned from this guy I know." I side-eye him.

When I was fifteen and Ryan and Eli were fourteen, we used to take Dubbs's truck and practice on the back roads of Maine when Dubbs was passed out, drunk. Ryan had learned because he had to pick up his dad whenever he called drunk from some god-awful place. Ryan taught himself, and then he taught Eli and me. Though, when Pop took us out for driving lessons, we pretended not to know as much as we did to give him the satisfaction of teaching.

We drive through Granite Harbor at fifteen after eight and take a left on School Road. The elementary school dead-ends the road.

Ryan, I'm sure, has been back to Granite Harbor Elementary many times in his career since we left the school, but it's nostalgic for me. The same musty smell from when I was a child fills me when we enter. Brings back both good feelings and bad. The large, cool hallway that houses each of the classroom doors takes me to my younger years. The trophy cases show pictures of past teams and athletes, past school board members, past principals. It's as if the child who walked the halls all those years ago is still the same but in a different body.

"This is weird," I say to Ryan as we make our way down the hallway. "I don't think I've set foot in here since we left."

"Warden Taylor!" a voice calls from behind us.

I turn with him.

"Ruby?" I say.

The redhead comes from the main office, bounding up to us. "Merit? Oh my goodness!" Ruby throws her arms around me.

I bring mine around her.

"I heard you were back in town. Taking care of this guy? Heard about the accident, Ryan, which is why I'm surprised to see you." Ruby turns back to me. "How are you? How have you been? I haven't seen you since … well, since you left Granite Harbor for California."

"I'm good," I lie. "Fantastic actually. Just helping out where I can." I casually put my hand to my stomach to the nonexistent itch that lives there—also called a lie.

Ruby eyes both of us and bites her lip. "Huh." She slides her phone from her back pocket. "What's your number, Merit? I'd love to catch up."

We exchange numbers while Ryan checks out the trophy case. Ruby Red was her nickname in elementary school because of her flaming-red hair and big smile. She was one of my only friends in elementary school and high school.

"You're a teacher here now, Ruby?"

"Principal, actually. We do this summer camp for the kids because of a grant we received about five years ago. It's specifically for science, and the warden service always comes out and gives us a great presentation. The kids love Warden Taylor." She stops. "Merit, didn't you become a marine biologist? I think Brand mentioned it sometime back when I ran into him at Ring's Pharmacy."

"I am."

She squeals. "Will you be here next summer?"

No.

Yes.

No. Maybe. Yes.

Probably not.

"I'm not sure." My stomach drops, and I don't dare look back at Ryan.

"I hope so, Ruby," Ryan calls out from the trophy case.

"Me, too," Ruby whispers as she links arms with me. She walks Ryan and me down the hallway to the gymnasium.

There are about seventy eager kids with about six camp leaders. And, when Ruby Red whistles with her fingers, the entire gym freezes into their favorite animal pose.

"Granite Harbor scientists! We have a special guest this morning. Take your seats on your dots, and we'll get started."

Several kids, about eight and nine, rush to Ryan.

"Warden Taylor, what happened? Why do you have that black thing on?" one kid with no front teeth asks, glasses sitting on the bridge of his nose. His eyes appear larger than they actually are.

Carefully, Ryan gets down on one knee to talk to him. "I had a run-in with a bear."

If the kid's eyes could grow any bigger, they would. They're huge now. The children's mouths are open as they stare at Ryan.

"You fought a bear?" one asks.

"Not really. I hit one with my truck on accident. He was a pretty big bear." Ryan shows the height and width of the moose with his hands. "Unfortunately, the moose didn't make it."

"My name is Blake. What do you mean, he didn't make it?" the smallest of the crowd of kids asks.

"He passed away, Blake."

"He went to sleep?" Blake blinks.

"No, he died."

"The moose died?" he repeats.

"Yes."

"And you didn't die." Blake reaches out and touches Ryan's good arm to confirm. "You're still warm." He stares at Ryan. "My uncle Lee died in Megunticook Lake." He's matter-of-fact. "His body was co-old. I got to touch it."

Ryan nods. "I remember."

"My mom says he was an asshole."

"Okay, campers"—Ruby walks up behind us—"time to get started."

Sixteen

Merit
Granite Harbor, Maine
Prom Night
April 2001

Ryan shows up at the house, and Eli answers the door.
Before Eli can say anything, Ryan pretends he's bothered that he has to go. "Can't believe you asked me to do this."

"Thanks, asshole." Eli holds open the door. "Merit, Ryan's here," he calls upstairs.

I take a deep breath and one last look in the hallway mirror.

Pop appears in the doorway of the room he and Mom shared and rests his hand at his waist, still in uniform. "You look just like your mother, Mer." He smiles.

I roll my eyes. "Pop, you're not going to cry, are you?"

"No, because that will make you cry, and we can't have you smearing that black stuff you put on your eyelashes, which you don't need, by the way. You're beautiful—"

"Just the way you are," we finish the sentence together.

"I know; I know. You say it all the time. I never wear makeup, Pop. Only on special occasions."

"So, how did this all work? You agreeing to go with Ryan and your brother and Grace?"

"Eli gave me fifty dollars and paid for my dress in exchange for me asking Ryan to go with me, so then we'd double with him and Grace."

"Huh. Well, if you're going to go with anyone, I'm glad it's Ryan, honey."

Me, too.

But, instead, I nod nonchalantly as if I don't care either way. If Ryan had asked someone else or gotten asked by someone else, it might have broken my heart a little. No, a lot.

"You need money?" Pop asks as I give him a peck on the cheek.

"Nope. I've got fifty dollars burning a hole in my pocket."

"You sure?"

"Pop, I've got it."

Quietly, he nods, takes my cheeks in his hands, and kisses my forehead. "I love you, Bug."

"Love you, too, Pop." I give him a tight hug. "Don't stay up too late, waiting for us."

He will though. He always does. I think the things he's seen in his life, in his career as a game warden, are things you'll never forget.

Rescuing adults and children from bodies of water.

Recovering adults' and children's bodies from water.

Recovering bodies of teenagers who'd tried to make it across the ice on their snowmobiles, drunk.

Arriving on the scene to car accidents.

Drug overdoses.

Pop has never been shy in showing us the photos. Does he try to protect us from the bad guys? Yes. But does he show us the realities of making poor choices? Never misses an opportunity. I think that's why Eli and I have stayed on the straight and narrow. We've tasted alcohol before but never taken full advantage of underage drinking, for fear of what it'll do to us. Or maybe because, since we live in such a small town, we know it will get back to Pop. And I'm not sure if we are more scared of paying for the poor choices or breaking Pop's heart.

In the two seconds it takes me to walk down the stairs, I allow myself enough time to overthink the situation of seeing Ryan in a tuxedo. Or him seeing me in my dress. I just march downstairs, grab my handbag, and look up. Staring at me are my brother and Ryan.

While I try not to look at Ryan, I can't help but steal a quick glance at his broad, square shoulders filling his tux. His stormy eyes with long eyelashes gaze back.

"Well, you don't look ugly, Bug. That's good." Eli smiles.

"Let's get this over with. I got an episode of *90210* I'm recording on the VCR." But, really, I'm dying in anticipation—not to watch the episode, but to kiss Ryan on the lips. To feel his hands slide around my hips. To feel him harden between my legs. My face grows warm. "You guys ready or what?"

While Eli gets in his truck, Ryan opens my door, and I try my best to act casual when I smell his cologne.

It's still light out when we pull out of our lane and drive to Grace's house in town. We follow Eli to Grace's. Ryan turns off his Jeep after we pull in behind Eli, as he jumps out and goes inside to get Grace. We drove separately at my request. There was no way I could spend an evening with Grace ogling over my brother.

I can barely breathe, and it isn't because of the dress.

"You're the prettiest thing I've ever seen, Mer," Ryan whispers, tapping his fingers on his steering wheel, looking straight ahead, his jaw tight.

I don't waste any time, and I lean over to place my lips on his cheek, but he turns, so my lips fall on his. I know we shouldn't do this. Not in broad daylight.

Damn you, daylight savings.

I feel his restraint. He knows I don't want Eli to know about us. But I can't help it. Not right now. I coax his lips open with mine.

"Are you sure?" he whispers against my lips.

I gently put my tongue in his mouth. At first, I'm soft, but as my need increases, and the ache between my legs deepens, I know we need to stop.

His hands slide to my hips, as he wants to pull me to him, but he stops himself. Pulls away. "I can't do this. Not in here. Not right now." Ryan takes his thumb and slides it across my lips, his look devouring me. "Because, if I do this right here, I'm not sure I'll be able to stop, Mer. And I really want to dance with you first."

I sink back to my side of the Jeep, my stomach in knots, twisting and turning with excitement.

"Here comes Ida." I try to push the red from my cheeks and fix my bangs, as if we didn't just make out.

"Hey, you two. Headed to prom?" Ida's black sunglasses shield her eyes from the spring sun making its way to light the dark part of the world.

"Yes, ma'am," Ryan says. "Where are you headed?"

"Uptown. Grocery store. Need to pick up a few things. Well, have a good time."

"Bye, Ida," I say.

Ida's timely interruption helped cool the tension, the electricity, in the Jeep. As Ida walks toward Granite Harbor Grocery, Eli and Grace come out from her house.

"That's a pretty dress," I say about Grace's dress.

"Liar." Ryan smirks.

"I mean, if you're into red."

Ryan laughs a slow, throaty laugh.

We pull into the packed parking lot at Granite Harbor High, and we all make it into the dance.

We take pictures.

We drink punch.

We watch the Malcomb grandsons get plastered.

We watch the principal take them outside.

"We should dance," Ryan whispers in my ear in the darkness as I watch Eli and Grace make out in the corner. "Come on. I promise you, he's not paying attention to us."

One dance. One dance, and no one will know any better.

"One dance."

It's dark in our gym, and many of the partygoers have left for prom after-parties. Or rather, one big party out at the beach.

But, before my body gets to his, he reaches for my fingers and gives me a quick tug. It's a tug that explains the need for me to be next to him. It's both forceful and soft. Our fancy fabrics give us a barrier, a safe haven, when our bodies touch. He firmly places his hands on the small of my back and sighs into my ear, sending chills down my spine. I rest my hands on his shoulders and keep my head next to his. In the most quiet, still way, Ryan drops his head, as if he's going to whisper something into my ear, but instead, he presses his lips to my neck, and he lingers there. I feel my knees grow weak.

My heart isn't skipping a beat, I think to myself. *If it skips a beat, that will most likely mean death. Or that I have some sort of heart condition.* I try to distract my mind from the way my body is responding to Ryan's touch.

I believe Ryan is holding me up and that my feet aren't touching the floor. And that he's taking me to a place that might lead to teen pregnancy. Pop has given us many lectures on safety, making the right choices, but never sex. I mean, he might have with Eli, but it's a subject that has remained untouched with Pop and me. Sex education can cover only so much. But I've seen movies. I know what happens.

"Ryan," I say breathlessly as his hands tighten around my backside, "let's go."

Sex education does not prepare you for the feelings, the hormones, that your body will fight against you, telling you it's all right and that it will feel good. Because Ryan's body against mine right now feels too good.

He walks away from me, leaving me in the middle of the dance floor, alone. He interrupts Eli and Grace and whispers something into Eli's ear. He comes back, tightly grabs my hand, and ushers me out of the gym.

At his Jeep, before he opens the door, he squares up against me, taking my jaw in his hands, gently moving my head to the side, and pushes his lips against my neck. I feel his teeth nibble against my neck, and I quietly call out—not out of hurt, but need.

Ryan stops. Drops his hands, moves back, giving us a few inches of space. Runs his hands through his hair. "Mer, we can't do this."

"What?" I reach out for him, beckoning him, my legs still spread just a bit, in preparation for what I want him to do to me.

He comes back to me, quick and hard, lifting the hem of my dress, exposing my panties. He stares. Marvels. His eyes then meet mine, and he crashes against me. I feel him adjust himself so that his sex meets my middle. Slowly, he moves against me. I want to pull my panties aside, thinking about how good this feels right now. He keeps his sex right at the top of mine and moves quicker.

"God, Merit," he whispers in my ear with restraint.

I spread my legs more. He reaches up and lifts my legs, hoisting them around his waist.

Softly, I come unglued in his ear as I squeeze my eyes shut, and white stars dance in my head.

His scent.

The feeling of him against me.

I feel the wetness in my panties.

But Ryan stops. "We're not doing this right here, Merit. We can't. You aren't losing your virginity in the high school parking lot."

"Don't stop, Ryan. Please," I beg, want slipping through my lips as I trail kisses down his jaw.

He throbs against me. "I don't have a condom with me. We can't."

I feel the head of his sex at my middle through his pants. I want him to remove what separates us, to feel him entirely.

I reach down for his zipper.

He sighs in my ear with one hand against his Jeep. The other one wrapped around my waist.

Slowly, I attempt to unzip his zipper, but I'm in the way.

Ryan freezes. "No."

"Please," I beg.

My legs tighten around his back.

"No." He stops abruptly, carefully setting me down on my feet.

My breasts ache, my middle aches, my head is foggy, and I can't see straight as my dress falls to its rightful position.

Zipping up his pants, he shakes his head, creating more space between us. "As much …" He pauses. "As much as I want to do this with you … God, as good as you look …" He moves closer. "Mer, I love you too much to do this with you in a parking lot."

The world stops rotating.

The sun stops rising. Stops setting.

Time is on hold.

"You-you love me?"

"Hey, guys!" The shadows of Eli and Grace make their way toward us.

Ryan laughs and explodes with a, "Hey!" It's artificial.

"You guys ready?" Ryan slides his hands together, trying to act normal but totally not giving off the normal vibe.

"Think we're going to call it a night and head to Grace's house," Eli says. But what he's really saying is, *I need alone time with Grace.*

"Curfew is midnight," I tell Eli as the older sister. "If you're not home by 12:01 a.m., I'm telling Pop." I say this only to protect my little brother, out of my distrust for Grace. I make sure she sees me.

I'm not sure what it is about her. Maybe it's her lack of eye contact with me. Or anyone for that matter. Her lack of words for Pop and me. Pop always makes sure we look people in the eye. Says it's a sign of truth. Confidence. It's respect. Apparently, the Ebscotts, Grace's parents, didn't teach her that. I shouldn't doubt her for that.

I'm so glad it's dark because my cheeks are flushed, and I assume my dress is more wrinkled than it was before.

"You two kids have fun!" Ryan says, still acting awkward as Eli and Grace load in his truck and drive away. "Oh my God," Ryan says, rubbing his face with his hands. He looks to me. "That was close, Mer. Too close."

Seventeen

Merit
Granite Harbor, Maine
Present Day

I stand back as Ryan talks to the seventy-plus kids about what game wardens do—from chasing bad guys in the woods to finding lost hikers.

A little girl raises her hand. "Warden Taylor, have you had to shoot a bad guy?"

"No. Thankfully, I have not."

Another child asks, "What about a tiger? Have you had to shoot a tiger?"

"No. No, I have not. Tigers aren't animals that live in our woods."

"What if he got loose from the zoo?"

Ryan smiles. "Well, then, I'd try my best not to shoot the tiger but instead try to get him back to the zoo as safely as possible."

Blake, the little boy from earlier, asks, "Warden Taylor, why don't you have hair on the top of your head?"

Ryan laughs a real, genuine laugh, and I feel the wall inside me crack just a little bit. The wall I've put up to shelter my heart. My protective barrier. I feel his smile deep within my own little cracks of vulnerability. The cracks I can't control. The cracks that have been building. Becoming bigger, exposing me a little more.

"Because hair would just get in the way. It makes being a game warden easier."

Blake stares, focusing on Ryan's answer but also pondering his next question. "My mom just uses a hair tie. She has another one if you want to have hair again."

Then the crowd gasps.

In walks my brother with Rookie.

Ruby excitedly rushes to Eli. "Thank you for coming," she whispers.

Eli nods and walks to Ryan, and the two men stand in front of the group of kids. Rookie pushes on Ryan's leg with his nose, and Ryan reaches down and gives him a good pat.

Rookie sits.

"These are my friends Eli and Rookie."

The kids so badly want to rush to Rookie, getting antsy while sitting in their seats, on their hands. But they know they can't.

"Hey, kids! Who knows what a K9 unit is?" Eli begins.

From the doorway of the gymnasium, I watch two of the most important men in my life entertain and educate our youth about water safety, making good choices, and following the laws.

If I'm being honest, Ryan is an important piece of my past. He owns many of my childhood memories, mostly good ones. Even the bad ones. And, somehow, watching him with my brother makes me want to fall even harder for him, seeing how he's overcome what he's had to in order to get here today. It doesn't mean that I have to fall in love with him again. But it means that I can still love him, appreciate his past, my past, because maybe things don't have to happen to us; they happen for us.

In groups of five, the kids come up and pet Rookie, and Ryan takes another larger group out to his patrol truck.

"Think you can help us keep the kids together at Ryan's truck?" Ruby asks.

"Absolutely."

"My name's Olivia. What's yours?"

I look down at her hand in mine. She's no older than seven. My heart twists and contorts as I see her fingers in mine.

I take in a big breath of air. "Hi, Olivia. I'm Merit."

She drops her head to the right and pulls her top lip back, exposing her toothless grin. She thinks on it. "I like it." We walk out to Ryan's truck. "Do you like tigers?"

"They're beautiful creatures," I say.

"Yeah, I wanna be a tiger when I grow up."

I don't dare laugh. "Why do you want to be a tiger?"

"Because they're pretty, and they run fast."

A little boy hits Ryan's sirens, and Olivia takes off.

"Bye, Merit!" She waves back.

"Bye, Olivia. Nice to meet you."

I watch as Ryan interacts with the kids. Picking them up. Showing them buttons on the vehicle, his computer that sits on the dashboard, and how he can work from anywhere.

"Whoa! Are those guns?" another little boy asks.

"Yes."

The kids in the truck look up and see the two guns locked to the ceiling of the cab.

"A shotgun and a rifle. But wardens only touch those when it is absolutely necessary."

The kids move on with their questions after a brief silence.

Kids pile out of the work truck, and one little boy pulls on Ryan's pants. "Warden Young? Who's that lady? Is that your girlfriend?"

Ryan's eyes meet mine.

There are defining moments in our lives when we question if honesty is always the best policy. Will the truth protect me? Will the truth hurt someone else? Or is the right answer the wrong answer?

Seconds pass.

And we're still staring at each other, and I feel his eyes on mine, staring right through me, cracking the wall a little more.

"She used to be. Now, she's a real good friend."

"So, she is your girlfriend?" the extra-smart little boy asks.

Ryan shrugs. A smile begins. "Yeah, buddy, I guess you're right."

"Good, because she's really pretty." He smiles.

"All right, campers! Back to the gym! Bubble Jim is up next."

The kids, with help from some of the camp leaders, pile back into the gymnasium, leaving Ryan and me alone by the truck.

I look over at Ryan after a long silence. "You're really good with kids." And I can't help but say, "You would have been good with ours."

I see the searing pain that starts just beyond his eyes, making its way down to his heart.

"Come on, Rookie!" We hear Eli calling.

We turn just in time to see Rookie barreling around the corner and straight for Ryan, who bends down and gives Rookie big love, putting his head to his fur.

"Hey, buddy."

Rookie rubs his nose on me, and I, too, reach down and love on him.

"Big baby," Eli says as he walks to the truck. "Really interesting to see him with kids now. The dynamic has changed. He used to be more work, work, work, and now, he's more interested in the little humans, ever since Emily was born anyway. I think Rookie has taken on the role of protective older brother."

"How do Larry and Rookie get along?"

Larry is Alex's Maine Coon cat; she brought him from Belle's Hollow.

"Two peas in a pod. I'm convinced that Larry thinks he's a dog, too. He sleeps with Rookie on his bed. Grooms him." Eli rolls his eyes. "It's pathetic."

Ryan's still loving on Rookie. I think it's his way of avoiding the conversation, maybe because old feelings have come up from what I said earlier.

"How are the shoulder and ribs?" Eli asks.

Ryan finally stands, sore. "Better."

Whether he thinks he's doing better or it's the pain medication, I'm not sure. I guess only time will tell.

"Drinks tonight at Angler's Tavern? I'm off at five unless something comes up."

Terrified, I don't look at Ryan. If I look at Ryan, it will seem more like we're a couple seeking input on plans. Plans that we don't have. Input that shouldn't involve Ryan *and* Merit. But rather, Ryan period. Merit period.

"I'm free," I say. Not, *We're free.*

I don't keep Ryan's agenda. His calendar.

"I'm good, too. No plans." Ryan follows suit.

Eli curiously eyes both of us. "All right then. You ready, Rookie?" Rookie's licking his nether regions. Looks up at Eli. Blinks. "All right. Truck." And Rookie bounds to the warden truck that's parked next to Ryan's. "About six?"

"Sounds good," I say awkwardly.

Ryan tosses the keys in my direction. He used them when he showed the kids around the truck.

"Warden Taylor, Warden Taylor!" Blake comes running out with a handwritten note. "I want to give this to you."

Ryan, with pain this time, barely bends over. "Hey, bud. What have you got there?"

"It's a picture of you getting the bad guy." Blake looks at Ryan.

"Thank you, Blake. Wow. I'll hang this on my refrigerator, so I can see it every morning before I go to work."

Blake smiles proudly, and then he grows shy and stares at his feet. There's another drawing behind his back.

"Do you have something else for me?"

"Yeah." But he's quieter about this one. After a few seconds of silence, he pulls the other picture from behind his back. "This is for your dog."

Ryan tilts his head to the side and takes a look. "But, buddy, I don't have a dog."

Blake grows uncomfortable.

I peek over Ryan's shoulder. It's a picture of a gray-colored dog. On the collar of the dog is written, *Heeewow.*

What?

"There's a dog that follows you, Warden Taylor." He stalls. "My mommy gets scared when I draw stuff like this."

I can't pull a thought together right now. I'm almost certain Ryan feels the same, if not even more overwhelmed.

"When I drew a picture of my dad behind my mommy one day, she started to cry."

Ryan touches Blake's shoulder. "What color was your dad in the drawing, Blake?"

"Gray."

"Yeah?"

Blake nods.

Ryan's quiet for a moment before he speaks. Ryan has never talked about Hero with me since his dad backed over him when we were teenagers. "Hero was my dog when I was a kid. I got him when I was your age. He went to heaven, just like your dad did."

Blake nods again. "Gray people are in heaven. That's what my mom told my grandma anyway."

"Yeah." Ryan touches the boy's shoulder again. "I think you and I both can use a hug right about now."

The boy, with ease, slides into Ryan's arms.

Tears start to form in my eyes. I think Ryan needs this. I think Blake needs this. Maybe things happen in the exact time that they're supposed to happen.

Maybe.

"Thank you," Ryan tells Blake. "And I have something for you. Stay put." Ryan opens the passenger door and grabs a plastic badge from the glove compartment where he keeps ten on hand at any given time because he loves kids.

Blake's eyes light up. "Thanks, Warden Taylor." Then, he turns to me. "Thanks, Bug."

My heart comes to a speeding halt.

What? What did he just call me?

Ryan looks at me, his face about the shade of white that I probably am. He looks back at Blake. "What did you call her, bud?"

Blake looks past me—or through me. I'm not sure which. "The woman behind you, she said to call you Bug." He stops. "She's a gray person, too."

My mother.

Knees weak, I just need a minute. Everything inside me wants to turn and look, but I know Blake can see things, hear things, that most people can't. A metallic taste in my mouth spreads, like a warm liquid.

I swallow.

To a child, it's so innocent. It's as simple as, *I see something. Here it is. It's gray. Sometimes, what I see talks.* That's it.

There's no overthinking it.

But, for adults, we tend to mash it up. Make it messy. Make it weird. Scary maybe. Through a child's eyes, it's uncomplicated. They say or draw what they see.

What Blake sees and hears isn't complicated. It's fact, it's concrete, it's evidence, and he just has the sensitivity and the openness to see it.

So, I don't scare him. I don't feed him the bullshit messiness that adults create around things like this. But I do bend down, take his little hand in mine, and thank him. I don't allow him to see the shock that's making my body vibrate. I allow him to see the gift he's given Ryan and me today.

"Thank you, Blake. You made my heart so happy."

Eighteen

Ryan
Granite Harbor, Maine
Present Day

Mer and I get in the truck. Shut the door. Sit. Wait for a moment to gain clarity of what just happened.

Still in my hands are the pictures Blake handed me. Hero in gray. The dog that made my life bearable. The times he protected me as I tried to sleep, waiting for Dubbs to come into my room, drunk. The cigarette burns happened when Hero was stuck outside.

I laugh out loud.

Merit looks over at me. Watching me.

She catches on. Giggles at first, but then starts laughing until she's crying. I let her cry. She needs to. She's crying for me. I know. I think, too, she's probably in shock. Neither of us expected Blake to draw the ghost of my dead dog. We also didn't anticipate Blake to talk about Rebecca, her mom.

"What the hell just happened?" she asks, more rhetorically.

I shake my head, knowing the heaviness of the situation, yet my brain can't quite comprehend the reality of it all.

"Do you need to do anything in town?" Merit asks.

"We could grab something to eat? Take it down by the harbor? Like old times."

Merit's eyes search the road. The harbor is a spot that means a lot to both of us. It's where we spent time as kids, trying to catch a break. Put life on pause.

Merit slowly nods. "Harbor, yeah."

"Grab sandwiches at Granite Harbor Grocery?" I suggest.

"Yeah."

It's just after eleven thirty a.m. As we drive down Main Street, it's not too busy in town yet. Though the tourists are starting to gather on both sides of Main.

"We could walk Main. We have some time to kill. We could wander aimlessly, like we used to as kids. With no agenda. No breaks. And time on our hands." Really, all I want is just time with her. Trying to bring back old memories maybe. Make her remember all the good times we had together.

She pulls into a spot near the post office.

"I'll run into Rick's and change real quick." I pause as a sharp pain shoots through my abdomen, knowing the pain medication is wearing off.

You've got to have pain in life, Ryan. That's the only way to know you're still alive.

"I'll go with you." Merit meets me at the sidewalk.

"Excuse me, can you point us in the direction of the harbor?" a woman in a large-brimmed straw hat with a white nose lathered in sunscreen asks.

Her husband, in a matching hat with hands stuck deep in his pockets, stands behind her, staring at our old buildings. "*Beauty-full* place you got here." He whistles through his teeth.

"The harbor runs parallel to Main Street. You can take a left down any of the side streets, and that will get you to the harbor." I motion with my hands.

"Thank you, Officer."

"You're welcome."

They cross the street and head down to the harbor.

We walk into Rick's, and I make my way to the counter as Merit peruses.

"Warden Young," Rick says. "What brings you in today?"

"I just need to use your back room to change."

"Absolutely. Come on back. Reminds me of when you guys were kids. But you're older. Taller. Much bigger now. I can remember when you had no front teeth and that dog always followed you around."

"Hi, Rick." I hear Merit say from behind me. "Do you still have double-sided tape?"

Rick is a talker. He'd talk your ear off all goddamn afternoon if you let him.

"Well, Merit Young, it is so good to see you back in Granite Harbor." Rick walks out from behind the counter to meet Merit. Rick is a walking encyclopedia of weird facts. Don't get him started on double-sided tape.

I smirk as I look back at Merit, watching Rick talk about the bonds of double-sided tape. Where it was invented and why it was invented. Quickly, she looks back at me, and I wink.

I mime the words, *Thank you*, and head to the back room.

On my way out, Boom, the office cat, is lying on the old staircase that leads up to Rick's living quarters above the pharmacy. Boom must be about ten years old. His broken meow sounds just like it did we found him.

Boom lost his right eye when he was a kitten. I was brand-new to the warden service and found him in a gutter just south of town on my way out of town. He'd already been missing his eye, but it was fairly fresh, so I put him in the truck with me. I had to run into the pharmacy to pick up a few things and brought the little guy in with me. I'd planned to take him to the Granite Harbor Veterinary Clinic afterward, but Rick seemed to take a liking to the little kitten and decided to take him.

I give Boom a quick rubdown on his perch. "Good to see you, old friend."

With a broken meow, he yawns, stretching out his paw.

"And that's why double-sided tape should be kept in every home." I hear Rick say.

Merit's eyes are glazed over. "You're right; I'll buy some."

Rick turns.

Merit's eyes grow big as she stares at me. *You owe me big,* she mouths.

I smile and nod. She meets me at the counter and throws down the double-sided tape, and Rick's assistant rings her up.

"Come again soon, you two," Rick calls from behind the counter.

We wave.

"Will do, Rick," I say.

Merit throws a little bag with double-sided tape in the truck as I hang my uniform in the cab part of the truck.

The sidewalks are quickly beginning to fill up as we make our way across the street to Granite Harbor Grocery.

"I've got it, Hulk." Merit beats me to the door. "What are you staring at?" Merit's head is next to mine.

"Isn't that the guy who was with Dubbs on the porch the other day?"

Merit squints. Watches the man. "That's him. I remember the scar on his cheek. What the hell is he doing back in Granite Harbor again? There's no way he's from here."

"I don't know, but we need to stop by Dubbs's house before we leave." Something tells me this situation isn't fucking right. I take a quick picture with my phone. Though grainy, it warrants a Google search later.

We take our sandwiches and walk down to the harbor. We take our seat next to our tree, just down a ways from the main traffic of the harbor.

"So," I start, "you rehabilitate river otters."

Merit finishes her bite as I take another.

"Did you know you wanted to do this straight out of college? That's a pretty specific job."

She shrugs. "I knew I wanted to work with marine life. River otters just fell in my lap."

"Like what you do?" I set my sandwich down and take a drink of water.

"Pays the bills. I've been at the aquarium for so long; it's what I know."

I nod. "And you feel comfortable in that?"

Merit takes a bite.

Violet Ugly

On one hand, she's always been a creature of habit. As if I have room to talk. Lived in Granite Harbor. Only moved to Hallowell because I have to live in the district I patrol. Never leaving Maine unless it's absolutely necessary.

But Merit moved from coast to coast.

"What's California like? It's not really palm trees, movie stars, and beaches, right?"

"Southern California is similar to that. I'm not sure about movie stars though." She laughs. "I live in the middle of the state. It's on the coast, like here, but the beaches are sandy. Doesn't get as warm in the summer as Granite Harbor. We get the fog. People are different. Not as friendly as they are here." She shrugs. "Could be because we know everyone. I don't know what an outsider's perception would be of our people, but I suppose"—Merit looks at our now-packed streets—"we must be doing something right."

Merit watches a family moving down the harbor, collecting shells, a dog in tow. She looks away as she takes another bite of her sandwich, pushing a strand of her fallen hair from her face.

"What?" She takes her napkin and wipes her face with her long, slender fingers.

I remember what those feel like. Her nails against my chest, my back.

"Nothing," I say, trying to push the thoughts from my head.

"Do I have something on my face?"

"No."

"Why are you staring at me like I have a deformity?"

"Well, you do. It starts right here." I reach over, take my finger, and slide it across her jawline. I watch her entire body change in slow motion.

Her body tenses.

Her breathing hitches.

And she freezes.

"H-how's my jaw a deformity?" she asks.

When I get this reaction, I know it's my fingers that do this to her.

Just as I'm about to tell her how her perfect jawline, her bone structure, is a deformity, Lydia walks up.

"Hey, Merit! I heard you were back in town."

Merit stands to hug Lydia.

When Lydia first moved to town, we slept together. Went on a few dates. My way of trying to rid myself of Merit.

"Hey, asshole." Lydia turns to me.

I almost choke on my water.

"I'm kidding, Ryan." She tosses a hand at me.

I deserve that. I am an asshole. She's not kidding.

Lydia bought a bookstore in town about three years ago, which was about the time I heard some guy had asked Merit to marry him. Eli had casually mentioned it in conversation one day.

I was angry.

Hostile.

Fucking pissed.

Jealous.

I'd have slept with anyone if that meant I could chase Merit from my thoughts. None of that worked. Not a fucking thing. Lydia and I especially didn't work. But we both knew that.

I watch as they exchange words, sentences in conversation, one I have no business being in. I turn my attention to the harbor and listen to the seals.

It's amazing how quick our town fills up every summer. We double in population but not size, making it hard to accommodate extra bodies.

"You, too." I hear Merit say.

"Bye, Ryan."

"Lydia." I nod.

"Guess she doesn't like you?" Merit asks.

I want to tell her. I want to tell her I slept with Lydia. I want to tell her what a whore I turned into after she left. But she knows. Telling her would only cause her more hurt. She left her job in California to come help take care of me. She wouldn't be here if she didn't care. We've got too much history together. By telling her that I slept with someone who didn't matter, how would that make her feel better? By telling her, I'd only be trying to clear my own conscience. So, I decide not to tell her. What would I say anyway?

Oh, Lydia? I let her suck my dick a few times. She's a great blow. But nothing like you, Merit. Never. Nobody has ever reached the level that you and I had.

That's why I always make it a thing, never to kiss any woman on the lips. Whether I'm fucking them or we're doing other shit. My lips have always been for Merit.

"Guess not. Want to take a walk?"

Merit stands and grabs her trash and mine.

"I can take our trash—"

"Shut it, Ryan. I don't want to hear it," she says.

I smile as I watch her take our garbage to the trash can.

"What's with Lydia?" she asks as she walks back.

I can't—no, I won't lie to her. "You want to know the truth?" I know it will kill her, but I also know I can't lie to her again.

She hesitates at first but then says, "No."

Nineteen

Merit
Granite Harbor, Maine
Christmas Eve 1995

Ryan's shivering on the porch. I have no idea how he got here. My heart wants to jump right out of my chest and grab him from the cold.

"Well, what are you doing on the porch? Come in," Eli says, standing in front of me.

I move back as Ryan walks past us. Hero at his heels.

I bend down and take Hero's face in my hands. "You're cold, too, boy." I put his muzzle in my neck and then stand and walk to the kitchen, grabbing a few dog treats.

The fireplace provides warmth as the Christmas tree lights twinkle, providing the only light in our living room aside from the fire.

"Where's your dad?" Ryan asks, looking at both Eli and me.

"Shower. Just got home from work," Eli says. "Ryan, it's snowing like hell out there. You and Hero walked here?"

Ryan bites his lip. Stares at the fire. "Dubbs finally passed out."

I can tell in the way that he sits, that Ryan's sore.

"What'd he do to you, Ryan?" My tone is terrible. Hostile. I want to take Dubbs, tie him to a pole, and beat the living shit out of him.

"Nothin'."

It's Ryan's go-to line. The one that keeps us out of trouble. The lie he tells us, so Dubbs won't come after us.

It's our first Christmas without Mom. I tried to make her potato salad and miserably failed. The ham is dry. The biscuits are burned. Eli said we could scrape off the top, but I'm tenacious, and I insisted that I make new ones. The oven dings, and I walk in the kitchen, hoping to give some space to Eli and Ryan. I hope Ryan tells him what happened. Ryan's always been so strong, too strong, and I know, one day, it will catch up to him. I know, one day, he'll fall apart. At least tell someone else what Dubbs does to him.

Hero's nails click across the hardwood floor, following me to the kitchen. He knows Ryan is safe here.

Hero sniffs the air and sits as I pull the freshly made biscuits from the oven.

That's more like it, I say to myself.

While I can't remake the ham and potato salad, at least the biscuits will be all right.

I hear their voices, Ryan's and Eli's, whispering so low that I can't make out what they're saying. Part of me is scared to know. Part of me doesn't want to know the beating Ryan took because I can't manage both my sadness without Mom and knowing that Dubbs is slowly killing his son, whether it be emotionally or physically. Deep down though, I know it's Ryan's spirit that will die first. He'll never show Dubbs that his kicks, punches, or cigarette burns hurt him.

A whine escapes my throat, and I quickly slap my hand against my mouth. Tears threaten my eyes, and I choke the sob back.

Enough, Merit.

Slowly, I release my mouth from my own hand. I look at Hero, whose head is cocked, ears perked. The biscuits are too hot to give him, so instead, I grab a few more treats, wondering when he and Ryan ate last. I bet the truth is, Ryan gave Hero what he found at his house, or he saved leftovers from last night's dinner at our house to split.

"You should stay with us tonight." Eli's voice sounds like a man's. Like a father talking to his son. "You don't want to go back there, so don't."

Hero chomps down on the treats.

I listen to two best friends dealing with problems that they shouldn't have to deal with.

Ryan asks, "How's Merit?"

I hear Eli sigh.

Does he really know how bad I hurt? While I try to hide behind the stove, the housework, school, I know I can't fool my own family. Or Ryan.

"Shitty," he whispers.

Ryan doesn't ask how Eli's doing. I guess boys don't talk about feelings to each other. Or at least, my brother and Ryan don't. Maybe that's boy code. Or man code. Or whatever.

I hear Pop's footsteps coming down the stairs, and quickly, I hide behind the biscuits, checking their doneness with a toothpick, hiding my face from his so that he won't feel my sadness.

Eli's right; I am shitty. All I want is my mom back.

All I want is for Ryan's dad to stop hurting him.

All I want is someone to tell.

"Hey, Ryan."

Hero groans deep within his throat as he runs at my dad, sitting at his feet.

"Hey, buddy." Pop gives him a good rubdown. "Merry Christmas. Did you get some treats?" he asks.

Why couldn't Ryan get a dad like mine?

"Smells good in here, Bug." He gives my shoulder a quick squeeze.

We all feel the weight of my mom's loss. The big black hole that screams her name. Pop tries to play the part of a happy dad, a law enforcement officer, but really, he's dying inside, too. I hear it when I'm in bed, and he gets home from work and gets in the shower late at night or in the mornings when it's still dark, and he's lying in bed.

"Dinner's ready," I say.

My mom taught me a lot about cooking. How to baste a turkey, how to get the biscuits to a golden brown, how to add salt to boiling water for flavor. How to cook with a Dutch oven.

Eli and Ryan make their way into the kitchen and seat themselves at the table that Eli already set.

Ryan helps me move the ham, potato salad, and biscuits to the square table. Hero has his own bowl of food, and I get it ready on the counter with ham, some potato salad, and a biscuit.

The four of us sit in our own sadness, and we wait for food to heal our hearts.

But it doesn't.

It sits like a wound.

An open wound that keeps breaking open. One that won't heal. One that needs attention. One that's getting infected. But I'd take a scab wound any day over grief. I'd take it over this knot in my stomach, a plague that spreads throughout my entire body when I wake up.

My mom won't be there to greet me in the kitchen.

Dubbs will continue to hit Ryan until he's old enough to stand up for himself.

We finish eating, and Pop does the dishes. He won't stand or take argument from me about doing them on Christmas.

We go back to the darkened living room where the only lights are the lights from the Christmas tree and the flicker of the fire.

The change of lighting gives me ease.

I watch Ryan as he eases down onto the couch. He looks in my direction because he knows I'm watching his every move. He doesn't flinch, which also gives my heart a little satisfaction, knowing that it might not hurt him to sit.

It's as if he says, *I'm all right. This is okay. I'll be okay.*

His face is stoic—not because it doesn't hurt, but for me and Eli. Dubbs takes it upon himself to hit Ryan where no one can see the marks.

When Pop, Eli, and Ryan watch the football game, I curl up in a ball at the end of the couch, next to the people I love most in the world. I chase sleep I know will not fulfill my need, but my eyelids beg for mercy. So, I give them some.

Hero sleeps by the fire, content.

Hollering.

I jump awake.

A man's tone.

More hollering.

My brain is trying to catch up to where the pieces of the puzzle fall.

Pop is at the door.

Eli and Ryan are behind him.

Hero is gnashing his teeth at whoever is standing in front of them.

"Just go home, Dubbs, and sleep it off." Pop is cool, like a morning layer of fog.

"I wan' my son."

"Go home, Dad. I'll be home tomorrow," Ryan says.

Hero growls.

"Chrissmas, for God's sakes. Home with me." His voice slurs.

What's inside me wants to explode. I want to rage against Dubbs. Scream at him. Give him every reason why he shouldn't have a son. But I don't. I just stand behind Ryan. His shaking body. His broken body. His resilient body.

But I do stare down Dubbs as his eyes roll back in his head, floundering for answers that he'll never find because he's too drunk to find them.

"Go, Dubbs. Now," Pop says in his official game warden voice.

Somehow, after a moment, Dubbs turns in the dead of winter with the cold and the snow. Without falling but in a zigzag way, he makes his way toward his truck, which is parked in our yard.

"You going to let him drive, Pop?" I whisper, though I'm secretly hoping he will and then Dubbs will kill himself.

Sorry, God.

I bet he'd have a funeral, and everyone would show. Not to pay their respects to Dubbs, but for Ryan. The boy who kept persevering, no matter the odds.

Before I get another thought in, Pop is on the phone.

"Sandy, this is Lieutenant Young. Dubbs Taylor is leaving my house right now, drunk as a skunk. Yeah. Yeah. Might want to nab him before he gets too far. Ten-four."

Sandy has worked in dispatch at the Granite Harbor PD since I was born. She'll send someone out.

Pop didn't arrest him for one reason. This I know because I know my dad. He didn't want Ryan to watch. He didn't want Ryan to see his dad get arrested one more time. Even if he is a dirtbag.

As I peek out the window, the PD catches up with Dubbs at the end of our road.

We settle in again and finish the game.

Ryan and Hero will stay with us tonight and he won't get hurt. Won't get burned. He'll be safe underneath our roof. Where there's no drinking, no yelling, and no violence. But there is the empty sound of my mother not cooking in the kitchen, not calling us for dessert, not humming a tune, not asking Pop to get the milk for Santa, who we stopped believing in about two years ago.

But we all fall asleep in the living room. Together. All four of us.

"Mer, you awake?" It's Ryan.

"Yeah."

"Worst-case scenario."

I smile, and my heart breaks into a million pieces at the same time. It's an odd feeling that love and grief can be so real in the same moment.

"I'll wake up tomorrow, and Mom won't be in the kitchen, making coffee." A burning sensation starts in my heart. My eyes almost succumb to the same burning and start to leak, but I don't allow the tears to fall.

I feel his hand slowly take mine, and this makes my chest ache. I squeeze his hand.

"That Dubbs will get arrested and be released tomorrow."

The crackle of the fire and the twinkle of the Christmas lights make me feel more at ease. Not because of what's happening around us, but because all the people I love most are under this roof right now.

I think, secretly, Ryan and I both know that worst-case scenarios can be full of truth, a big truth. But also, what's equally freeing is, we can walk through those truths together.

I scoot down on the couch, laying my head next to our hands, connected.

"You're safe, Ryan."

"I know."

Hero groans contently and stretches in front of the fire.

Twenty

Merit
Granite Harbor, Maine
Present Day

We're on the porch. It's almost four in the afternoon. Ryan said he should just check on Dubbs. Why he has compassion for this man, I'll never understand. Ryan seems to have a spotty memory. Perhaps it's the old friend in me, the girl who wanted so badly to keep Ryan safe. That part of me doesn't want Ryan to forget. And that same part of me wants to remind Ryan of the cigarette burns Dubbs gave him on his twelfth birthday. The ones I cleaned, so they wouldn't get infected. The only reason I'd found out about them was because the pain was almost unbearable, and Ryan almost couldn't take it. He made Eli and I swear that we wouldn't breathe a word.

I look through one of the front windows of Dubbs's house, pushing back the memory. It's actually relatively clean. Picked up. With a couch, a recliner, and a coffee table. A television. Even a flower. A dead one at that but still a flower.

"What?" I ask as Ryan jumps off the front porch and walks to a side window of a bedroom.

"That's not like Dubbs."

"The flower? I know."

"No, the fact that it's dead." He peers in the window.

I lean off the porch and watch him. Ryan jumps back up to the porch and tries the front door.

"How long's it been since you've been inside?"

He shrugs. He knows, but he's not willing to share. Not that it matters.

There is a lamp knocked over in his room. The door opens, and the stale odor of cigarette smoke fills my lungs.

"Big change from the last time I was here. There was shit everywhere." I follow Ryan inside.

He's wearing his game warden hat right now. His investigative nature has the best of him. Ryan's looking for something.

"What are you looking for?"

He stops. "Something happened to Dubbs. I don't think he left this house willingly."

"He shouldn't be making bad debts. Karma's a bitch."

Ryan carefully places his finger against his lips because he hears something.

It's a phone. A ringing phone.

We follow the ringing and find a flip phone in a wire basket along with a pack of cigarettes and a set of keys.

"He definitely didn't leave willingly." Ryan picks up the phone, but we hear footsteps and talking outside.

He grabs me by my arm and pulls me into the pantry, shutting the accordion door behind us.

It's a cramped space, and my backside is against the front of Ryan's body. The same body I've touched with my hands—the seventeen-year-old body, not the manly body that rests behind me. I'm careful not to move because I don't want to bump his arm or his ribs.

"Are you all right?" I whisper.

"I'm just fine."

I feel his good hand attached to my waist, and my entire body breaks into chills, remembering the ache inside me that he caused. Him between my thighs, carefully pushing and thrusting in a way of love.

There's a tiny crack in the accordion door that we can see through, to Dubbs's phone that we left out on the counter.

"It's here. I got it," a man says into his phone.

It's the man from the porch the other day.

"Fucking liar," he seethes as he shoves his own iPhone in his pocket. He looks around and stares straight at the accordion door, as if he can see right through it.

Ryan's grip on my waist tightens. His fingers press into my skin, and I feel it between my legs and in my breasts.

He takes a step closer to the door we're behind, but his phone rings which makes him stalk to the front door.

Ryan and I stay put until we hear the front door shut. Until we can't hear footsteps anymore. Until it's quiet, and all I hear is the blood rushing in my ears.

Ryan's hand is still on my hip.

A big part of me wants to stay put, to feel him against me again. The other part of me screams, *No.*

But Ryan's grip changes. It tightens and loosens and tightens and loosens.

My breath hitches.

With his broken ribs and a shoulder injury, this isn't the best-case scenario—for him or for me.

Desperately, I want to rest my hands on the door in front of me and allow myself to be in this moment with Ryan.

It will only end in heartbreak, Merit.

It won't end happily.

You can't get past the past.

I don't know if it's the increasingly warm pantry or his breaths on the back of my neck, but I fall forward, resting my hands on the accordion door, just as I shouldn't.

I hear the air suck between his teeth as his hand opens up, as if I'm giving him the go sign. His good hand slides across my waist, down my backside, against my jeans. So badly, I want the jeans to be removed.

I get lost in his touch, as I always do, and allow my eyes to close for just a moment.

Stop, Merit, my heart says.

Ryan turns me around to face him.

Face him.

Face our past.

Face what happened.

He takes his hand and places it on the spot between my neck and cheek, against my jaw.

Chills spread across my skin, against my own will. As if I can control what my body does when Ryan touches me. As if I can control what my body says it needs.

The light from the outside seeps through the long crack of the door. His jaw is tight, his eyes wide.

There isn't space between us.

Ryan's hand slowly moves from my jaw to down my chest to around my breast, and my nipples grow uncomfortably hard. His hand drifts down between my breasts to my stomach and my waist, as if he's remembering not only what my body looks like, but also what it feels like beneath my clothes. But he doesn't look anywhere but my eyes. He's gentle and firm at the same time. His jawline tightens as his hand moves back up to my chest and then to the back of my neck, and he pulls me to him without question. I feel his firmness at my stomach, and I feel his lips against my ear.

My hand moves to his good shoulder while I'm careful about his ribs. I push my body into him, my traitorous body defying what my head is saying.

Stop.

Don't do this.

But my heart says otherwise.

"Merit, I will always belong to you. And I'll wait as long as it takes."

His lips barely graze my lobe, and then they slowly make their way down my neck.

I let out a sigh as my nipples grow hard again.

Urgency grows inside me.

Desperation.

The intimacy between us right now, the way our bodies stand, tells a story that extends just beyond our reach.

How will it end?

But again, my body has defied me. It has its own mind. Slowly, I slide off my shirt, desperately wanting his touch.

His.

It's always come down to him.

Ryan's look changes. As if I'm giving him something, a secret. A second chance. He grows protective as he helps me pull it over my head and drops it to the floor of the tiny pantry.

He pulls me to him again, but this time, he takes my mouth. He gives my lips a purpose as he pushes against mine. My tongue pushes into his mouth. The familiar, yet new mouth. A mouth I spent time exploring, defining the limits. A mouth that has been between my legs, a mouth that I never quite got enough of, and a tongue that is magnificent.

"Oh my God, Merit," Ryan whispers against my mouth. He rests his forehead against mine. "Please," he begs, "take off your bra."

And, just like that, my body defies me. I reach back and unclasp the hook. One thing it seems I've always been cursed with is big breasts. Big for my body anyway.

Ryan moves me against the wall, so he has more stability. He takes me in, his eyes still wide with curiosity yet familiarity. His good hand rests against the wall over my head.

"There's a reason that our timing is off. That I'm in the arm brace. That my ribs are healing. Because, Merit, right now, all I want to do are all the things I shouldn't." He kisses the spot just under my earlobe, trying not to bend his waist, knowing the pain will meet his nerves.

I feel some of the weight of his body against mine. I feel his ever-growing hardness, and air escapes my mouth, pleasure disguised as surprise.

Gently, he takes one of my breasts with his hand and puts it to his mouth, and I almost come off the wall as the ache between my legs only worsens.

"Ryan," I sigh as my head falls back against the wall, and I struggle to find air.

His tongue flitters around my nipple, and then he softly bites down.

Then, he takes my other breast with the same hand but not before meeting my eyes with his. "Is this all right?" He's breathless, his look hooded, as if he might not be able to control himself.

I nod quickly, withering against the wall as if my free will has disappeared and I don't know what my body will do next. This time, not so gently, he takes my nipple between his teeth and flicks it with his tongue.

"Oh, God." The ache only worsens, and I feel myself growing wetter and wetter.

But I reach down and give him the help that he doesn't need, taking my breast into my hand. I watch him as his mouth takes as much as it can. I grab the back of his head. I want to tell him what I need. I want to tell him what I want.

My head screams, *Merit, you've got to stop. The last time you fell this hard was for the man standing in front of you. And then he broke your heart.*

Then, his lips trail kisses from my breasts to up my chest and against my collarbone until he finds my mouth again.

But life has a funny way of working itself out because Ryan's phone starts to ring.

His head falls to my neck. His breathing is ragged, and I feel his heart slamming against my chest.

It takes us both a minute to regain whatever reality sits just outside this pantry. And the truth that lies just outside that.

"It-it's your work phone, Ryan. You have to answer it," I say, trying to catch my breath. My mind is spinning.

Ryan peels his body from mine. Stares at me and then looks down at my half-naked body.

I go to grab my shirt, but he holds me back from grabbing it, still staring.

"This one-handed shit really sucks." Ryan looks at me. "Warden Taylor," he says as he stands over my body, staring down at my breasts and then to my eyes.

Badly, I want to reach up and run my fingers along his jawline as he talks to whoever is on the other end of the line.

But I don't.

Though I can't feel him anymore because he's given us some space, the ache between my legs hasn't left.

I reach up and cover my breasts with my arms. Ryan gently pushes my arms away just after he takes the phone between his cheek and shoulder, adoringly looking down at me.

Smiling, I roll my eyes and feel my face grow hot.

I try to regain my thoughts, staring up at Ryan. This isn't, will not, be easy from here on out. There's no smooth sailing, and I will have to face my past, our past, head-on from here. I will have to take a look at us, what happened, my part. Eventually. Soon.

Twenty-One

Ryan
Granite Harbor, Maine
Present Day

It's been two weeks since the pantry incident. Dubbs is still missing. This isn't unlike him though. He did it a lot during my upbringing—if that's what you'd call it. Besides, it was better when he was gone.

But what keeps the situation in the back of my mind is the guy who took Dubbs's phone. Why? And why the hell can't we find him?

After we left Dubbs's place and when we got home, I tried a Google search with the uploaded grainy photo that I had taken with my phone with the word Maine. I've narrowed it down to three.

Luther Waker from Tyler, Texas. A black man.

Ronan Fields from Augusta, Maine. A white man.

Bruce Watts from Boston, Massachusetts. A white man.

Clearly, he's not a black man, so I removed Luther from the list and had dispatch run a search on Ronan Fields and Bruce Watts. Watts has no priors but a creepy penchant for unicorns, according to his Facebook page, but nothing else is out of the ordinary. Fields, on the other hand, has a criminal history longer than the state of California. From drug trafficking to felony drug possession to money laundering. The list goes on.

What would Fields want with Dubbs? Did he owe money to Fields? Hell, I just gave Dubbs five grand. That should have fucking covered what he owed. But what if he owed more? What if it wasn't enough? What the hell would a guy like Ronan Fields want with an old, drunk fisherman? Sure, he did drugs occasionally, definitely gambled, but not felony-level shit. He didn't mess with the underworld. The fucking thieves that send the lower-level thieves to prison for the crimes that the big thieves committed. *Was my dad working for one?*

We've just finished at my last doctor's appointment. The ribs are pretty much healed. My shoulder brace is off but not without physical therapy.

This also means that Merit has a decision to make. She can leave now. She's free to do whatever the fuck she wants.

Go back to California.

Stay here with me.

I sure as hell don't want to force her to do something she doesn't want to do. I don't want to bring it up right now, but I'm not sure I can help myself.

She finally stops laughing from a one-liner joke I told.

Merit sets down her Diet Coke.

Since that day in the pantry, we've done our best to avoid what's clearly never left our minds. I think she thinks it went too far. I get it. It's like after a night of drinking where you don't remember much, only bits and pieces. Like coming out of a fog, scared to death that what you did will happen again, terrified and excited, all at the same time.

She's distant with her body.

And I accept that—not always willingly, but I do.

I know she wants more, just like I do. I think, though, her guard has come down. I just hope she stays forever.

I take the straw wrapper and twist it around my finger. "What are you going to do now that I'm healed? Now that I can go back to work?"

Her smile slowly dies, but she tries to keep it light. She shrugs. "Guess I'll go back to California and help save the otters." She puts the straw to her lips again.

If that's what she wants, I'll pretend to be fucking happy, but I'm not.

I should ask her to stay.

No. No, I shouldn't.

If I ask her to stay, that's putting too much expectation on her. Maybe that will force her to make a decision she's not ready to make. Not yet.

I nod.

"You booked your flight yet?" I'm trying to act casual, but my stomach is a big clusterfuck of knots right now.

"No." She takes another sip of her Diet Coke. "I'll do it tonight." There's a long pause. "When do you go back to work?"

"Tomorrow, I suppose. I'll call HR."

"You mean, Faynette?" She smiles and throws a sugar packet at me.

"Maybe I'll luck out and get someone else in the office." I lean forward on the table, staring her down.

Merit's top dips down just before her milky-white breasts begin. It's a white top with some sort of design on it. Her jean shorts are of respectable length. I can't imagine that Brand or Eli would allow that to be any different even if she is a thirty-five-year-old woman. And a beautiful fucking woman at that.

She stands, and her legs go on forever. "Ready?"

"Uh, yeah." I stand, not expecting to leave so quickly.

"Looks like there's a summer storm coming through. The clouds are beginning to move and change, turning darker, more ominous."

We make the drive back to Hallowell, my mind spinning in a million directions. I'm sure hers is, too.

I can't let her leave this time without her knowing what she means to me.

You have to.

No. No, you don't. You don't have the right. You broke her heart. You made a choice. Lie in it. Don't do that to her again.

Tell her.

No, don't.

The rain starts to tap against the windshield. I'm driving this time, which is different. One hand on the wheel, I want to reach over and put my hand on her bare skin. Between her legs. Claim her without words.

Tell her.

"Mer, I can't let you—"

Her phone rings.

Motherfucker.

"Hang on." She puts the phone to her ear. "Hey, Abbey. Yeah." She pauses and looks over at me. "He's doing a lot better." Pauses again. Listens. "Yeah. I'll book a flight home when we get back to Ryan's place."

Ryan's place. It sounds awful, coming from her mouth.

Home, not Ryan's place. I want it to be her home. *Our* home. But we're not the same people anymore. Not in the least. She's got her home. I've got mine.

"I'll send you my itinerary. Sounds good. Okay. You, too. Bye." She hits End on her call.

My heart is slamming against my chest, like I'm running out of time. Like it's the fourth quarter with thirty seconds on the clock, and I can't quite pull out the win.

"Stay." That's how it comes out.

"What?" she asks.

"Stay. With me. Stay here." I swallow the remnants of saliva.

Merit takes in a deep breath, looks down at her hands, and then out the window.

The rain pelts.

The truck hums.

And time lags.

Merit finally says, "I can't, Ryan. You know that." She's still staring out the window.

"Yes, you can." Thank God, for timing because we just pulled into the driveway of my place. This conversation needs both my eyes, both my hands.

"There's too much water under the bridge," Merit says, resting her elbow on the windowsill.

I turn off the truck and turn my body toward hers. I can't breathe, and I struggle with the words that need to be said, knowing full well they need to be spoken and that I can't hide behind the facade that we've created anymore.

"Let's talk about it. Let's talk about all the shit, Merit." I explode inside.

Her head snaps back at me.

The rain pours.

Her look burns right through me. She's fucking pissed.

Good.

Merit gets out of the truck, slams the door, and marches inside as the rain bounces off her skin.

I slam the door and follow her inside, just as mad. More mad at myself than anyone. Mad as fuck that I let this get so far into this hole of denial.

"Stop," I command at the entryway. My voice is low and loud at the same time. "Don't run away, Mer, not this time."

Her wet shoes on the hardwood floor stop. She turns on her heel.

"Talk to me. Please." I shut the door behind me.

"Fuck off, Ryan."

"No." I stalk toward her as she starts to move toward her bedroom. "Stop. You don't get to run anymore!" I yell. "Just stop!" I take her shoulders in my hands.

Tears start to stream down her pale cheeks, and she wipes away the evidence. I try to touch her, but she pulls away, still standing, facing me, her arms wrapped around each other.

Dropping my arms at my sides, I try to act casual. But I can't.

She comes at me full force and pissed, and I'm not sure what to do.

Punch me.

Kick me.

Do something.

Anything. Just stop pushing me out, I want to say.

She rips my shirt from my jeans and lifts it up, exposing my stomach and chest.

I've never seen Merit so alive, so angry, and so sad. She takes her finger and touches each cigarette scar. "I took care of these. Cleaned these. Made you better. Helped you heal," she says through a clenched jaw. Her touches aren't soft.

I close my eyes, remembering how we both spent my twelfth birthday. "I remem—"

"Shut up. I'm talking." She pulls my shirt up over my head with my help.

Merit turns me around so that my back faces her. My head drops.

"And this scar. Remember that one, Ryan? When you asked my brother and me not to tell anyone while your dad hurt you?"

Her finger runs the length of the scar. "And then, three months before I left for college, we slept together. Finally." Merit's voice is quivering now.

I want to turn around, take her inside my skin, melt into her. Allow her worries, her fears, to become mine. But I deserve this.

She continues, "These wounds, these scars, are marks of your resiliency, but sometimes, internal wounds take far longer to heal. I'm sure you know all too well about that." Her voice ends abruptly.

I breathe.

It's quiet.

"I watch you," she starts. She clears her voice of pain.

I can't see her, but maybe it's better this way. My back to her allows her to speak her truth.

"I watch you with children, and I can't help but wonder what our child would have been like. What type of dad you would have been." She's barely hanging on now.

Something inside me cracks. Maybe it is for the little boy I was. So fearful, yet not afraid at all. Because I had to make split decisions that would dictate whether I made it out alive or not. Fight or flight.

I try to turn around, but Merit's hands stop me.

"I need you to hear this. I need you to hear me when I say you broke me, Ryan. You broke me when you asked if the baby was yours. You broke me when you asked me to make an appointment. And you put me over the edge when you walked out the door. You killed me that day." Her voice is muffled and broken with tears. "You turned into someone else that day. You became someone entirely different, not the boy I had grown up with."

Tears—fucking tears—start in my eyes. I feel every ounce of her hurt, if not more. Every fucking day, I've wanted to take back what I said. What I did after that. A rampage of women, filling my emptiness with sex. Something had to cure me. I was broken. *Why would I sabotage Merit and take her down, too?* Merit has been the only one to get through to me.

I allow her words to break my heart, just as she deserves.

"But you know what I did, Ryan. I carried that child to term. I left for college and carried the baby to term because this child deserved the best regardless of her parents' situation."

Slowly, I turn to face Merit. My stomach is somewhere in my throat, and I can't breathe. Her eyes meet mine.

"I carried that baby to term," she whispers, fidgeting with her fingers. "I fought through morning sickness, through early morning classes, surviving on saltines and any protein I could manage to choke down." She laughs only a little, and then her face turns to heartbreak. "But there were other plans for Destiny." Her voice breaks.

God, I want to hold her so bad. "Please, Mer, tell me what to do."

I try to reach out to her, but she shakes her head.

"No, you need to see in my eyes the pain of the day Destiny was born. I want you to hear this."

I stand, my body numb, listening.

"Destiny Rebecca Taylor died inside my body one day before I had to deliver her. The doctor recommended I deliver normally." Merit nods and wipes her nose with the back of her hand.

You weren't the boy she needed when she was eighteen, but you can be the man she needs right now.

"So, I did. I delivered our daughter on November 9, 2003" She pauses. "It's weird. I was holding this beautiful baby girl, who just looked so peaceful, just like she was sleeping. So innocent. As if nothing was wrong and she was perfectly fine. But the problem was, deep down, I knew she wasn't breathing. I knew, when I placed my hand on her tiny little chest, the heartbeat had left a day before."

Tears start to fall against her pale cheeks and mine, too.

There aren't any words to fill this void inside her.

Merit shakes her head and looks blindly out at the rain. "There are days when I can see her running in the sunshine. There are days when I can see her, feel her against my chest. I see rainbows a lot. I like to believe that's Destiny. The day she was born, the rain on the ground sat for days prior. Pooled in parking lots. Sat in gutters. It rained a lot. I'd like to think that was God's way of showing his sadness. I know I felt it." She pauses again, looking down at her hands again. "I had her cremated. The day when I went to the mortuary to pick her up, the torrential four-day downpour just stopped the moment I had to get out of the car to go pick up our daughter for the last time, and a rainbow as big and as bright as Destiny was just appeared out of nowhere." She nods again, now staring back out at the rain. "I like the rain, but I like the rainbows, too."

My chest is heavy like cement. I feel nothing, and I feel everything. "Can we sit down on the couch?" I beg.

"Yeah."

We move to the couch and sit down, numb. I look at Merit, a beautiful, strong woman who has managed to survive life. Who lost her mother. Raised her brother and me. Took care of her dad. Who lost our daughter. Alone. And scared to death.

Our backs resting against the back of the couch, I slowly reach over and slide my hand into hers, just like when we were kids. Merit was there. Every step of the way. Present for me. And, the one time she needed me, really needed me, because she walked through her mother's death by herself, I wasn't there.

"Mer, there aren't enough words …" I take a minute because the tears start to come again. I will never tell her why I did what I did that day. Try to explain myself. Ever. Thinking of her going through the pregnancy alone, holding our dead child alone—these are wounds that don't ever heal. "I'm sorry." But I break down, and I don't dare pull my hand from hers, so in the open, my tears fall.

We sit in silence and allow the weight of grief to pull us into oblivion.

Twenty-Two

Merit
Hallowell, Maine
Present Day

Ryan's been crying intermittently for an hour or so. Never once in my life have I seen him cry. I've seen him walk through a lot, just stoic. Ryan's gone into the kitchen to make some tea. I know he's crying for me. He isn't crying for Destiny. He didn't know Destiny like I did. He didn't feel her heartbeat from the inside. He didn't feel her movements. Her kicks to the ribs at three in the morning. He didn't feel the weight of her cheeks against my chest. He didn't get any of that.

I've never talked to anyone about it. Ever. I've pushed it away to a place unseen, and let it sit there while I've tried to mask the pain. The heartache. The anguish of going home to the off-campus one-bedroom apartment to unworn baby clothes I'd purchased. Nobody knew. Eli didn't know. Pop didn't know. Ryan didn't know. A crib I'd saved for. Books I'd bought. I'd planned to keep Destiny. I couldn't *not*.

After college, I dived right into my work at Monterey Bay Aquarium. One night, Abbey and I got tipsy. I told her I'd lost a baby. But that was it. Grieving can be easier when you're not alone.

The doctor who had released me after post-baby care recommended a few counselors. But I'd been through grief before. I did manage to make a few trips to the psychiatrist, but that was it.

He walks back in with tea. He's also not a tea drinker, which would explain the Gatorade in his hand, as he sits down next to me.

"I have to go back to California," I say.

There's a long breath. He doesn't answer. He just sets his drink on the coffee table, leans back, and places his hands behind his head, staring at the ceiling.

"Is that what you want?" he asks. "I'll do whatever you want, Mer."

What we want and what we need are two completely separate things.

"I want a cheeseburger every day. I don't need one. I want a bigger car. A better house. I don't need them. I want for Skittles to go back to their original taste. I don't need it. Because I'll survive without these things," I say.

I want you. I don't need you, Ryan. Besides, you're not mine to keep.

But what if the *want* becomes a need? A need so deep that it shrouds my happiness, picking it apart piece by piece. A need like water. Air. Food.

I needed Destiny. I needed her, wanted her, like the air that I breathe. Because something inside me died when she did. Something so profound that it made me walk in my own depression for a few years. Passing classes only barely. Graduating by the skin of my teeth. I think Eddie hired me because of my summer internships, for my work ethic, because it most certainly wasn't my grade point average.

"I need to book my flight," I say casually.

I've had a lot of years to process this. Ryan's only had an hour.

"Violet," he whispers, sitting forward, pulling on my hand.

The remnants of our childhood pull at my heartstrings. I'm taken back to a space in time when the world was more alive, more full of color.

"Just hold still, Mer." He pulled up my shirtsleeve. "It's violet." He stopped, stunned.

I rolled my eyes as he glanced back at my arm and then back to me.

Ryan was ten and I was eleven.

"It's about perspective, Mer. It's a bruise. It hurts, but the way you got—"

"It's ugly."

"Who would have thought you'd take a hit from Dubbs? He was so out of his mind. I'm sorry, Mer," he whispered in the most apologetic way.

He'd meant to hit Ryan again. But I wasn't having it, so I'd stepped in front of him and taken his punishment.

"Violet is an ugly color." I tried to squirm from his grasp.

"Violet Ugly is a beautiful color, Mer. It's you."

I'm convinced that Ryan calls me Violet when he sees my courage, even when I can't.

On that day, when Dubbs's fist met my arm, I thought I'd die later; it hurt that bad. But it just made me madder. It made me think about every time Ryan had come to our house with a new bruise hidden under his clothing, a new burn. I felt his pain.

I feel his large hand over mine, which brings me back to the present moment.

"One last time," is what I say.

I pull him from the couch. His tall, strong body unfolds and towers over mine. He's persevered. Survived. I think my family was put in place to help Ryan. People make awful choices. They hurt others. They do bad things. But some things are just out of our control, and we're left without power and with a whole lot of pain. What are we expected to do with all of it anyway?

Ryan's eyes are still stained from tears and guilt. Gently, I take him by the hand and pull him to his bedroom. I close the door behind us. One last time, I'll make love to Ryan. We'll reacquaint ourselves with each other's bodies as adults and not as kids.

We'll make love against the world.

Against our differences.

Our similarities.

Our guilt.

Our sadness.

Our grief.

Against the people we once were.

We'll make love for the last time. Because two people who once loved each other and experienced heartbreak at the level we did need two different, more solid people, in our lives to help us pick out the bones of our past.

Two broken puzzle pieces don't match.

I take my top and slide it over my head, exposing my nude lace bra. I slip off my shorts.

I hear air escape through his mouth as his eyes take in my body.

He reaches up and pulls off his shirt, exposing his defined chest. I assist with his pants because the anticipation, though I need to take this slow, is sweltering through my body. I pull my hair from my ponytail, allowing it to fall against my back, shoulders.

A large green-and-blue bruise sits where his ribs took the hit from the steering wheel. The only remnants of the accident from just a month prior.

He puts me in control of us, of what we're about to do. I know he's being gentle with my heart, only doing what I'm ready for. But I can tell by his boxer briefs that he's ready.

I push him to the bed, my hands on his hips, and look up into his dark blue irises. His long eyelashes are still a bit damp from the tears.

The backs of his knees meet the bed, and he sits.

"Are you all right?" I ask, but I'm not looking for an answer.

His answer will depend on my next move because hearts take longer to heal than flesh wounds ever will.

I slide myself on top of him and saddle him. I feel his length at my opening, the only thing separating us a thin piece of lace. He spreads my legs so that I'm flush against him.

"That's it," he says. Ryan is far more experienced in the sex department.

I gasp as I feel this large, hard bulge between my legs, and I start to move.

With one careful movement on his part, my breasts are out, in his face.

I've forgotten how good sex can be.

I've forgotten how good sex can be with Ryan.

He takes each breast in his mouth, carefully taking his time with his tongue.

Caresses.

Gives.

Tugs.

Ryan pulls my breast from his mouth, and then I rush his mouth with mine, taking my turn. My overdue turn. Ryan has always been magic with his tongue in the way that he kisses and the way that he moves it between my legs.

I want so badly to pull my panties to the side and allow him to feel my wetness, but I don't. I'll let the eagerness build as I move slow and steady against his hardness.

His tongue has become slower, softer, and he pulls back while his lips linger on mine, and I get drunk on this. Ryan's arms move from my hips and wrap around my shoulders and back. My breasts push against his chest as his kiss deepens, growing again with urgency.

I thought I could help it, but I can't. The ache has grown too much, so I slide my panties to the side and let him feel my wetness.

"Oh my God, Merit." He ends my name with a pronounced T.

When these words reach his tongue, I drink them in, knowing I'm the only woman who can do this to him. I'm the one giving him this reaction right now.

I spread my legs further, trying to feel all of him as I slide myself up and down his shaft.

"Fuck," he hisses in my ear as he stands.

Holding me in position, he turns and lays me down on the bed, pushing me up toward the headboard. He towers over me as he slowly slides my panties off.

I know he feels the ache the same way I do.

"What do you want me to do to you, Merit?"

My legs move to the sides, so I'm wide open for him, giving him a full view and full rein. "Start with your fingers."

He falls to my side and looks at me with confidence. His hand slides over my erect nipples, and he takes one breast in his mouth, watching me, as I, too, wrap my hand around my breast. He tugs and flicks with his tongue. Over my stomach, his hand glides and then to the inside of my thighs, skipping the part I need most and building anticipation at the same time.

His hand makes his way to my middle, opening me up with his fingertips.

I watch as his face turns hot as he feels me, the wetness. He doesn't have to say a word; we both know. Ryan takes his finger and gently pushes against my hot spot, and then he slides the same finger deep inside me.

He pulls out.

And pushes it back in.

I close my eyes and put my hand around his, as if I'm assisting with this matter, needing to feel what he's doing to me.

His finger goes faster but not too fast. He pulls out and takes a second finger inside me, and I reach for his shaft and take him in my hand.

"Don't touch. I'll come," he commands. "I just want to watch you, Violet." He kisses my mouth again, his tongue stretching deep within me.

Between his tongue and his fingers, my hips start to move, a sign I need more, or I'll explode. Ryan seems to know this because he pulls his fingers out and moves down to between my thighs. He pulls back the lips of my opening.

"Ryan, please," I beg.

His tongue starts at the base of my hotness and moves upward, pushing toward my hot spot.

My legs begin to quiver.

"Oh, God, Ryan." I grab the back of his head, pushing him deeper to me.

Ryan's fingers hold my folds open, and he gives a few last licks before he climbs up my body and takes my mouth in his.

This time, I'm the forceful one. My nails dig into his back, and I pull my head from the pillow and cling to his body. I manage to shimmy out from underneath him, and he follows my lead. On my knees, I feel him flush against my backside, his hardness against my back and my bottom.

Chills reverberate throughout my entire body, and he grabs my breasts from behind, owning them, taking me and bending me forward, trailing kisses down my body.

I fall to all fours as Ryan's shaft rubs against my backside.

"Take me right now, Ryan." My words are forceful.

With that, he uses his fingers to find the warm spot from behind and guides himself to my ache.

"Fuck," he says as I feel his dick at my opening. At first, he probes in and out and in and out, just barely entering me. "What about a condom?"

I shake my head. Ryan wouldn't put me in a spot to get a disease, and I'm on the pill.

"Enter me now, Ryan."

He plunges into me and lets out a loud groan from behind me.

"Oh my God," I say as I feel him filling me. I spread my legs a bit more, so he has better access. "Are you watching?" I ask.

"All of it."

He keeps one hand on my lower back and one hand on my hips.

But, in one pull, he flips me over like a rag doll so that I'm facing him. He's on his knees over me.

"I can't stand not being able to see your face." He crawls on top of me and eases himself inside me. "I need to watch you."

The walls of my heart begin to cave.

It makes it too hard, watching the man I love come undone, the man I need to leave.

Two broken puzzle pieces will never match. Remember that, Merit. Don't forget.

But I'll do it. I'll look him in the eye, give him what he needs, and pay the consequences of heartbreak later. I'll do it because that's what we do for love. I'll do it because that's what I've always done for Ryan.

"I'm losing you, Mer." His voice is vulnerable as his hand touches my chin.

I allow him to feel me just as I feel him.

His weaknesses. My weaknesses.

His heartache. My heartache.

His sadness. My sadness.

All the air leaves me, all the things I've tried to control over the last seventeen years. My feelings. My heart. My love. The preventative measures I've taken to protect my heart from this last twenty minutes have disappeared as I've taken him in once more.

But I'll still have to leave, I think as I stare up at this man who I know loves me with every ounce of who he is.

The answer isn't, *I'll stay and love you forever.*

The answer isn't, *Don't worry; I'm not going anywhere.*

The answer isn't, *We will work it out.*

My answer has to be, "Just make love to me, Ryan. One more time."

I've never seen a more broken man than the one before me. After I speak these words, his actions do not match the terror in his eyes. They don't match the heartache, the sadness, the grief I know too well.

But he makes love to me, scooping me up from the mattress and resting me on his lap, allowing my knees to fall on either side of his hips. I move on top of him, uncontrollably, unwavering. As tears slide down my cheeks, he watches them. Each one taking their position on my breasts, my stomach, his shoulders, his chest. With his arms around me, we move together.

Once, there was a boy I made love to, a caged boy who thought himself damaged.

Once, there was a man I made love to, and I left my heart at his feet as I walked away.

Twenty-Three

Merit
Granite Harbor, Maine
Spring 2002

I tap my foot on the bathroom floor and chew at my thumbnail, wanting to throw up but trying to refrain.

It could be negative, and that would be great. That would be fantastic. That would make everything a whole lot better.

Throwing up would be bad.

Morning sickness.

What if it's really morning sickness and not the fact that I'm eighteen years old and watching a pregnancy test?

"Oh, God," I groan as my stomach turns and twists, and my heart races.

My dad is going to kill me. This is not the future he wanted for me. This is not the future I wanted for myself.

College will be out the window.

"Oh, God." I stand and pace the bathroom floor, taking my temples and rubbing them.

No, no. It will be fine, I think to myself. *I have Ryan. We'll be okay. Ryan will make this all right. He'll talk some sense into me. We'll make a plan to get married. We'll get our own place. I have a job at Café by the Sea. Betty Lee will understand and give me extra shifts until my belly explodes.*

"Oh my God." My hands begin to shake.

Just breathe, Merit. I rub my sweaty hands on my jeans.

I glance at the test still lying on the bathroom counter, waiting for it to spit out my future.

Our future.

Ryan will make everything okay.

He'll make it okay.

He'll make it doable.

I glance at the test again.

A plus mark.

It's a fucking plus mark.

That can't be good for a teenager leaving for college. For a woman who had no plans of having a child, I can't be good for a baby.

This could be good for a married couple wanting to have a child.

This could be good for others.

Not for me. Not for us.

"I'm-I'm pregnant?" I say out loud, more to convince myself.

I run to the toilet and throw up the cereal I ate this morning. Several times until there's nothing left, I throw up.

Wiping my mouth with the back of my hand, I crouch down next to the toilet and try not to cry.

I feel guilty for crying.

I feel sorry for this baby.

This was not my destiny.

A knock at the door makes my insides explode with fear. A door I'll have to eventually walk beyond. Face life. Face the looks of others. The disappointment. The shame.

"Yeah?" I yell through the tears that want to fall.

"Mer, you've been in there for twenty minutes. What the hell is wrong with you?" It's Eli.

My stomach drops. My brother. The one whose life isn't falling apart. The brother who still has his senior year ahead of him. He has Grace. And prom. And a future.

We're fundamentally different now.

Mom, I could really use your help right now, I pray quietly to myself.

"Ryan's here," Eli says. "We're going downtown."

Fuck. Shit. Not now. I'm not ready to face him. Not ready to tell him. Playing this game I've asked Ryan to play, the *don't tell my brother that we're dating but kind of not dating* game.

Ryan's life is about to change, too.

I stand, dizzy, and I grab the counter to steady myself. "I'll be out in a minute." I wipe my nose on the back of my hand again. I grab the pregnancy test and examine it closer. *Pregnant.* "Shit."

I grab all the evidence of my life change and throw it in my purse, unlocking and opening the bathroom door. I drove all the way to Augusta to buy one. There's not a chance in hell I'd buy a pregnancy test at Ring's Pharmacy or Granite Harbor Grocery. I'd make the gossip ring in thirty minutes, tops.

"Hey," Ryan says from the hallway at the door of Eli's bedroom.

"Hey," I say. I slip into my bedroom and shut the door behind me.

There's a knock. A soft knock.

Ryan peeks his head in.

Tears start to burn at the corners of my eyes, my back to the door.

"Mer, you all right?"

No.

"I'm fine." I hear the door quietly shut behind him.

There's hesitation in his steps.

Don't you dare cry, Merit. Stop it this instant.

"Mer, what's wrong?"

I feel his hand slide up my arm. I wince.

"Violet?"

Please don't call me that anymore, I want to say, and I'm not sure why I don't want him to call me that anymore.

I turn to face him. We've committed this act together. He has to know.

"Ryan," I sigh and reach into my purse. My hands shaking, I hand him the pregnancy test.

He takes it in his hand and stares down at the test and back at me. "What's this?"

"It's a positive pregnancy test, Ryan," I whisper.

He sits on my bed. Stares.

He'll make this okay. He'll tell me everything will be all right now. He'll take me in his arms. Tell me he loves me and that we'll get married and that he'll take shifts at the harbor during his senior year.

"This can't be right," he says.

"What?"

"We wore a condom, Mer. This can't be right."

I've had a whole three minutes to process this before he knew anything. A whole three minutes to figure out what I can't seem to wrap my head around, so I'm no use in assisting with the understanding department.

Any minute now, he'll make this okay. Right?

I'll just wait.

We don't say a word.

I join him on the bed. Not the same one that got us into this predicament. That was a bed of blankets at the harbor. In the darkness, below the moon's light, where he pushed, and I took whatever he offered, unable to get enough.

We shook when he finished.

I didn't know what an orgasm was until two days after we made love. When he used his fingers and then his tongue under my summer dress. It was just past noon, and we were in the shade of an old evergreen, a secluded place just past the harbor.

Maybe I'm romanticizing the situation we're in to avoid the current situation altogether.

Ryan's head rests on his hand, still staring at the positive pregnancy test. Silence fills us like air, consuming us. Questions we can't answer. Answers that are just beyond our reach perhaps. A situation we shouldn't be in. And yet the silence is too deafening to hear anything else. Not the sound of the blood pumping from my heart to other parts of my body. My thoughts, too, have become quiet.

The silence turns eerie. Cold. Dark.

Then, he says, "You're sure it's mine?"

It takes several minutes for my brain to comprehend the question he asked. It takes me a minute to round up what's in my head to answer the question I'm not sure he really asked in the first place.

"What?"

"You're sure it's mine? The baby."

My thoughts are just a step behind my mouth.

"What do you mean?" Truly, I don't understand what he's asking.

Is he asking if I've slept with someone else? Is he asking if there's another father?

Just a step behind.

Disbelief can squander. Flounder. Like a fish out of water. It can flip and flop on an old deck, waiting for someone to do the right thing. Waiting for someone to understand the predicament and take action.

But anger starts first. Just at the end of my spine and quickly reaches my chest and then my mouth. Then, it registers.

"You're asking if I had sex with someone else?" The disbelief meets my tongue, and reality pours in.

He doesn't answer. He knows the truth. He knows it. I know it. And God knows it.

"I just want to be sure—"

"What?" I'm still trying to register, compute.

He shrugs, like it's no big deal.

I whisper my next words because I'm afraid, if I don't, I'll sound like I'm yelling. Even though I don't want to yell. I keep calm for Eli's sake. Because Eli doesn't know a thing about Ryan and me.

"Ryan, you were my first. And you think I'm just going to mess around with someone else?"

Ryan shakes his head, placing his elbows on his knees, still holding the pregnancy test. "You've got to get an abortion. I can't have a kid right now. I'm a junior in high school, Mer."

I can't breathe.

I need to throw up.

The room spins.

And I can't manage a rational thought.

I'm alone in this world full of people with a tiny seed inside me.

The sound of my pulse can be heard in my ear.

A loud ringing.

"Besides," I hear him say, "you're not the only one I'm sleeping with, Mer. Come on, you know there are no guarantees in life."

It's hard for an eighteen-year-old girl to hide pregnancy, especially living in a small town. Hiding the overindulgence in soda crackers and soda. Blaming it on a bad flu—in spring.

I drove to Portland two days ago to do what I needed to do, wearing a wide-brimmed hat, large black sunglasses, and red lipstick. I couldn't have a child on my own. I wasn't ready for one. I hadn't been to the doctor yet. Fear was my keeper. I couldn't give this child the life it deserved.

I sat in the parking lot, tears streaming down my face as I stared at the brick building.

You understand right? I touch my stomach.

I can't give you the life you're owed.

I'm sorry.

Looking in the rearview mirror, I wiped my mascara away, pushed my sunglasses over my eyes, and marched into the clinic.

I didn't expect the clinician to check for a heartbeat.

She did.

And hers—I just knew she was a girl—was strong.

I wept quietly as I listened to the sound of her heart.

The music of her beat.

"Are you ready, Miss Young?" the clinician asked.

I lay there, on the sterile chair, shirt up, my stomach exposed, listening to the most beautiful sound I'd ever heard. I believed this girl had been made with love. I believed this girl would overcome. And I believed she and I were meant to be.

Tears rolled.

My heart ached.

I wanted so badly to do what I had come to do.

But love won. A mother's love won.

Without a shred of fear, I said, "No. I've decided I can't do this. I'm keeping my baby."

The clinician sat back. Smiled. "All right then. Let's schedule your next checkup."

I began to wonder on my way back, with this child growing inside me, what clinicians felt when they were asked to do things like abortions.

Do some women use it as a form of birth control?
Do some women do it without a second thought?
Are some women like me?

I supposed we all wore a different conscience as people made by God. I supposed we all walked this world differently. But, when I heard that strong little heartbeat, I knew this little girl was my destiny. And, whatever that looked like, it didn't matter because we'd figure things out together. I had to be her strength until she could stand on her own two feet.

I drove two blocks down to Books Galore and bought a day-by-day pregnancy book. Without my mom, without Ryan, I'd navigate this on my own.

Twenty-Four

Ryan
Granite Harbor, Maine
Spring 2002

Something's wrong with Merit, I think when I see her ash-colored face coming from the bathroom.

"Hey," I say, fear building in my body.

"Hey," she says and walks into her bedroom, shutting the door behind her.

Something's definitely wrong.

I tell Eli that I'll meet him downtown, that I have to talk to Merit about a school project. We don't even have the same classes. She's in all the AP classes, the smart-kid classes, and she's a senior, but I don't care what he's thinking right now. I need to check on Mer.

Eli leaves, and I knock on her door before I enter. I've seen her naked, so if she's changing, it would be all right. More than all right.

"Mer, you all right?"

"I'm fine," she lies.

"Mer, what's wrong?" Hesitantly, I walk to her, not knowing what she needs right now, but I take my hand and slide it up her arm. "Violet?"

I feel her body flinch at the name. Something she's never done.

"Ryan," she finally says, reaching into her purse. She hands me a white stick that looks like a thermometer.

Does she have a fever? Is she sick?

The problem with the thermometer is, it doesn't have a place for numbers. I want to tell her that she needs to get her money back or get this one fixed, but I'm not sure what she's trying to say with this.

Oh. God.

Just for clarification's sake, I ask, "What's this?"

"It's a positive pregnancy test, Ryan."

I need to sit. I need some stability behind me to hold me up because, all of a sudden, I feel light-headed. I manage to get to the bed and stare at the pregnancy test.

"This can't be right," I say, grasping for reality. *This cannot be reality right now.*

"What?"

"We wore a condom, Mer. This can't be right."

This isn't bad. This is an okay thing. So badly, I want to pull Merit in my arms and tell her we'll be just fine. That I can take my GED, and I'll get another job. That we can find a place in Granite Harbor together. That we'll have a life together. We'll get married. And everything will be all right.

But that's not what she wants.

She wants the West Coast.

She wants college.

She's been dreaming of this since we were kids.

I look at her open closet door and see pictures of the school she wants to attend in California. Marine animals. Otters. Whales. Dolphins. Exotic fish. Near her light switch, she has a University of San Diego pennant. The one Rebecca bought for her. I glance at her nightstand to see a picture of the Young family.

This dream she's worked for all her life. I can't stand in the fucking way of all that. I won't let anything hold her back from a life, a good life, that she's been building with her smart-girl classes in high school. I won't let anything stand in the way of that. Having a baby and staying in Granite Harbor would keep her here. And, as much as I want her to stay, she can't.

"You're sure it's mine?" Every fucking word kills me.

Silence.

I see her face contort as I try to stare her in the eyes, proving my question is valid. Real. It isn't. I know Merit loves me.

"What?"

I see the pain written on her face. The insult. The sadness.

"You're sure it's mine? The baby." It rips me to shreds. *Fight, Ryan. For her sake.* "I just want to be sure—"

"What do you mean?"

Merit's eyes meet mine. If hearts could crack, mine just did. All over the floor, making a mess of things.

Turn off your love and lie to her fucking face. Because you owe her this.

Heartbreak can be telling. Heartbreak can be seen and not heard.

This I experience with Merit when she says, "Ryan, you were my first. And you think I'm just going to mess around with someone else?"

I shake my head.

Fucking fight for her future because she won't do it, and you know how bad she wants this. Fight.

"You've got to get an abortion. I can't have a kid right now. I'm a junior in high school, Mer."

I see the walls go up. Her heart snaps shut. All in a matter of seconds.

"Besides"—I put the nail in the coffin—"you're not the only one I'm sleeping with, Mer. Come on, you know there are no guarantees in life."

I know this statement alone does its job. Does what I intended it to do. I see it in her face. The disbelief. The hurt. Sadness. Then, anger.

This will be the last time Merit will face me again. I feel it in my gut.

179

I follow her to Portland. Watch her as she sits in the car and cries.

It will be a long road. But she'll get to where she needs to. Merit Young always does.

I watch her as she leaves the appointment, wiping her face dry, a few papers clasped in her hand. I wonder what they say.

The truth is, I haven't been sleeping with someone else. I could never do that to Merit. And I've never regretted telling that lie. I'll take this information to the grave.

I guess I have faith that life will work itself out. If I'm not meant to have Merit, then I'll have to live with that. But I know she is meant to fulfill her ambition. Her goals that she's dreamed about since we were kids.

I watch as she gets into her Jeep and shuts the door.

I wait.

I follow her when she pulls away from the curb and drives to a bookstore not far from the clinic.

She walks out with a book, but I can't read the title.

I hope it is a read that keeps her mind busy. Passes the time. Makes up for the heartbreak I've caused.

This is for the better, I tell myself and pull away from the curb.

Merit Young will be all right. Eventually.

Twenty-Five

Ryan
Hallowell, Maine
Present Day

I jump awake.
    A dream she's gone.
I reach for her.
But the warmth of her body is non-existent.
There's nothing left but her scent.
The darkness is too blinding. I fumble for the light.
All that's left in her wake is a note.

> *Two broken puzzle pieces will never fit together. We're better left alone.*
>
> *Love,*
>
> *Violet*

My heart starts to hammer against my chest. My body starts to sweat. I grab my cell phone and throw it against the wall, fucking pissed at myself for allowing her to slip past me without a good-bye.

Some things are better left alone.

Some things are better left in the dark.

And some memories are better left unremembered.

I hear the swoosh of blood through my ears. I look down at my naked body, what it felt like to lie with her again. Feel her skin against mine. Feel myself inside her. Feeling her in my mouth. Fulfilling her needs in a way no other man can. I wanted to be gentle with her last night. Take my time. Show her things and do things to her that I only wanted to do to her.

But our hearts needed fixing.

So, we both took what we needed.

My dick grows hard almost instantly, knowing where it's been. I don't dare wash my body. Wash her remnants from me.

I have to let her go.

Again.

I can't fix this.

Three Days Later

It's morning. The birds are chirping, and I want to tell them to shut the fuck up. But I don't. Feeling almost hungover, I'm reminded of where Merit isn't.

It's my first day back on the job. I arranged to get busy as soon as possible because I need to stay busy. Keep my mind moving forward, not allowing myself to think of her.

I take a shower and remember Merit's body on top of mine, moving in the moon's light. Panting. Her hair dangling against my balls as I reached up and took her nipples between my fingers.

I need relief.

So, I lean forward and stroke myself with only thoughts of her until I come.

This won't make it better. The heartache. But it will keep my dick from hurting.

I grab a towel. My phone starts to ring.

Please, let it be Merit.

I look at my phone. It's Dubbs.

"Dubbs?" I say.

But there's nobody on the line, just a lot of static.

"Dubbs? Can you hear me?"

The static grows louder and then click.

Silence.

I dial the number back. But it goes straight to an automated voice mail. I told Dubbs to get that set up a while ago when he got the damn smartphone. But he never listens.

I try to shake the nerves that the phone call caused.

Where the hell is he?

Why couldn't I hear him?

Was it really him who hung up?

Did he finally make it home?

I make a mental note to check his house again on my way home. He's probably on the boat. Fishing. But Ronan Fields's name is at the back of my mind. I'll also stop by The Angler's Tavern and see if Felix has seen or heard anything.

I'm on my way to a spot just south of Hallowell, about a half hour down the road. ATV accident. The driver was flown out just before two in the morning. They aren't sure if the driver will make it.

I see Eli's truck as I step out of mine.

"I see the uniform still fits." Eli smirks.

He walks over to my truck as I gather my tools from the cab.

A knot in my stomach has been building since Merit left. I haven't been able to eat or sleep much for that matter.

Does he know about Destiny? No doubt he doesn't know, or he'd have tried to kick my ass already.

"Merit make it back all right?" I ask, trying to act casual.

I've wanted to text Merit several times. Call her. But I know it's space she needs. I'll give it to her for as long as she needs it. Even if it means forever.

"Yeah. Made it back yesterday. What's going on with Dubbs?" He changes the subject.

I shrug as I put my tripod on my good shoulder, my ribs letting me know they're still there with a slow, dull ache. "Hasn't been home in a week. Not like him though. Did Mer tell you about Ronan Fields?"

He nods his head. "Mentioned it. Why does that name sound so familiar?"

"I know. I said the same thing. He's got a laundry list full of drug charges. Some felonies. Some prison time."

We get to the overturned ATV.

"How old is the driver?" I ask Eli as I set down my stuff.

"Twenty-four. Blood test confirmed his blood alcohol level was .31 Touch and go at Maine Medical Center."

I set up my stuff to re-create the scene.

"Is it good to be back?" Eli crosses his arms, standing across the trail.

"Yeah. Feels good." Anything to distract me from Merit and her scent that I'll leave on my sheets for as long as I can. I'm reminded of the ball of knots in my stomach as it growls. "How are Alex and Emily?"

My chest tightens when I say Emily's name. Destiny would have been almost seventeen years old.

"Good. Alex just finished another novel. Got to go meet with some book publisher in New York City."

I hate cities. I hate lots of people. That's probably why I live here. More power to Alex.

"I'll probably go with her. Have Pop and Meredith watch Emily." He pauses. "You all right, bro? You seem off."

No, I'm not all right.

"All good."

But, really, I can't talk about Merit with him. I can't say that I'm in love with her and that she's left for the last time. That she's all I fucking think about.

Eli nods. "All right. Well, I'll let you get to it, asshole."

I smile. "Later."

It feels good to be back in the warden truck. It feels good to wear the uniform again. It's what I know. It's what I've done for my entire professional career.

My phone sounds.

It's a text from Sadie.

Fuck. What the hell does she want?

> *Sadie: Heard Merit left. I'm available and at your service, Warden Taylor. I'll have on your favorite pink nightie tonight if you want to show up at my house.*

Sadie's the type of woman I need to be clear with. She's also the type of woman who can go all night long, which would take away the itch I've been feeling since Merit left. But, since she left, there's no fucking way I'd be able to walk away from Sadie's and feel all right about fucking her. Because that's all it would be. Sex.

> *Me: No, thanks.*

I set my phone down and get to work on the scene.

I pull into Granite Harbor and head to Dubbs's place. It's after four, so the tourists are tucked in nicely to their cottages or inns or have left town completely.

I park on the side of the house under the evergreen where needles used to drag across my window as a kid. One day, when I decided I'd had enough, I went out and took a saw to the branch that billowed just over my window. Cut the fucker down.

My key dangles at the doorway as I push it open. "Dubbs?" I call out just in case he decided to come home.

If he had a choice. If he wasn't taken.

I walk through the entire house, passing the pantry closet where I wanted to make love to Merit. Whisper my name in her ear. Tell her how good she felt against me.

But the house is still. Quiet. There's no one here, and the house clearly hasn't been touched in a while.

As I go to leave though, something catches my eye. In the corner of the living room, behind the front door, I see Dubbs's pocketknife. Something he never leaves behind. Not in a million years. He'd leave me behind before he left his pocketknife.

Examining the pocketknife in its current position, I don't touch it. I inspect the way it's sitting, in the way it was most likely placed, slid, or thrown there. It's open and stuck between the baseboard and the cheap laminate floor, which tells me there was force involved in getting it from point A to point B.

There was a struggle. Dubbs isn't on a fishing trip. There's something totally fucked up going on here.

I need to find the address for Ronan Fields. I'm sure I can find something on him to pay him a visit.

It's after five thirty when I set my keys down on the counter. I pour myself a shot of whiskey and sit down at the kitchen counter.

There's a knock at the door, which is odd. Nobody ever comes to Hallowell unless it's Eli.

God. Merit?

I run to the door, trying not to look too eager when I pull it open.

"Are you"—the guy whose delivery truck says *Great Option Deliveries* looks down at a sheet of paper—"Ryan Taylor?"

"Uh, yeah."

He walks back to his truck and pulls out a crate. He walks back to my front door. "This is for you. Just sign here."

"Wait, I didn't order anything."

"Here's the note the buyer wanted you to have." He hands me the note with the crate.

The delivery guy, a young kid, is clearly in a hurry because he drives away like NASCAR might be in his near future.

A whine comes from the crate. With big black eyes and two floppy ears, a German shepherd puppy stares back.

"What the fuck?"

The puppy in the crate cries, tilting his head to one side.

I set the crate down and let him out, and he immediately attacks my face with his tongue.

A smile tugs at the sides of my mouth. "What in the hell?" I say to myself as I open the note.

Dear Ryan,

I didn't intend to get you a puppy. But, when I saw the ad … the couple getting rid of him had named him Hero. I couldn't not call the number. I met the little guy and the couple who had him. I asked them why they'd named him Hero because I knew you'd be curious, too. They said he had come with the name. They explained that they had to move out of state and that they couldn't keep him.

I know how you feel about dogs, Ryan, so spare me the bullshit lines. You need Hero, and he needs you. It's about time you start loving again. Besides, it will give you something to do.

Merit

My chest aches at Merit's words. I let my hand fall, the note still in my grasp. I watch the little fluffball chase a bug in the front yard. It's been a long time since I had something to care for.

I run my hand over Merit's name, knowing this is where she touched as she signed the note. My stomach growls, and I know I need to eat, but I don't feel the least inclined to do so. Hero runs toward me and barrels into my feet. Then, he barks, as if the shoe is the culprit for his fall.

I pick him up, and he begins to lick my face.

"You like bad guys, Hero?"

He tilts his head to the side, both ears folding over.

"Me neither," I say. "We'll make a K9 out of you yet." I push his head down under my chin and feel his fur against my neck.

I set the crate inside but not before taking Hero back outside to see if he needs to do his business. Inside the crate are puppy food and a check from Merit, labeled veterinarian services.

I laugh. She knows better. I rip up her check, knowing why she wrote it. She didn't want me to bear the costs of a puppy when it was her decision that I needed one. I set out a bowl and fill it with some food, and then I get him some water.

Watching him wolf down his food, I think he might just have a place here, but I know Merit already knew that.

Twenty-Six

Merit
Monterey, California
Present Day

"I t's good to have you back, Merit," Abbey says from the front of my desk. She's just walked in.

I smile. "It's good to see you're on time."

She rolls her eyes. "Someone needed to be responsible after you left. Besides, Eddie would have noticed." She sets her bag on her chair.

"The apartment looked good, too."

She shrugs. "I missed you. It's not the same order when you're not around. There's a big black hole."

I stop typing the email to Ryan. I just want to know how Hero is doing.

Strictly platonic. Just a brief message.

I've been back for three days. Maine seems like a dream, a distant memory that has become a composition of my current favorite life moments and a few of my not-so-good life moments. I close the email.

"What did I miss?" I cross my arms in front of my computer and lean forward.

"I'm totally done with men."

My eyebrow pulls up.

Abbey's eyes meet mine. "No, I'm serious. Totally done."

"What happened?"

She fidgets with her fingers and pretends it's not a big deal, but I can tell by her face that it is a big deal.

"I met *the one*."

"Where'd you meet him?"

"Organic One actually. I was shopping for anything that doesn't walk on two or four legs, and he was standing between the mushrooms and the broccoli, contemplating the price."

I listen.

"Get this: he was raised Mormon, too."

"It's fate," I say sarcastically and force a laugh. One I don't feel in my heart.

Abbey does, too. "He's thirty-five. Runs an internet business. Works from home."

I deadpan. "An internet business? You know that's vague, right? It could be anything, Abbs. Porn. Illegal drugs. A scammer."

I feel as though I've let down my friend. Clearly, she needs me to be the sounding board for good decision-making.

"Actually, it's a food company."

"A food company."

"Yeah, come here."

I walk to her desk as she pulls up his website. "Seven Days a Week, it's called. They prepare meals with recipes and then ship them all over the United States. You can order single meals or meals for your whole family."

We both scan through the site.

I don't see any mention of prostitution, porn, or illegal drugs.

"When did you meet?" I ask.

"The day after you left. Without you to cook, I needed to adult and go buy some ingredients for recipes I didn't know I'd make."

"Wait. You went to the store without knowing what recipes you'd make? Abbey, it's the opposite. You look up recipes and then go to the store to buy the ingredients."

"See? This is why I need you."

Part of me knows she's kidding. Though her mom did most of the cooking when she was growing up, I know Abbey did manage to make a few things.

"If I had done all the research and looked up the recipes first, I'd have missed my chance to meet Ruben."

I slide onto the desk, facing Abbey. "Ruben, the was-Mormon, huh?"

She laughs as she clicks around the website. "Look. Here's a picture."

He's your typical all-American guy with blond hair and blue eyes.

"Handsome. But how do you know he's the one?"

She sighs. "Remember that time you caught me eating your entire birthday cake out of its container when we first moved in together? It was the middle of the night." Abbey never forgets anything. Ever.

"No."

Her shoulders drop. "Oh. Well, anyway, he was doing the exact same thing one night when I caught him."

"Abbs, I hate to say this, but that doesn't constitute fate or forever."

She shakes her head. "No, it's what he said." She's quiet, almost embarrassed or shy. "Do you remember what I said?"

"I have no idea, Abbey. It was midnight, and all I heard that brought me from my slumber was the sound of someone rifling through the fridge—or burning down our apartment."

Abbey clears her throat. "I said, 'Cake is my weakness. Take it or leave it.'"

I stare at her, waiting for further explanation.

"That's it. Sealed the deal."

"But, Abbey, you're deciding your fate based on a few bites of cake? We're talking about the rest of your life here."

Abbey pulls her hands from the keyboard. She's methodical when she chooses her words. Thoughtful. "Mer, it wasn't the cake. It was my heart. Sometimes, the heart knows what the head doesn't. Sometimes, my head doesn't allow me to follow what my heart is saying."

For some reason, her words, this time, they cause a burning sensation in my stomach, and they make my heart pick up pace.

"Why'd you come back?" Abbey asks, knowing full well her question is loaded.

"What do you mean?" I cough to clear my throat, not ready to answer her question.

"Why'd you come back to Monterey, Merit?" she asks again. Louder, as if I couldn't hear her the first time she asked the question, though I think she's just being sarcastic.

"Ryan was healed. He was released to go back to work." I shrug, trying to be diplomatic, fact-driven. I think that's why I appreciate science so much. There's usually a right answer.

Abbey laughs. "Liar."

"What?" I stand.

"You came back because you weren't ready to face your past with Ryan."

"You don't know everything about us, Abbey."

"I know enough to know true love when I effing see it. I know you enough to know that you're in love with Ryan, and that's why you haven't been able to find a guy out here since college." She leans back in her chair, crossing her arms, staring back at me.

I don't know what to say to that. My mind spins. My eyes burn.

"Sometimes," she whispers after a long silence between us, "it's destiny that brings people together."

Fuck.

It's the mention of her name that tells me I am supposed to hear what Abbey is offering. It's like subsequent events that fall into line in a matter of seconds that have actually been in the making for the past seventeen years. Some things that I don't want to hear.

Moment one: I was supposed to experience heartbreak.

Moment two: I was supposed to come to California pregnant.

Moment three: Abbey was supposed to be my lab partner in our general biology class.

Moment four: I was supposed to leave for Granite Harbor each time I was called.

Moment five: I was supposed to hear the exact sentence spoken at this exact time from the person I needed to hear it from.

Moment six: I am supposed to make the realization that Ryan is my destiny.

Moment seven: I am supposed to realize that I need to heal before I return.

My eyes start to burn in meeting each of these moments.

"Hey, you all right?"

I don't know, Abbey, I want to say. I don't know because the rug has been ripped out from beneath me. I'm unstable and unsteady, and I have nowhere to land.

Yes. Yes, you do know, Merit. Move on. Just like you've always done.

"Yeah."

Abbey laughs. "Mer, I've known you a long time. You're five shades of white right now, and you look like death."

"I do not." I reach up and touch my face.

"Have you slept since you've been home, Mer?"

I have to think about it.

"And who were you about to send the email to?" Abbey smirks.

"No one."

"Liar."

Damn it.

"How'd you know?"

Abbey rolls her eyes. "I'm a trained researcher. These things come easy to me. Why are you sending the email?"

"Because I bought a dog for Ryan," I confess.

"Why?"

"Because he lost his."

"Why?"

"Why what?" I'm getting pissed.

"You're right; I didn't plan that question out. Look, you're not sending the email because he lost his dog. You're sending the email because you care about him. And"—she shrugs—"if I'm being real honest, you're still in love with him."

Grab at a straw, Merit. Grab at something to pull you out of this.

Why do I pick these people to be friends with?

"Things happen, Abbey, that have separated us. People make decisions. Say hurtful things. It's not that easy."

"Until you can get past all the stuff, you won't be able to move forward, Mer. Trust me. That's why life with other guys you've dated didn't work out. That's why, on Friday nights, you hang out with Ethel and Lucy. That's why you haven't been able to get past whatever happened between you and him. It's keeping you in the exact same spot as you were when all this shit went down."

Truth. It hurts. And festers in my gut like a wound that won't stay closed, busting open at the smallest touch.

This is coming from a Mormon whose mom is overbearing. Whose dad left her mom for another woman. Who can't seem to find what she's looking for.

Maybe talking about what happened might change the feeling in my chest. I haven't told a single soul aside from Ryan just recently. I trust Abbey. But I'll wait because I hear Eddie making his way down the hallway.

Then, his head pops in. "Gotta say, Merit, it's good to have you back. Really made Abbey step up, tell you that much." He side-eyes Abbey as he walks to the copier.

I missed him with his shaggy silvery-white hair and board shorts, the sound of his flip-flops echoing off the stone cement flooring down the long massive hallways of the aquarium. I missed his not-in-a-rush, carefree demeanor. His advice.

"Good to be back, Eddie."

"Liar," Abbey whispers in a tone so quiet that Eddie misses it, and I almost do, too.

"Board meetin' next week. Mer, can you—"

"Already done, Eddie. Board packets are printed. Research attached to our agenda item."

Eddie turns from the copier. "Did I tell you how much we missed you?"

"Yes, Eddie." Abbey rolls her eyes with a smile and gives me a wink.

Eddie leaves after his copies are made.

"I need a break," I say to Abbey. "Be back in fifteen."

Abbey isn't paying attention to me, and she types away on her computer.

I walk down to our river otter exhibit, and my hands meet the glass as Lucy and Ethel show their excitement to see me.

I assume Leon, Ethel's baby, is in the birthing den, as he's still blind and immobilized until about the fourth week.

"Heard you did well, Mama," I say to Ethel as my hand slides across the glass while she swims. "That's a girl. I missed you, too."

Both Lucy and Ethel glide through the water next to the glass.

Ethel jumps back out of the water and goes to her birthing den, most likely to feed Leon. Abbey said Leon was on an every-three-hour feeding schedule.

In the early hours of the morning, the aquarium is quiet. It's so quiet that you can hear the smallest of noises as I try to tread lightly on the cement floor. It's impossible.

I walk up the stairs and out the side door labeled, *For Staff Only*.

Taking in the cold, salty morning air, I meet a railing that runs the length of the building. The Pacific Ocean is below my perch.

This is where I come to find my right place in the world. Where I feel closest to my mother on the West Coast. Where I feel more human. Out here I feel safe, away from the world.

I slide down the side of the cement wall and watch the white caps move along the ocean's surface, such a small movement for such a large entity. The space between the bottom and the water's surface, the vastness, makes me feel so small. I take pleasure in knowing that I'm not the only person in the world. There's the ocean, the sky, the stars, the planets, and so much more, and I'm just a tiny piece of this world.

What if, in this big world, there's a space for happiness for me? A tiny slice that sits just beyond my reach. A place where I can sit and be comfortable in my own skin. Rest. Have some peace.

"I knew I'd find you here," a voice says.

Twenty-Seven

Ryan
Granite Harbor, Maine
Present Day

"I don't think Dubbs went willingly," I whisper to Eli over the bar crowd.

It's Friday night, and Angler's is packed. It's also tourist season, and it makes for uncomfortable Friday nights.

"You think Ronan Fields took him?" Eli sets down his beer.

"Strong possibility."

"What's the connection?"

"I don't know yet, but I'm having Lindsay in dispatch run criminal history to see what she can find. Who the fuck knows?" I take another sip of my beer and set it down.

Merit's in the forefront of my mind, and it's hard to focus because of that.

"Another beer?" Felix asks both Eli and me.

"I'm good. Thanks, Felix." I throw a ten down.

"Nah. Thanks, man." Eli grabs his wallet.

Shannon, one of the cocktail waitresses, walks up behind us. "Eli. Douche bag." The douche bag reference is for me.

I've done a lot of fucked up shit in the past. Broken hearts. Things I sure as fuck am not proud of.

"Hi, Shannon," is all I say.

She ignores me. Whispers something under her breath.

"I've gotta take Hero home."

Eli laughs. "I still can't believe she did that. Got you a dog." He shakes his head.

My hands start to sweat. I want to ask him if he's talked to her. If she's all right. She hasn't—and probably won't—return my texts and calls.

"Have you talked to her?"

Eli quickly shifts his head toward me. "You haven't? Does she hate you again?"

I peel at the label of my beer. It's not hate. I know it's love. It's hard for her. But there's no way in hell I'll explain it to Eli right now.

"We just haven't connected."

"She's good. Made it back all right. Same Merit. Something up with you two?"

Peel label.

Don't respond.

I can't lie to Eli. I've spent years denying how I fucking feel for this girl. *Get truthful, Ryan.*

"I love her, Eli."

Although the bar is loud with chatter, it's silent for Eli and me.

Finally, he says, "It took Alex several times to point this out to me." Another long pause. "You wouldn't tell Merit no if she agreed to help. You needed the help. It was more Alex's idea than mine to get you in the same house together."

My heart starts to beat fast. Hands still sweating. I continue to peel the label.

"Seeing you guys together this past month, I felt like a fucking idiot for not seeing this sooner." Eli takes the last of his beer.

Maybe, when you're in it, you don't think others can see it. Or maybe it's because we've spent so long hiding, running, from it.

I stand, taking what's left of my beer.

"Remember when I was working the Stehl poaching case a while back?" Eli switches gears as he throws some cash out on the bar, too, and puts his wallet away.

"Ryan, Eli, thanks." Felix holds his hand up to say good-bye.

"Thanks," Eli and I say in unison. He follows me to my truck.

"No. Who's that?"

Eli opens my truck door and lets Hero out of his crate. He pulls a few treats out of his pocket and picks up Hero. Holds him like a baby as he squirms to lick Eli's face.

I lean against the truck, nodding.

"One of the inmates we interviewed for the case said to talk to Stan at The Bill." He shrugs. "So, I did. Seems he knows a few things. Wouldn't hurt to check and see if Stan knows anything. Especially, if Ronan Fields has an extensive criminal background."

Eli lets Hero lick his face and then puts him back in his crate.

"I'll do that."

"I'll go with you."

I shake my head. "I don't want you tangled up in this mess. You have a wife and daughter. No."

Eli stops. Turns. Smirks. "Wait a minute. You value my life more now that I have a wife and daughter than when I didn't?"

"That's right." I open my truck door.

"When you headed over to Portland?" Eli walks to his truck.

Tonight.

"Tomorrow."

"All right. Later," Eli says as he climbs into his truck.

"Later," I say and shut my truck door.

I head toward Portland.

I sit outside The Bill in my personal truck, watching the clientele filter in and out, profiling the comings and goings, getting a feel of what I'm walking into. It's a dive bar. With a padded red door. What it's not is, sophisticated. Classy. Upscale. And the neighborhood was my first indicator.

But it's the perfect neighborhood for intel.

Hero is passed out on my lap. Too much running in the woods today. I stroke the soft spot at the base of his ears.

I take out my phone. Stare at the screen. Wanting to text her.

All of a sudden, the passenger door opens.

What the fuck?

Hero doesn't budge.

Eli.

"How in the fuck did you find me?" My heart is neatly put back into my chest, finding its original pace.

"You didn't seriously believe that I bought that line of bullshit about you leaving tomorrow? And, when you lie, it's all over your face. Just so you know. Work on that shit, would you?" He quietly shuts the truck door, careful not to wake Hero, who is still sleeping.

I smile. "Un-fucking-believable."

"Surveillance?" he asks, looking at the front door of The Bill.

A man taller than normal in baggy green jeans and a Pink Floyd T-shirt looks behind his shoulder and walks in.

"You ready?" I ask, putting the sleeping puppy in his crate with a blanket.

But Eli's already out of the truck.

We make our way across the street and can already smell stale pretzels, booze, and cigarette smoke.

There are a few patrons playing pool and a younger couple sitting at a table in the corner. The guy in the Pink Floyd T-shirt is at the jukebox.

Eli and I sit at the bar.

"What can I get ya?" the bartender asks.

"You Stan?" I ask.

He leans on the bar, one arm stretched out, rag in hand, his eyes narrow, his eyeglasses held around his neck with a rubber strap. "Who wants to know?"

"I'm Ryan. This is Eli."

He doesn't budge.

I slide the grainy image of Ronan Fields across the bar. "You know this guy?"

The bartender stares at me and then at Eli. Taking in our haircuts, facial features, our nail beds, our character. He probably knows our drink preference just by looking at us. I hope this guy is Stan. If he isn't, I'm sure Eli would have tipped me off.

Finally, Stan breaks eye contact and looks down at the picture, putting his glasses on his face. "Ronan Fields," he whispers.

"What's the guy do?" I ask.

Stan slides the same picture back to me, and I slip it into my pocket.

He walks to the other end of the bar to help the guy in the Pink Floyd T-shirt, who curiously eyes us. "You don't wanna know."

Stan makes a whiskey on the rocks. It's an expensive whiskey, which strikes me as peculiar, taking in the guy's choice in clothing.

Stan leaves us at the bar, cleaning glasses, cleaning counters.

Eli and I each order a beer, trying not to make us look out of place or too obvious.

The guy in the Pink Floyd shirt lights up a cigarette and occasionally looks up at us, sipping his whiskey like he's got all the time in the world.

Stan eyes us as Eli and I shoot the shit. A totally fake facade. Talk sports as the old box television sits at our end of the bar, playing ESPN highlights.

It's been forty minutes. I know Hero will need to piss soon. He did do a lot of running with me today out in the woods, so maybe he's still asleep, and maybe he'll be all right for another twenty minutes.

Finally, Pink Floyd finishes his drink. Takes the last drag of his cigarette and throws money on the counter. Nods at Stan. Walks past us and leaves.

Ten minutes after he leaves, Stan walks back over to us.

"Look," he whispers, "whatever beef you have with Ronan Fields, he's not a man you want to mess with. He's got eyes everywhere."

"What does he do?" I ask again.

Stan leans closer. "He's your best friend if you're willing to run drugs for him. But, the moment you fuck him over, consider yourself dead."

"Where can I find him?" I pretend to take a drink of my beer.

"Runs in and out of Mookey's on Tuesday nights. Bar down on Seventh. Other than that, I dunno."

Eli pipes in, "You know the guy in the Floyd T-shirt?"

Stan smirks. "I know everybody who comes in and out of my bar. Guy works for Fields. Better be careful and make sure he's not following you. You might be on some sorta list."

"He's got my dad, Stan. So, yeah, I'm probably on a list somewhere." I take a long pull of my beer. Because, now, I'm fucking pissed.

Stan stops wiping the counter. "What's his name?"

"Dubbs Taylor."

Stan thinks for a minute. "Doesn't sound familiar. Anyway, how do you know Fields has him?"

"Just a hunch." And then I tell Stan what I saw with Ronan at Dubbs's place that day.

"Oh, fuck." Stan takes a deep breath and rubs the back of his neck, throwing his cleaning rag on the counter. He leans in. "If you saw Fields and your dad together, he's as good as dead. Fields never does his own dirty work unless it's personal. He'd bring in a minion before he put his name on any evidence. The only person you'll see him with ever is his old lady."

"It could have been a chat about the weather." I shrug, trying to get more intel, clearly knowing it wasn't a chat about the weather.

Stan laughs. "Your dad's missing, right? Wasn't a chat about the weather."

Eli stands, and this time, I follow his lead, trying to figure out my next move with the new information.

We each throw a twenty-dollar bill down on the counter.

"Thanks, Stan," I say, and we make our way out of The Bill.

My alarm sounds and I hit snooze, already awake, needing a few more minutes before I get in the shower.

It's Merit who's first on my mind. It's been a week since she left. I want to call her again.

Give her space, Ryan. For fuck's sake.

Hero is passed out in his crate. He's not too bad through the night, but I still let him out every two hours to piss.

I can't help but wonder how she's doing. I used to wash my worry away with other women. Use them as a tool to my advantage. Now, with Merit's return to Granite Harbor, everything has flipped the fuck around.

In my nightstand, I have a picture of Merit, Eli, and me when we were barely teenagers. Merit has on her big, beautiful smile while Eli has me in a headlock. We're all smiling. I kept this photo and slept with it under my pillow during times when fear ran rampant through my body, just waiting for Dubbs to drunkenly bust through my bedroom door. I wasn't so scared when the old

Hero was there. But, when Dubbs killed him, I knew it wasn't a safe situation. It never was.

The photo captures what most kids should feel all the time. Carefree. Excitement.

I've always felt I have to look over my shoulder. It wasn't until I finally stood up to the fucker when the fear subsided. Finally, at sixteen, when I grew old enough, strong enough, to stand up to a man so full of hate, the fear went away. But then I was left with some sort of inadequacy. Like I wasn't good enough. And I knew goddamn well that, when Merit left, I'd never get her back. Women, just like alcohol to some, just like drugs to others, seemed to fill that inadequacy with a false sense of ego. But, woman after woman, the fix changed. It didn't meet my ego's expectations. It didn't anymore. I wanted to be fixed. But nobody had taught me how to deal with shit.

Screw.

That's what Dubbs taught me.

One night, he said, "You want to know how you deal with life, shithead? You don't. You just keep runnin'."

I rub my thumb across Merit's face on the picture. She felt a lot of responsibility after Rebecca died. But the level of the responsibility never took away her smile. A smile that told you she would be all right, no matter what.

I know Merit will be all right. She'll make it through life. I just hope she doesn't settle.

Twenty-Eight

Merit
Monterey, California
Present Day

"When I hired you, there was something about you that I knew would never fail. Like a machine, I knew you'd be the one to take over once I kicked the bucket or went crazy enough not to make decisions for the aquarium." Eddie slides down against the cement wall next to me as we stare out at the Pacific. "But I also saw you were runnin'."

I smile—not to appease Eddie, but because he knows more than I think he knows.

"Kid, you've been runnin' from shit your entire life. You're the type who has walked through life too scared to rock the boat because you don't want to deal with the damage if it all falls in the water." Eddie pauses. "But, when Abbey brought you here, I knew there was somethin' special about you. Sometimes, we run because it's easier." He pauses, rests his elbows on his knees, and picks at his callous hands.

Seals bark in the distance.

I take in his words and allow them to settle in my skin, my heart, though I'm not sure I want to hear them.

"Abbey calls me Eddie for what I did to her mom. Can't change it. Shit happens." Eddie clasps his hands together. "She runs late because she knows I won't fire her. She's my daughter. She's snippy with me because she's still hurt. I get it. Sometimes, we run because we're tired of dealin' with a pile of shit. Guess I was tired of dealin' with a pile of shit." Eddie nods. "So, I left. Strayed from my marriage. The Mormon Church can be very unforgiving to people like me. But what I found out is, it wasn't the Mormon Church at all. I just couldn't forgive myself. I know God ain't that bad. In fact, I'd say the dude is pretty forgiving—if you ask an old hippie." Eddie smiles. There's a long silence that falls in line with the sea line, right where the sky meets the ocean.

"What I'm tryin' to say is, life doesn't have to be one big consequence, kid, if you want to be happy. You've just gotta figure out where you hurt and get on with the healin'."

"How?" I whisper as if the word is spoken with someone else's mouth.

"Stop runnin'."

When my mom died, I dived into taking her spot. Maybe more to keep her memory alive, but if I'm being real with myself, it was because it kept me moving forward, so I didn't have to look at my sadness.

Every time Ryan came over with another bruise, another cigarette burn, I'd put all that hurt into fixing him.

When I got pregnant, I ran.

When Destiny died, I ran from anything that made me feel.

A sob chokes in my throat, and when it manages to make its way up through my mouth, there aren't any tears. There aren't any words. There's just a hole in my heart that a sob is trying to protect. Because dealing with life on life's terms isn't as easy as running.

My life has been calculated. Carefully scientific. Set up so that I don't have to feel anymore. Even when I told Ryan about Destiny. Stoic. All these little things are met with my memories of me.

Push it down.

Don't feel.

Keep moving.

It will only hurt.

Protect your heart.

I feel a pat on my arm.

"Stop runnin', kid."

"What if I can't, Eddie?"

"I think you just did." He takes the outside of his thumb and wipes a single tear falling down my face.

"What about you and Abbey? You'll be all right?"

He shrugs. "As long as I show up for life, I think we'll be okay. But I couldn't do that until I stopped runnin' from all the shit I'd caused."

"How will I know?" I look up at him as he turns away.

Eddie stops and turns back. "There's a moment when you'll know. You'll stop runnin'."

"Hi, Merit. I'm Dana." She extends her hand from the plush chair she's sitting in to me on the comfortable sofa.

Therapists probably shouldn't make sofas so comfortable for patients. I assume they want to get their patients in, cured, and get them on their way. Dana won't be able to do that with her patients if she keeps this sofa. I should tell her this.

We shake hands.

Slowly, she leans back in her chair, arms crossed in a relaxed way, as if we're two old friends catching up after years apart.

We're not. Another wall of armor.

"What brings you in today?" She has a pen in one hand while a pad of paper rests on the small table between us.

I'm not sure. I mean, I know. I think. I know why I called. It was the right thing to do.

I haven't said two words to Dana, except, "Here's my insurance information," and, "I filled out a questionnaire that asked about self-harm and depression."

"I lost a child."

Slowly, Dana nods. "I bet that hurt."

I chew on my bottom lip and bite hard enough, so the tears don't fall. "I don't want to cry. I want help."

"When did this happen?" She leans forward to grab her pad of paper. Probably how she'll diagnose me. Write down descriptive words that are used only by therapists in the psychology field. "The notepad is just for my own notes. I hope that's all right?" Dana's smile is soft. Inviting.

"Seventeen years ago."

Dana nods again.

Is there a secret code word for nods?

One nod: keep talking.

Two nods: wow.

Three nods: huh.

Four nods: call security.

Does Dana have a secret phone line to 911? What if she has a crazy person that she didn't know she was dealing with?

"Bet it's been hard to walk through this. Have you seen a therapist before, Merit?"

"No."

"Did you tell anyone about it?"

"No. Except the father, Ryan."

"When?"

"Recently."

Dana takes down the information.

"I want to be free," I whisper breathlessly. Saying this is the most honest thing I've done for myself in a really long time. "I'm tired." My voice grows hoarse. "Tired of being angry. Tired of fighting myself. Tired of grieving." I bite my lower lip again.

Don't cry, I tell myself.

"Whom are you angry with?"

That's a really great question, Dana.

I fill my cheeks with air. Let it out. "Myself. Ryan. My mom. For dying."

"Can you tell me what happened?"

I tell her the story about Destiny. The same story I told Ryan. I don't want to carry this around with me anymore. The conversation, the retelling of a story with an awful ending, feels more freeing every time I tell it.

Dana's pen sits in her hand like a cigarette of a seasoned smoker. Light. Careless. Free.

"Can you tell me more about Ryan?"

How much time do you have?

I tell her the story of a girl who called herself Violet Ugly. A girl who grew into a woman, internally bitter and angry. A girl who loved a boy and he loved her the best way he could. A girl and a boy who made decisions based on what they knew at the time. I tell her about a young girl's dream to go to San Diego to become a marine biologist.

"Did you achieve that?" she asks about the last bit.

"Yes."

Dana jots down another note.

I go on, and I tell her about a young woman who lost her mother at eleven years old. Who tried to care for her brother, her father, and a boy she loved from a very young age.

"That's a lot to take on for an eleven-year-old girl."

Is it?

I don't know. I don't know the truth anymore.

What's easy? What's hard? I just did what I thought was right. What I needed to do.

So, we sit in the quietness, nestled deep in the confines of her office, protected from the world, as her statement lingers, hovering in the space around us.

"Yeah," I finally say. And the emotion of this answer pushes at my chest like the finger of a person who's mad.

Push.

Hurt.

Push.

Hurt.

It's the first time I'm willing to accept that my childhood wasn't what I thought it was. Maybe pain does this. Forces us to see what we've been avoiding for years. For the first time in my life, in a person's office I don't really know, I'm willing to see the truth that, when my mom died, my dad checked out for a bit, my brother hid behind whatever he could, kept busy, and I turned to Ryan because he needed me. That I willingly took over the position of Rebecca Young and that I didn't allow myself to grieve.

"So, when you lost Destiny, I'm sure that hurt just as bad, if not worse?" Dana asks in a very kind way.

I don't allow myself the tears. Once more, I push them down. Just like I've always done.

"How did you deal with it, Merit? Her death? How did you get through it?"

There it is. The one question I've never been asked about my daughter's death. About my mother's death. Because here's the truth. "I didn't," I whisper.

Tears start to fall uncontrollably, as if the grief is met with shock. As if I'm just realizing this for the very first time.

"I'm sorry." I push forward from the sofa and put my head in my hands. The pain in my chest is so severe; I'm sure my heart will fall at any moment.

Please fall. It will be easier than the pain, I tell myself.

Dana leans forward and touches my knee. "Why are you sorry, Merit?" she asks.

I shake my head.

I don't know.

So, I'm honest. "I don't know why I'm sorry."

The sobs get stuck in my throat.

Destiny's scent.

The heaviness of her body on my chest, right where it belonged.

My mother's arms. I was curled up in them in her final days.

I feel as though I'm stunted—emotionally, mentally. Stunted by grief that I wasn't willing to face and heartache. The pain in my chest grows, cracking in segments, just like a windshield. Section by section, the cracks push and move.

"I just pushed it down. I pushed it down, so I could keep moving forward," I say with a strained voice.

"I think you pushed it down because you didn't have the tools to deal with death."

The sobs come out one last time, and the hurt in my chest moves.

I rock and cry.

For Destiny.

For my mother.

For me.

As I drive home from Dana's office, the sun is glistening off the Pacific. The grief has met me where I am. But the hope is that maybe I don't have to carry this baggage around with me forever. Baggage that I didn't know I had. The secrets I didn't know I was keeping.

For the first time in a long time, I see hope. Even though everything with Dana was exposed, someone else knows. Someone else knows, so I don't have to keep all of these things tucked and folded into me like I need them. Keeping them for myself, to harbor the worries, the trouble, the grief, so no one has to see the ugly truths about Merit Young.

I couldn't see enough to know how much Ryan cared for me. Loved me. I couldn't see enough of me to know that maybe Eli didn't care that Ryan and I wanted something more than just friendship. Perhaps I was too focused on what others thought of me.

As I drive along the coastline, back to my apartment, the pain in my chest loosens. Just maybe I'll be all right after all. Maybe I won't, but this is a damn good start.

Twenty-Nine

Merit
Granite Harbor, Maine
Summer 1995

My head rests on my mother's chest, her heartbeat solid and slow. Her chest moves as she breathes. I want to match her heartbeat, her breaths, because her dying isn't something I want.

If you'd asked me, God, consulted me about any of this, I'd have told you no. It's not supposed to happen like this.

Dubbs, he should die. He isn't kind. He's a bad man. And yet he lives. God, why?

My mother mutters something, and I look up to see her eyelids are closed, just the way they've been for the past three days.

She hasn't said anything, and I make a note that, if I'm to die an untimely death, I want to die at home, just like my mom.

Her bedroom window is open. There's a breeze that makes the white sheer curtains billow gently.

So, God, if you'd asked me, I'd have given you my opinion, and said, Don't take the good people. Take the bad ones, the ones who hurt people, the ones who do bad things. Don't take the innocent ones.

But God clearly didn't hear my plan.

I push my face into my mother's frail chest, needing her scent. Needing her arms. Needing her body against mine. A mother's love should never be taken for granted. But I guess kids don't know that until their mom is gone, and all that's left are traces of ash and pictures.

"Mommy"—my voice is quivering, as I know what's coming— "I know you want to stay here with us. I know. But, if you need to go, I understand. I won't be mad." But the tears start to burn my eyes. "I can take care of Pop and Eli." *But who's going to take care of me?* "Mommy? I love you."

There's a low rumble in her chest. Hopefully, she hears me.

Something inside me tells me to go get my brother and Pop. Although I don't want to leave her, nestled on her side, I have to.

I pad down the hallway to get my brother and Pop.

"Is it time?" Eli asks, terror written in his eyes, asking the question we've all thought about but not spoken out loud.

"I think she's close," my lips barely get out. The heavy ache in my chest burdens my body.

Pop somehow is already in my parents' room when Eli and I walk in. He's sitting on the bed with her, stroking her face.

If I ever had a picture of what love looked like, a snapshot of what real love was, I'd take this one right here. My dad and mom.

Losing a mother is hard. But losing a love is also hard.

Pop is on one side, and Eli and I get on the other side of her.

The only sound there is are two birds at the window, calling, singing, maybe letting God know that heaven will have another angel soon.

I don't say anything out loud because I'm too embarrassed, and Mom won't be able to answer me anyway.

Will someone meet her at heaven's gate when she arrives?

Is it a long trip up?

Will she know where to go?

Will she have someone to guide her?

Does she need a change of clothes?

I guess not. Since people are buried in clothes and there's no toothbrush or a fresh pair of underwear, I assume she won't need them.

What happens to her body? What will Pop do with it?

"Where will her body go after she dies, Pop?" Eli asks.

But Pop can't speak because his eyes are full of tears. And love. And sadness. But they don't fall. When I see this, it tells me that I can't cry, that I need to be strong for Pop. My brother.

Mom hasn't talked in two days. Before that, there really wasn't much communication either. The medicine the home nurse had given her kept her quiet. Comfortable. At ease.

Still, Eli's question lingers. Pop hasn't answered it yet.

"Mom … Mom wants to be cremated." His voice is strained, his jawline tense, as if maybe to keep the tears at bay.

We're bright kids—or so Eli and I have always been told. That means, they'll burn her body, and all that'll be left are ashes.

I wonder if Mom can hear us. I wonder what she thinks. Her family planning their final good-bye.

"Mommy?" My lip quivers as I pray she'll answer me. That this will all have been a bad dream or that she'll miraculously recover right in front of us. And it will be a miracle.

Isn't that what you're supposed to do, God? Create miracles?

I feel Pop's hand on my back. I don't want to upset him more than he is, so I burrow down against her legs, against her light-pink summer sheets. The ache in my chest rises again. I close my eyes and allow myself to drift. Dream.

That she isn't sick.

That she's sleeping.

That she'll wake up soon.

That we'll go get ice cream.

That she'll tickle me and apologize for her absence lately. That all this is fatigue.

I pray.

I'm awakened by Pop's voice, a slow, soft, "Merit."

But there's something in his voice that's familiar and not at all familiar. Maybe it's his tone. I'm not sure.

My eyes open. The room is darker. The window is shut. The birds are quiet.

"Merit." I hear my dad's voice again.

I fell asleep.

"Mom. Where's Mom?"

I sit up, and I'm facing the opposite direction I fell asleep in because, when I turn my head, my dad is still by her side. My brother isn't anywhere to be found.

"She's gone, Bug."

"No, she's not. She's right there, Pop."

My insides build with nerves. My stomach begins to twist. My heart starts to pound in my ears.

"She's gone, Bug. She went to heaven," my dad says, reaching out for me.

"No, Pop. No. No. No." I scramble to her side.

Her body is still warm. She can't be dead. I nuzzle my head into the side of her neck, but her breath is gone. Her chest no longer moves.

I move my hand to her chest and wait for the slow rhythm of her heart.

But the beat can't be found.

I tuck my feet underneath me, my shoes on her sheets. I can't help the incessant sobs that begin to come from my mouth. My body involuntarily giving everything it can.

Death isn't easy. Nor is it fair.

I don't think I'll survive this one. The way my body feels.

It's just my mom and me on pink sheets as the room falls away.

She's not cold, I tell myself again.

Bodies turn cold when they die. I've seen it on television.

The detective always says to the other detective, "Body's cold," when the body is clearly dead.

I lie here with my mother until someone touches my shoulder.

Time is a well-oiled machine. It moves forward, no matter what happens. It doesn't stretch. It doesn't shrink. It certainly doesn't pause.

"Rusty is here to take Mom." It's Eli's voice. "Come on, Bug."

I refuse to cry. Tears won't bring back my mom. Tears only bring more sadness. I can't afford that. I told my mother I would take care of Pop and Eli, so that was exactly what I'm trying to do.

When I want to cry, I push my tongue to the roof of my mouth and tell myself it's all a dream. That Mom never existed. Or that she's in the kitchen. I put myself to work. Do laundry. Finish dishes. Make lunches. Hang clothes. Clean a room.

I push all the sadness deeper, tuck it away, lock it in a box, and never let it come out again. I won't allow myself down *that* rabbit hole.

When someone dies in Granite Harbor, it seems like the whole town mourns.

We have an endless food supply. Really, I'm sure that Jenny Love's seven different casseroles will sit in our freezer for a long time. Everyone knows Jenny Love can't cook worth a crap. It's the thought though. We live on Milton's famous chili, the one he makes every year for the Chili Cook-Off for the Fall Carnival and Ida's award-winning homemade raspberry cobbler.

Granite Harbor mourns with us. The Maine Warden Service mourns with us. The chaplain, Katherine Bernstein, the second warden chaplain in the state of Maine, sat with us right after Mom's death. Gave her eulogy. Told me it was okay to cry. She's also the same chaplain who sits with families when a loved one goes missing. A lost hiker. A snowmobiler who falls through the ice. When the mission becomes body recovery rather than a search effort.

But I don't dare cry.

I am afraid I won't stop.

The wardens are here now to talk with my dad. I know they're here for support.

"Has she cried, Brand?" Katherine asks my dad as I sit in the dark hallway of our house.

Warden McCullen and Warden Brash sit with my dad on the couch in the living room

"Yes. When Rebecca first passed. Sat with her body until Rusty came. Nothing since." Pop looks down at his hands.

Katherine nods. I remember her voice from the eulogy she gave at my mom's service. It was soft. A voice I wanted to get lost in. A voice I wanted to hide behind and soak up. One I wanted to remember in moments of panic. Moments of chaos. Moments such as these where I'm not sure where to turn.

As I listen to her talk softly in the living room, I tiptoe to the end of the hallway from my room, deeper into the darkness. I take a cleaning rag to the floor and start in one corner, quietly scrubbing.

In the darkness, I clean because I can't stay still.

In the darkness, I hide, so I can't see my feelings.

In the darkness, I run, so I don't have to face the world.

I'd rather not.

But it's what I do.

Does Katherine need a daughter? Her kids are grown, but surely, she needs a broken little girl who's trying to put the pieces back together.

"Hey."

"Jesus Christ!" My heart leaps out of my chest.

"Cleaning?" Ryan whispers. He nods and sits down next to me. My heart is still pounding.

"You scared me," I breathe.

"I know. Sorry. You all right?"

"Yeah." But, really, no. "Where's Eli?"

"Sleeping."

I look down at my watch. Yeah, he should be. It's late.

"Why aren't you sleeping?" I ask.

"Can't."

I nod. My head falls against the wall as I try to put my body back in working order.

"Did you hear that Michael Bradden shoved asparagus up his nose yesterday at school and was taken to the hospital?"

I smile. Michael Bradden is a jerk.

I pause. "He shoved asparagus up his nose?"

"Well, he might have had some help." Ryan shrugs. Smiles.

"One of these days, Ryan, you're gonna get caught."

He's quiet. "Not today."

We listen to the voices in the living room. The whispers are therapeutic, and we know they're whispering about my mom. About us.

"Do you ever think about your mom?" I ask.

He thinks for a moment. "Not really. Guess you can't miss something you never had or something you don't really remember."

"Do you ever get mad at her for leaving?"

Ryan breaks eye contact with me and stares at his lap. He shrugs.

The silence stays with us. Sits down between us. Takes its time.

"I'd be mad, Ryan. If it were me, I'd be mad."

Thirty

Ryan
Portland, Maine
Mookey's Bar
Present Day

Eli wouldn't let me go alone. It's one thing, working with your best friend; it's another thing to try to fight crime without him knowing.

We're at the bar at Mookey's.

"What do you want?" the bartender asks from the register.

"Whiskey on the rocks," I answer, knowing full well I won't drink it.

Eli sits two stools over.

I arrived first. He arrived fifteen minutes later.

Mookey's is known for its tough location and its even tougher clientele. Located just south on the coast, the railroad tracks run parallel to the bar. Rumors about Mookey's in Portland floated in and out of Portland since we were kids. Bodies have been discovered on trains. Bodies have been discovered in the ocean not too far off from Mookey's, tied to cinder blocks. All the evidence of these murders—sometimes solved—has almost always led detectives back to Mookey's.

The bartender eyes me like he knows something, or maybe it's the fucking nerves in my stomach. I put the whiskey to my lips from the glass he slid down the bar to me just as Eli orders a beer.

I pretend to put the brown poison in my mouth but keep my lips tight, so it doesn't get in.

A guy two rows down from me, in his late sixties—or he could be younger; it's hard to tell with these guys if they've beaten up their bodies with the stuff they put in it or if they are actually the age that they look—flicks his cigarette into the clear ashtray.

The whiskey, still on my lips, burns as I set the glass down on the bar.

Merit asked me why I needed to find Dubbs.

"You should let him be," she said. "Find his own way out of the mess he's in."

But it isn't in me. It's not because he's my biological dad. It's not because he deserves the help. It's because no person deserves to go unlooked for. Not even Dubbs. Because I can guarantee, nobody in Granite Harbor knows he's missing. He didn't contribute to our small town. He didn't support the Fosters when they lost their home. He never attends the Fall Festival or the Christmas tree lighting in December. Doesn't help when someone's down and out. He's a dick. Plain and simple.

Has he been running drugs for Ronan?

Did he decide to use the product for his own testing?

Maybe Ronan found out.

Maybe Ronan hadn't noticed in the beginning. But the supplies got bigger and bigger, and the money wasn't being made. And it all traced back to Dubbs.

Stan at The Bill said though that it had to be big, whatever it was, for Ronan to be seen with Dubbs. Stealing the supply doesn't seem big enough. Not for what he does.

There's got to be something more.

My phone sounds. It's a text from Eli.

Eli: We're fucking game wardens. Why the fuck are we here, in a bar I don't want to even piss in?

I shove my phone back in my pocket and pretend to take another swig of my whiskey. I look at the guy who's a seat over. He's watching the box television that sits at the end of the bar. *What's with dive bars and box televisions?* Fucking surely, they can afford better. Especially with the drugs and money that roll through this place. Money paid to be silenced. Money paid for drugs. Money paid for taking lives.

"You got another smoke?" I ask the guy.

"Fuck you."

Ah. Right.

A fight breaks out at the pool table behind us.

"Fuck you, Abe. Fuck you!" one man shouts to the other. "Spit on your motha's grave."

"Those are fightin' words, asshole," Abe says. "Don't talk about my motha. She was your motha, too, Pauly."

Another man stands between them.

The guy at the end of the bar sits, still staring at the television. "Don't botha. They do this all the time. Fucking idiots." He takes another slow drag of his cigarette.

I turn back around and see Eli do the same.

The guy at the end of the bar rolls a cigarette to me. It was just a fucking conversation starter. Now, I've got to smoke the goddamn thing. I didn't think this through.

"Thanks … I didn't get your name."

"Lou."

But the fight behind us starts to escalate. I look at Lou. He's still facing forward, watching an infomercial.

"You fuckin' told me that I'd get my share!" Pauly yells at Abe. "You didn't even give me half."

"I gave you what I was told to give ya, asshole."

"That's not what Ronan said."

"Who do ya work for? Me or him?"

When Lou stands, Mookey's falls silent. It's only the television that sounds.

He walks over to Pauly, pulls a five-dollar bill from inside his leather vest, and shoves it in his face, and Pauly watches it float down to the beer-stained floor like a starving dog. "Take the fuckin' five and shut the fuck up." He leans in closer. "And, if you don't, I will fucking kill you and put your ass on the train to Massachusetts. Got it, Pauly?"

"Yeah, yeah, I got it." Pauly's hands are up, but when Lou walks away, he scurries for the small amount of money. The money that he knows won't give him the high he needs.

"If I hear a fucking peep out of both ya tonight, I will kill you both myself." Lou walks back over to his stool at the bar, picks up his cigarette, and resumes his stare at the television.

"You seen Dubbs around? Asshole owes me some money," I say, starting the conversation.

Lou's in the midst of a long, thick drag of his cigarette. He's still staring at the television. Then, he slowly turns his head to look at me. "Owes you money? What for?"

"Doesn't matter."

Lou smiles. Puts his cigarette out in the ashtray. His greased-back hair, more salt than pepper, matches the aging lines on his face. The lines that tell me he's lived a much harder life than he's had to. That drugs and law-breaking have been his forte for the last thirty years.

He drops his head to the side, and a peculiar look he gives. "Can't trust narcs, pretty boy. Your money is as good as gone." Takes a sip of his drink, the ice, with several clanks, converges at the side of the glass. Lou doesn't break my stare, as if he's trying to read me.

Good guy.

Bad guy.

I've never been accused of being a pretty boy. Angry? Yes. Intimidating? That, too.

I pretend to take another drink of my whiskey. I know my boundaries. I know my boundaries as a warden. Know my boundaries as a man. Know which envelope to push and which not to. Merit. She's the only one I'll fight for. Not for Dubbs. Not for information. I'm not willing to risk Eli's life, my life, to find Dubbs. This is logical. This makes sense.

But there's a question I know I need to ask. One last question that will put me on Lou's radar. Not because I know Lou, but because I know his type. Short fuse. Angry. Mean. No moral compass. He wouldn't think twice to take Eli and me in the back and shoot us. Put our bodies on the train to Massachusetts, just like he said he'd do to Pauly. And this doesn't intimidate me. What scares the living shit out of me is hurting Merit again. Breaking her heart. Her having to find out that her brother and I were killed. But I have to ask it. "Know where I can find him?"

Lou's got a lazy eye. It's not one that's really noticeable, but it's most likely something that law enforcement officers pick up on. His hands, too, are riddled with arthritis. I can tell from his knuckles on his hands; they're big, swollen almost. Probably something he takes pain medication for—and not the kind he gets from the doctor. The kind that is purchased on the streets. The kind that kids get ahold of, get addicted to, and die from. The opioid addiction in Portland is fucking awful, and it's assholes like these guys, like the Lous and the Paulys and Ronans of the world, who get kids addicted.

Now, I'm fucking pissed.

"How much does he owe you?" Lou lights up another cigarette and takes a long drag, and the tip of it ignites into a bright orange glow.

"Doesn't matter." My anger is getting the best of me.

Chill the fuck out, Ryan.

I feel my jaw tense.

Eli slaps my arm. "Hey, man. You know where the restroom is? I've gotta piss."

Eli can tell I'm pissed.

Lou looks over at Eli. "Outside," Lou answers the question that Eli intended for me.

Eli turns and walks out the front door of the bar.

"Won't get your money back. He was taken care of."

"Why?" pops out of my mouth.

Lou's cigarette again hangs loosely from his lips now. He doesn't break eye contact with the television. He's done talking.

Fuck.

Eli walks back in the bar and sits at his spot, two seats down from me. We both know it's time to go. Lou's not budging.

I stand and throw a hundred on the bar to let the bartender know I'll be back and that I expect the drinks to be stronger than the criminals who drink them.

Not long after, Pauly walks out the front as I wait for Eli in my truck around the corner.

Pauly's a car over, facing the brick wall, pissing.

I wait for him to finish.

I get out of the truck as he zips up. "You know where I can find Dubbs?"

"Who's askin'?"

"He owes me money. Tell you what. You tell me where he's at, and I'll give you half of what he owes me."

I know he'll fall for this. He's the coward criminal. The type who will lie to get himself out of trouble. The type who will throw his pack under the bus if it means less jail time for him. He's stupid and loose-lipped.

Pauly uses the same line Lou did. "Can't trust narcs."

"I know. But I need my money."

Pauly will cave. For money, he'll do just about anything.

"He's dead."

There's no feeling behind Pauly's words. As if I somehow already knew it would end like this. His words have no effect on me. They might later. But, right now, they don't.

"What happened?"

This is where I know Pauly will get squirrelly. Try to backtrack. Try to leave.

"I don't talk about shit I don't see."

I grab a hundred-dollar bill from my wallet.

Pauly's eyes grow shifty, looking from the hundred-dollar bill back to me. He attempts to take it, but I pull it back.

"What happened?"

"Shit! He's gonna come after me, man, if I say a fucking word." Pauly's talking more to himself than me right now.

I push. "What happened?"

"Fuck," he whispers under his breath. Rubs his forehead. Looks at the money again.

I can tell he's got an addiction. This hundred-dollar bill will get him loaded on the streets, a high I know he needs because I can see he's jumpy. A little paranoid. With a wad of cash in his front pocket, I wonder why he didn't leave sooner. It seems like they use Pauly to be the gopher in their operation. A pawn. The delivery guy. A guy who sits back and sometimes pays attention when he's not faded on whatever he can get in his body.

"Narced out the boss to the police. Boss put a hit out on some sort of law enforcement officer."

"What?"

Pauly's legs shake. "Can I have my hundred dollars now?"

Why the hell would Dubbs care about a hit on the LE? He hates law enforcement.

"Who was the hit for?"

"Fuck, man, I don't remember his name." Pauly grows more nervous. His hands fidgeting.

"No answer, no money."

"Come on, man, told ya why he got killed."

I go to put the money back in my wallet.

"Come on!" Pauly is crawling out of his own skin. He reaches up and scratches his forehead for an itch he probably doesn't have. He thinks. "Robert T-something." He thinks again. "No, no. It was Ryan Tanner. No! Ryan T-Taylor. Can I please have my money now?"

Thirty-One

Merit
Monterey, California
Present Day

I start the text with, *Hey.*
  I delete it.
 I start again.

> Me: *It's me, Violet.*

I delete it.
I start again.

> Me: *Hi. Just checking in on Hero.*

I delete it.
I rub my forehead and chew on my thumbnail as a ball of nerves builds in my stomach.

"Be honest. Be open." I remember Dana's words.

I want to hear his voice, not read his words—if I'm being honest.

It's been two weeks since my first therapy session with Dana. Some sessions, I just sat and cried.

Dana said, "When you cry, it's just the grief letting you know you're not done yet."

Some sessions, I didn't want to be there. Some sessions, I didn't want to end.

But, today, the sun is shining, and I'm looking out the window that overlooks the Pacific.

"Hey." I hear Abbey's voice.

I turn to look at her. "Hey. You look like hell," I say.

"I feel like hell." Her bag is pushed behind her as she walks toward me.

"What happened?"

"No more tequila."

"What happened to just two drinks?"

"Oh, yeah. That." She pauses. "Ruben left early. We'd gotten into a fight. From what I remember."

"What was it about?"

In the hallway, we walk toward our shared office at the aquarium.

"Honestly, I don't remember. He was late for our date. I knew the bartender. Told him to pour me a shot of tequila. Then, another. Then, another. By the time Ruben arrived, to my recollection, I used a few choice words. He got pissed. Told me he was taking me home. I wanted to stay. He wouldn't have it. Woke up in his empty bed this morning with a massive headache."

I don't offer any advice to Abbey. I can't in situations like these because I'm not qualified to offer sound advice. Probably due to my track record of failed attempts at love or not trying at all. Not even with Ryan. Not after what happened.

"Did you call him?" I ask.

"No."

I cave. "Maybe you should. Clear the air."

We reach our office.

But, before Abbey walks in, she turns to me. "Maybe you should call Ryan. Clear the air. Sounds like great advice to me."

The mention of Ryan's name from someone else's lips reaches every sore spot and every right spot in my body. I do want to call him.

"I've gotta get me back, Abbs. I've gotta get me back before I make that call."

Her eyes grow big, as if my answer has caught her off guard. "That is the most honest answer I think you've ever given me." She stops. "Whatever you're doing, it seems to be working."

Abbey turns to walk to her desk when she sees the flowers. She turns and looks at me. "I need to make a phone call." She doesn't have to read the tag to know who they're from. She sets her bag down in her chair, slips her phone from her pocket, and breezes past me. "I'll be back soon."

I smile, a tinge of jealousy at their ease to forgive so easily.

Is it that easy? Were words exchanged last night that will leave marks, scars, on their hearts for years to come?

Maybe there aren't scars. Maybe it's the mind's ability to keep tally, to keep track, and every time the heart says it's time to forgive, the mind snaps shut. Maybe that, too, is a layer of protection. A way the mind preserves the heart, so it won't die a broken one.

Eddie watches his daughter walk down the long corridor before he enters our office.

"Hey," I say, leaning against my desk. My feet crossed. A smile on my face.

Eddie stops in his tracks. "Is that … is that a smile from Merit Young? Holy shit." He pulls out his flip phone.

I laugh. "What are you doing?"

"Sending a text to the world. News flash: yes, Merit Young does smile."

I chuckle again as he shoves his flip phone back in his board shorts.

"Anyway, do flip phones have the capability to text?"

Eddie smirks. Walks to the copier. He peeks back over his shoulder and smiles. "It's just real good to see you smile."

A reminder pops up on my phone: *Dana @ 5:30 p.m.*

"I'm going to feed Benny."

He's the new river otter we received from SeaWorld. They've got too many, so they sent one up here and two to San Francisco to rehabilitate. Benny and two other river otters had been caught in a fishing net and severely dehydrated when a fisherman came across them. Benny had some fairly severe cuts, caused by the nets, that needed care.

Benny's in our quarantine enclosure when I toss a few mudminnows to the rock. He swims to the rock, hops up, and eats the fish.

"Hey, Benny. How ya feeling, big boy?"

He waits for another fish, up on his back two wide, webbed feet. I watch him as he stands and then dives back into the water, twisting and turning up toward the surface and then back toward the bottom. Benny pops back up out of the water, still waiting for another fish. I toss a handful of small fish and some carrots. Though he'd rather have fish, carrots are a close second.

The medical staff at SeaWorld didn't think Benny would survive. He had severe lacerations to his webbed feet and hind legs. In fact, when he had been found, they'd thought he'd already expired. But, with modern science and technology, Benny made a comeback they hadn't expected.

Benny nibbles on the carrots, one by one.

"Got to keep you healthy, buddy."

My phone begins to ring. It's Alex.

I answer the phone with the hand that doesn't have fish guts on it. "Hey."

"Hey, Mer."

"Hang on. I need to wash my hands. Just did a feeding."

Behind the stairs of the enclosure is a hand-washing station. I wash my hands and grab the phone from where I put it down on the makeshift shelf above the sink.

"Sorry." I wipe my hands on my pants as I hold the phone between my shoulder and cheek.

"No need to be sorry. You are doing your job. Sorry to bother you at work."

"No bother. What's up?" And then I panic. *Why is Alex calling me in the late morning on a Tuesday?* "Everything okay?" Panic festers deep in my stomach.

"Everything's fine. You've just been on my mind lately, and I wanted to call you."

His name pops from my mouth without control. "Is Ryan all right?"

There's a long pause.

A long pause can mean several things with Alex. It could be that she's simply choosing her words wisely, sensitively. Two, she's got news, but she's not sure how to deliver it. It isn't bad news either—all the time. Three, she's embarrassed to talk about it.

"He's fine," she finally says.

I can breathe.

The fear in the pit of my stomach disappears.

"He's been really different since you left. But that's not what I called you about."

"Oh?" From the other side of the glass, I watch Benny slide agilely through the water. As if he's posing for a picture or being playful. I put my hand to the glass.

"So, your brother and I were talking about wills—"

"What?"

Alex sighs. "Mer, if something happens to us, we have to have a plan for Emily."

Right. That's the responsible thing to do. Have a plan.

"Oh, right."

She's hiding behind words. I can tell.

"Come out with it, Alex."

She sighs. I know she's picking at her nail right now, probably chewing on her thumb. "If something happens to Eli and me, we want you and Ryan to have custody of Emily."

"Ryan and me? As in … together?"

"Well, yeah. You're family."

"But we're not together, *together.*"

"It doesn't mean you have to be. Co-parenting. And, Mer, it's just in case. It's a just-in-case plan."

"Of course," I whisper into the phone. My mind still attempting to catch up to speed.

"I'll send you some documents via snail mail that you need to sign. Nothing big, just some documents that explains what will transpire if something happens to us. Money. Etcetera."

There's a long silence on my end.

Did our parents have a plan when Mom died? Of course, we'd live with our dad, but was there a plan if he died?

For whatever reason, the grief pops up again. Masked behind the current situation with Alex. Funny how grief does that. Hides. Stays hidden for days on end. Then, someone brings something up, and there's grief again, smiling from across the room, waving, as if an old friend. One you've dreaded. One you own a past with. One you seem to shake but can't get rid of.

"Merit?" I hear Alex's voice.

"I'm here." Really only half-listening.

"I'll put the documents in the mail today. Call me when you receive them, and we can go over them. Ryan's already signed them."

Did you hear that, Merit?

He's already signed the paperwork. Meaning he's okay with this. He's already committed to this decision. Or maybe it's just Emily. Maybe it's me, too. Because, if we have to co-parent, he's up for it.

When Alex says his name again, something in my body shudders. It's hidden beneath the hurt, and it comes to life. Maybe it's my heart, allowing me to feel again. Feel like a woman that God intended me to be. A woman who doesn't need a man, but a woman who wants a man.

"Send me the paperwork, and I'll sign it."

"Thank you, Mer. Oh, shit, Emily's up from her nap. I've gotta run."

"Yeah, run," I say.

There's silence on her end.

"Mer?"

"Yeah?"

"Funny how life keeps putting you two back together."

"Yeah," I sigh. "And, Alex? Thank you for asking. It's an honor I don't take lightly."

I hang up and rest my back against the cement wall.

Ryan infiltrates my mind with his hands. His scent. His bare chest against mine. How his lips feel against me. On my body. On my lips. In unspeakable places. There's something that's in his touch, in his way, that commands my need for him. It's not something I've admitted to needing in a long time.

I've always told myself, I can do things on my own. Handle my own business since we lost Destiny. I've never relied on anyone else to pick up the pieces. But maybe, with this piece of vulnerability I see in front of me, it's not a need but a want.

When we made love a few weeks ago, it was for my heart. Ryan did it for me, knowing I'd leave. Knowing I had to leave. But also knowing it was what we both needed. The connection, although seventeen years had passed, was there. More intense. More present than it'd ever been. We made love in our own wake

234

of memories—if not for our past, then for our future, which was uncertain. We stayed in the moment, drunk on feelings and passion. We pushed.

It's just past five thirty, and I'm meeting with Dana.

"Maybe you ought to do a trust retreat? It's something where you rely on a team. There are several in our area," Dana suggests.

I laugh. "Like what? I close my eyes, fall back, and trust someone will catch me?"

Dana shakes her head. "Something more. Like a retreat. I have some in mind. I'll send you a few links."

"Do you think I have trust issues?"

"Do you think you have trust issues?" Dana is seated in her chair. The chair she always sits in. The red chair made of velvet.

Her *think chair* is what I call it.

I toy with my fingers, more able to look at myself, my actions, and my past that has brought me here to Dana's office for reoccurring visits.

"I feel like, if I protect myself, my heart, from hurt by keeping them at a distance, becoming too vested in them, then I won't be too hurt when they leave or let me down."

Dana takes down a few notes. I'd love to see that notebook. What she writes about her clients. Or maybe it's an ongoing grocery list, a to-do list. Or maybe technical terms in the field of psychology for diagnoses.

"I feel, if I keep walls of separation up, then I won't get hurt again."

"So, it's fear-based?" Dana suggests. "From my experience, anger, jealousy, and sometimes sadness are fear-based, right? You were angry with Ryan for what he'd said to you."

Smirking, I say, "Well, yeah. Wouldn't you be? He asked me to have an abortion, Dana. I think that I have a right to be angry to some extent."

"So, justified anger?"

I jerk my head back. My face grows warm as I feel her words crawl up my throat. "What's that supposed to mean?"

"Exactly what I said. You're justifying your anger. That's what's helped you cope. Justified anger." She stops and holds up her hand. "Hear me out. You're angry because why?"

"He hurt me." My words are clear.

"And, when it hurt, when he spoke those words, said those things about the abortion, about another girl, what emotion did it all come down to?"

"I don't know." My voice is louder.

My head is swarming with past feelings and present thoughts. As if I'm trying to climb my way out of a dark hole without a flashlight.

Help, I want to scream.

But I can't. Because the only way out of this one is through the dark, by myself.

"Fear. You were scared. Terrified of losing him. Terrified of the infant that was growing inside you. Did you ever stop to think there might be a strong connection to your mother's death and what happened that day with Ryan? Perhaps you were fearful that you couldn't be the mother Rebecca had once been. Or worse, that Destiny would lose you in a way you lost your mother."

Tears start to fall.

My past meets my future in a collision. An explosion of truth and sadness. For the first time in my life, it's clear.

And the truth falls from my eyes and splatters against my work shirt. The truth I didn't know existed. Until now. My vision is blurry as I try to stare at the glass vase on Dana's coffee table that separates us.

My perception of reality has been thrown off. What I knew about myself this morning when I woke up is the opposite of who I see sitting here with Dana in her office right now. A person I don't know. A person who has been in her own body for thirty-five years has no idea of who she is.

I grab a tissue from the box next to me and wipe my eyes.

"Why did he hurt you?" she asks in a softer tone.

I shake my head and whisper, "I don't know."

"Maybe he had a reason. Maybe there was a purpose for it. Perhaps. I could be wrong. But, from what you've told me, it certainly doesn't seem like his MO with your past together."

My hands fall to my thighs. Weightless and without feeling, I stare at the woman across from me. She, too, is a different person than the one I met just a few weeks ago. My mind is spinning in all different directions, unable to focus on a single thought—or the spinning thoughts are too quick to grab.

"You asked me to help, Merit, and that's what I'm trying to do. I'm trying to help you get down to the causes and conditions of why you sought me out. That's my job."

But I didn't know it would hurt like this, I want to say.

Thirty-Two

Ryan
Granite Harbor, Maine
Present Day

"You think Dubbs is really dead?" Eli asks and then takes a swig of his beer.

I'm caught off guard by Dubbs's actions. *Why would he have gone to the police and told them about the hit on me?* He's my father, yes. But being blood never stopped him from putting a cigarette to my skin. Kicking me in the ribs when I was too loud during the Red Sox game. Punching me in the back when I didn't get my chores done. It was clear he was incapable of love.

What doesn't surprise me is that he didn't come to me first with this information, that Ronan put a hit out on me. We never had the best communication unless it involved a closed fist or other appendages used as weapons.

"No," I finally answer. "Something about all this seems wrong. There's no body. I won't believe it until I see a body. And why the fuck would Ronan have a hit out on me?" I set my beer down at Eli's kitchen table. Eli's across the table, Alex sitting next to him. "I don't know Ronan Fields. Think I'd remember his name if I arrested him."

Pauly wouldn't answer that question when asked. Killing a cop is a federal offense. Even a hit out on a cop is punishable with prison time. But proving it would be almost impossible without evidence. But Ronan, or one of his minions, was careless with information because Dubbs heard this somehow.

"But why would they keep him alive? What could he give to Ronan and his clan?"

I shake my head. "I don't know. But something tells me he isn't dead." I look at Alex, concern on her face. "I'm sorry, Alex, for bringing Eli into this."

"Don't know why you're sorry. It was his choice to go, and I understand why. I'd probably do the same if it were Bryce."

Bryce is Alex's best friend from California.

I stand and take my bottle to the sink. "Give Em a kiss for me?"

"Drive safe, Ryan," Alex says.

"Yeah, watch out for bears, asshole." Eli laughs.

Smiling, I call Hero, who's curled up by the fire, clearly comfortable but eager to go home, too. He does his puppy hop over to me, and I pick him up and take him under my arm.

My phone chimes with a text message as I say my good-byes, and my heartbeat rises.

Please, let it be Merit, I think to myself as I leave.

I need her voice. The voice that held steady through our formative years. The voice that never wavered.

People will do just about anything for money, but I'd do anything for Merit.

I slide it out from my pocket. My heart jumps out of its rhythm as I read the words across the screen.

> Sadie: Home alone again. Come by if you can. I'm lonely and in need of you.

I feel it in my dick. And not because it's Sadie, but because I picture they're Merit's words. Remembering what she felt like. Her tears as they fell down her face when I connected with her in ways I'd never been able to connect with anyone.

I want to feel relief. Relief from all this shit with Dubbs, with Merit. I just need a break. Sex helps with that. Sex without strings attached was a drug I relied upon for years. Used it. Took it when I could. At lunch. In the morning. In the restroom at Angler's. I see the pattern now. I knew Merit wasn't coming back those years ago, that I'd fucked everything up. I'd used sex to take away the loneliness. The sadness. It wasn't my childhood that I tried to escape. That was survivable. I used sex to forget Merit. Tried for years to find someone else. Sex was my solution for a long time. Until the day it didn't work anymore.

Until my fucking heart said, *Enough already.*

Sex would feel real good right now, my ego says.

But, when it's over, you'll be in the same place you started, my gut says.

You deserve this, Ryan. Merit said she wasn't coming back anyway, my ego chimes in.

You save lives, ego says. *Help recover bodies so loved ones can have closure.*

Progress can be slow, but it's worth the wait. You keep doing what you're doing, and you'll keep getting what you're getting, my gut yells.

Merit makes me happy.

Hero makes me happy.

Being part of an entity I believe in, the Maine Warden Service, makes me happy.

I text Sadie back.

> *Me: No more. I'm done. I can't do that anymore.*

I can't keep running.

Sadie texts back.

> *Sadie: Fuck you.*

I laugh as I throw my phone in the pocket just below my dashboard. I flip on my headlights and drive the hour home to Hallowell.

I need to move back to Granite Harbor. I make a mental note.

Granite Harbor has always been home. Even if I had a shitty upbringing, the Young family always made up for it.

241

Maine Warden Service Headquarters
Augusta, Maine

"Chief Markel, thanks for taking the time to see me." I slide into the mahogany chair on the other side of his desk.

His glasses sitting on the bridge of his nose, he scans through some documents.

"Sergeant Taylor, what brings you in this morning?" He doesn't look up from his work.

Usually, our daily work doesn't involve the chief, and the only time we ever have to meet with him is for serious reasons that can only be handled by the chief. That has been never in my case. But, if we want something done, we need to go straight to the source.

"Superior job on the Lago case. I read through your scene reenactment. Top-notch."

"Thank you, sir. But I'm here this morning to ask about Ronan Fields.'"

The chief stops. Looks up and meets my eyes. "Oh?"

"It's been disclosed to me that there was a hit taken out on me."

He's quiet.

"That true?"

The chief removes his glasses from the bridge of his nose and stares. "Where did you hear this?"

"I'm sorry, sir, but I cannot reveal my source."

The chief sits back in his large leather chair.

I clasp my hands together. "It either is, or it isn't, Chief. It's that simple."

"Sergeant Taylor, if there was a threat put on your life, I sure as hell don't know about it. I haven't heard a word on this."

I shrug. "Rumor is, Dubbs came to law enforcement and snitched out a man named Ronan Fields and that Fields killed Dubbs."

It isn't a secret that Dubbs is my father. The Maine Warden Service is aware that my father isn't on the good side of the law.

"I'll make some calls and be in touch with you by the afternoon."

"Thank you, sir." I stand and shake his hand.

I trust the chief, but I've also got to stay diligent in protecting myself, and finding Dubbs has become my mission.

I'm walking through the main floor of headquarters when a hand jerks my arm from behind and pulls me into a dark closet. The door shuts behind me, and my back hits the wall.

Lips meet mine. Soft lips. Hands meet my dick through my pants.

This would be an easy out. Allow my mind to escape just for a few minutes because that's all it would take.

There are two things I know for sure. One, these lips don't belong to Merit. Two, I can't do this with anyone else. Not anymore.

My zipper is eased down, and I can feel her hand against me, pushing herself closer to me.

Fumbling in the dark, I pull her hand from my dick and push her off of me. "Stop, Faynette."

Though I can't see her, I know she's standing in front of me, fucking pissed.

There's a drawstring light to the left of the small closet, and she pulls it on.

She pulls her shirt open, exposing her gray lacy bra and her overflowing tits. Faynette unhooks her bra and allows her tits to fall. Quickly, she takes my hands and pushes them over her tits, against her erect nipples.

I slowly pull away, trying not to embarrass her. "Faynette. Stop. I'm not doing this with you. Get your shirt buttoned up." I take a deep breath, putting my hands on my hips, as she buttons her shirt back up. "Look, I'm in love with someone else."

I've never said those words out loud. In fact, I've never said those words. *In* and *love* were never part of my vocabulary.

"I've never taken you for a man with willpower, Ryan," she says hastily as she finishes her buttons. "I've never taken you for a man to be in love. A nomadic heart and good with his dick? Perhaps." She shrugs. "A troubled childhood and a shitty life are what made you."

My head jerks back. "What did you say? How the hell would you know what my childhood was like?"

Faynette crosses her arms. "Looked through your file. Look, I had to know what I was getting into before I slept with you."

I laugh. "Are you fucking kidding me? You looked through my file?"

"Ryan, all you're good for is a great fucking lay. You'll never commit. Don't fool yourself. You're going to live a long and lonely life, afraid to commit to anyone. Because, one day, you'll be old. You won't look the way you look today. You'll drive your warden truck until you're sixty-five. They'll force you into retirement because you can't seem to keep up with technology. And then you'll think, as you sit on your porch, drinking your Ensure, *I wonder what happened to Faynette.*"

As I hear this come from her mouth, I realize she doesn't know me at all. "Well, you've got one thing right, Faynette. I'll work until I'm sixty-five. But you, on the other hand? I'm not so sure. You've just sexually harassed me."

She laughs out loud, dropping her head, and then stops. "You can't prove that. Nobody will believe you."

"That's the thing about body cams. They're so damn little that you just can't see them."

Faynette's mouth falls open.

I turn and grab for the door handle. "The thing is, I told you no, and you kept coming at me. I wonder what the chief will think when he sees this. I'd probably start packing your things."

I leave Faynette in the closet as I quietly shut the door behind me. She'll need a minute.

Will I turn over the body cam?

Not unless I'm told to do so.

I don't want to embarrass Faynette.

But, if I'm asked, I'll be truthful. The camera will corroborate my story.

Thirty-Three

Merit
Monterey, California
Present Day

After leaving Dana's office, I go straight home and to my room. The house is quiet, no signs of life, which means Abbey and Ruben most likely made up.

I close the door to my room and walk to the large window, crossing my arms. The sun is setting over the Pacific. This is why Abbey and I picked the place years ago. Our bedrooms both face the ocean with big, spectacular windows that give us the view of the outside world that we get to visit as spectators.

The leaking colors of deep reds and dark oranges spread across the sky, thick and rich like honey.

Two people holding hands make their way down the beach.

A man with a gray beard shuffles down the sidewalk.

Seagulls call.

A woman runs, as if trying to beat her time from the previous day.

Tally, from Tally Man's Florist, sweeps his front walk.

Time moves whether I'm moving forward or not. Time moves. People go. The world keeps spinning.

I realize I've been stuck. Stunted by trauma I didn't think I had. A perception of reality I built based on false truths I told myself.

Lie: My mom's death hurt, but it didn't break me.

Truth: It did. I just didn't allow myself to feel it until now.

Lie: Holding my dead child in my arms was just a fact of life. Shitty things happen.

Truth: My heart broke in two pieces that day.

Lie: I'll get over Ryan.

Truth: I was and still am terrifyingly in love with him.

The sun has reached the end of the show, but the encore performance is just as stunning. The sun has left behind the sea, traveling the same distance to another part of the world. In the sun-soaked clouds, I see the outline of an angel.

I wonder if it's my mom letting me know that she's with me.

I wonder if it's my Destiny playing in the clouds.

Or maybe I'm just as crazy as I seem.

I walk toward my full-length mirror in the corner of my room, the darkness beginning to pour through my window. I see my face with enough light that's left. The woman staring back at me is unrecognizable. I don't know her likes, her dislikes, what she enjoys, and what she doesn't enjoy because I don't remember the last time I've enjoyed something. But I do remember the way Ryan made me laugh about a month ago. I remember it in my heart. I remember the sun beating down on my shoulders in the softest way, the way my body relaxes when I'm with him. The way his smile covers half of his face and the way his dark blue eyes look back at me, asking me to give him my forever. I remember that. But I didn't enjoy it until this moment right here. Right now.

How many other moments have I missed?

How many other times have I missed the pure feeling of joy because I wasn't able to feel it?

"How many?" I say to myself while staring into the mirror. Frustration and sadness take over my chest, and I feel as though I can't breathe. "Breathe," I say out loud. "Just breathe."

I was unaware that my heart was trying to take care of itself. Preserve itself. Protect itself.

These words come to me. They're not my own. *Fear not of what you haven't lived and come to what you love.*

Tears fall from my eyes, trailing down my cheeks like softly written words.

You'll grieve your mother. You'll allow yourself the time.

You'll grieve your daughter in a way some only know.

And then you'll be free.

Grief is ever-changing. Binds and moves freely through our lives until, one day, we remember something that brings the tears back. Hang on to these moments, the unfamiliar voice says.

For Destiny, it was the way her perfect little lips formed at the close of her mouth, the way her long eyelashes rested on her cheeks. The way she looked so peaceful, though her tiny little soul was gone.

The way my mother used to make everything okay. No matter the situation, if Mom was there, everything would be okay.

I'll never forget when Frankie Pullen's body was pulled from the lake when I was seven. Frankie had sat next to me in kindergarten at Granite Harbor Elementary. His family had been ice-fishing. Frankie had fallen through. The Warden Service had spent countless hours searching for him.

Pop took that one especially hard.

Finally, a week later, they'd recovered his body from the lake.

When my mom tucked me in that night, I asked her why God hadn't saved him.

Her answer was, "Mistakes happen. God can't control the awfulness in the world. Things happen in life that are beyond our control, too. And, if we can accept that answer, then we can gain a little slice of peace in our lives."

I guess it comes down to causes and conditions. If I can accept this answer, then maybe I can be free.

The image in the mirror stares back at me as I catch glimpses of our childhood, Ryan and me. Together. Moments I remember. Moments I'd rather forget. Regret. Promise. Truth. Two different people. Separated by defining moments that somehow, along the way, divided us.

You have lost, Merit.

You have loved.

You've been broken.

But you've also been put back together. Somehow, the people you love have given you words along the way that have led you to this exact moment right here.

Seize it.
Define it.
Own it.

I reach up and wipe my face, pushing the wetness back into my hair, and I use my sleeve to wipe my nose.

When I stare back at my reflection, now, there are two of us, Young Merit and I.

"I'll take it from here, little Merit. I'll love again. I'll try. And I'll try to bring down the walls that guard my heart. But it's time you go, little Merit. When the tears want to come, don't worry; I won't fight them. I'll allow them to fall. I'll be okay."

With that, my younger version of myself smiles back, disappears. The current version of me appears, and for a moment, I see my mother. Not next to me, but in me. Her eyes, her mouth, her hands. It's as if I can feel her in this room with me. A warm sensation comes over me, followed by a peace I've never known. I'm in the moment. Quiet. Calm. Fulfilled. I feel an overwhelming feeling of acceptance. That I'm exactly where I'm supposed to be.

A tear starts down my cheek, and it's not made of sadness, but for the first time in a long time, it's faith. I know, without a doubt, that I'll be all right. No matter what happens in my life, I'll be okay.

I turn and grab a blanket from the foot of my bed, and I curl up and go to sleep.

When I wake up, it takes me a minute to gather my thoughts. Collect them. Store them and try to remember what I was doing last night. I haven't slept that good in a long time. I'm refreshed. Collected. Still at peace.

Through my big bay window, the sky is bright and blue, which tells me it's the next day. I glance over at my bedside clock, which reads *9:52* a.m.

I haven't slept this late in years. Since before college, since the night Ryan and I made love. We woke up late. He and I were wrapped in each other, our bodies, our skin stuck together, like the bond we'd started as children. I remember that morning. He didn't want to leave. Didn't want to leave my body, leave it untouched.

Although sore, we made love more. He touched me in ways that old lovers bend for compromise, stretching the strength of love, knowing that, in the end, all we need is one another.

I reach for my phone just as I remember his touch against my breasts. His hands between my legs and the rhythm of his pounding heart against my chest.

It's Saturday morning, and I highly doubt Dana is in the office, but I call her anyway and leave a message, asking to meet with her, telling her I've got an idea and that I need a second opinion. Ask her if I can come in on Monday, and thank her. I hit End and ponder how quickly this all happened. After all, it's been only two weeks since I've been meeting with her. But it doesn't seem odd. It only seems right, fitting. I think everything has a way of working itself out in God's time and that all the pieces fall together in exactly the right time that they're supposed to.

People are meant to meet.

Advice is supposed to be given.

Timing is perfect. We just need to be open to the fact that it's not always going to be in the time frame that we want.

So badly, I want to call Ryan. I want to tell him all the mistakes that I made. Apologize. But, most importantly, I want to love him in the way that he deserves to be loved. Show him what it's like to love without hurt. But I'll wait. I need to wait.

I throw on my jogging pants, a sports bra, and a tank top. I wash my face and head to the beach. I want to get back to running, to taking care of my body.

I walk down to the parking lot of our condominium and take a right, which leads right down to the beach.

It's been a long time since I've thrown on these shoes to do something other than work. Stretching, I touch my toes and pull at my elbows, making sure my body is warm. I take the running path that runs parallel to the water's front, knowing my body will feel it later.

Monterey Bay has given me a temporary home for many years. It has provided me an escape, a place to hide from issues I didn't know I had. It's given me a place of reprieve, but it's never been home. Nor was San Diego. Home is where snow touches down at the beginning of December. Where the sun rises over the ocean and sets among the evergreens that surround our beautifully broken small town. Where families suffer in silence and are loved through it. A place that shuts down when locals get married and where funerals mark time. A place where memories become fixtures of feelings, both good and bad. Where the whole town gathers around during the Fall Carnival, the annual Christmas tree lighting ceremony, the Mudd Run in the springtime. A place where every single person has known you since birth.

My breathing quickens, and I know my body will start to talk soon. But I find a rhythm with my breaths.

I look up just in time to see a woman with gray hair, almost purple in the morning sun, and a little girl with my color hair, walking hand in hand. The little girl turns to me.

My heart seizes, and emotion comes over me when her eyes meet mine, but my legs keep moving.

"Destiny! Look at this seashell," the grandmother says.

I stop in my tracks at the mention of the girl's name.

When I turn to face them, I'm a bit past them, but the grandmother, this time, catches my eye. If my mother could have reached the age that she'd be today, she'd look like this woman.

They both stand there, waving, as if it's my mother's way of saying, *We're okay, Merit. I've got Destiny until you get here.*

I wave back, and then my fingertips fall, emotion filling me with happiness, love, acceptance. After a long while of staring at each other, I watch them walk away, slowly disappearing into the haze and mist the ocean provides.

Timing is everything. A sob chokes in my throat. My mom had to go first to be there for Destiny when she arrived in heaven.

I'm overwhelmingly moved as I realize we get what we need when we need it if we're open to the idea of acceptance and forgiveness.

And then Eddie's words come to me. *"There's a moment when you'll know. You'll stop runnin'."*

250

Thirty-Four

Ryan
Hallowell, Maine
Present Day

It takes a lot to scare the shit out of me, but the black sedan makes the hairs on my neck stand at attention, and I notice it in my driveway before I notice the light on in the kitchen. Could be Eli, but I don't see his truck.

The light's on so clearly, so whoever's in there isn't trying to be sneaky. I do, however, turn the Track My iPhone switch on just in case the person inside drags my body somewhere.

I reach under my seat and pull out my handgun. I load it and crack the windows for Hero, who's passed out in the front seat of my truck.

I move quickly as I get out of the truck, knowing what Eli and I have done lately, working with shady people to get some answers. I send a short text to Eli.

> Me: *You and the girls all right?*

He texts back.

> Eli: *Eating dinner together. Yeah, what's up?*

I push my phone back into my vest and make my way to the front door. Quietly opening the door to my house, I say, "Hello?"

"In the kitchen," says a woman's voice. A voice that reflects a lifetime of cigarette smoke, a life vested in hard knocks. It can be only one person. She knows where I live. Maine is a small place.

Somewhat relieved, I shove the gun back in my holster and come around the corner to see my mother sitting at the dining room table.

Her face is bruised, cut, her hand bandaged.

No matter if she raised me or not, disappeared and left, leaving me with a man who sided with the switch, his fist and feet to carry out discipline, no woman should ever look like this.

"Hi." Her voice is more hoarse than it was seconds ago.

I walk to the counter. "What are you doing here, Mona?"

Her eyes fill with tears as she bites her bottom lip, staring at her fingernail paint that's chipped away like splattered paint. Her hair is wiry and two-toned, dark roots and blonde ends.

Four times, I received calls from my mother.

One: on my sixth birthday when she came back and wanted to be a mom again, and then she left a week later.

Two: she tried again when I was ten and left two days later.

Three: at sixteen when she needed money.

Four: and the last time she called me was when I was twenty-eight. She'd landed in jail for the hundredth time.

It wasn't a secret to me or to Granite Harbor that my mom couldn't lay off the powder.

"Spare me the shit and the sob story, Mona. Why are you here?" I set my phone down on the counter with my keys.

"It's bad, Ryan, real bad." She picks at her nails. "You need to get out of here. He's after you."

"Who's after me?"

"Ronan. He wants you dead."

"Why?" My heart picks up pace, but as I breathe, my anger grows.

She chokes out a sob. "Look, Ryan, you need to get out of here."

"No." Confidence refines my tone. No man will ever intimidate me. I decided that at sixteen years old when Dubbs took his last swing at me. "Why would he care, Mona?"

"I knew you'd be here, slut, once again trying to prove you're the mom you never were." An unfamiliar voice sounds from behind me.

Mona starts to cry.

"You stupid bitch," he says to her as he comes into view.

Ronan Fields is tall with dark brown hair that's slicked back like a dated car salesman. Dresses like he's a few minutes late to the party. Dresses like he doesn't have a few minions working under him. Dresses like people would underestimate him. Chalk him up to a man who takes orders, not gives them. And maybe that's what he wants. White polo that's a size too small. Dark jeans.

"Please don't touch him. Just take me," Mona says.

I slowly edge my hand back to grab my gun.

Ronan laughs as he walks through the dining room, opposite side of the table from Mona, his gun in his hand like it's an added appendage. He looks at me. "Take your gun from your holster, unload it, and give it to me."

My skin begins to crawl.

Don't let him get to you. He wants to see you get pissed off. That's what cowardly criminals do.

"What do you want, Ronan?" I ask. "What is it that you want from me so badly?"

Mona sits, chewing her thumbnail, tears still streaming down her face. She doesn't look at either of us.

"You don't know?" He smirks. "You didn't tell him?" Ronan looks at Mona again.

"Let Mona go," I say—not because she's my mother, but because I'm a warden. My job is to get everyone out alive, including the bastard with the gun.

He laughs. "So she can run to the police and have them surround the fucking house before I kill you? No fucking way, not a chance."

"She wouldn't do that. You've kept her doped up for years. Brainwashed her. Come on. She wouldn't betray you."

He mulls this over for a minute. "You know, I've tried over and over to figure this out. Played scenarios in my head. How the timing would have been just absolutely totally fucked up thirty-three years ago."

My phone rings, and it interrupts Ronan. It's Eli. After two more rings, Ronan gets impatient.

"Shut that fucking thing off when I'm talking to you." Ronan grows furious and then fires a shot into the ceiling.

My heart begins to pound as my eyes slowly meet his.

You will not intimidate me, fucker.

Mona begins to whimper. "Just let him go, Ronan. Please." Her fingertips are white from her own pressure as she balls her hands into fists.

I silence the phone.

A text message shows up on my screen, but I don't break eye contact with Ronan. I don't want him to know I've received one. But, when Ronan's own phone begins to ring and he looks down, I look at my phone. It's from my lieutenant, not the chief.

> *Shreeves: Do not go home. Ronan will be there, waiting for you. We are on our way.*

Too late.

Ronan shoves his phone in his pocket. Taps the gun to his head, another intimidation ploy. "Where was I at?"

"You started with thirty-three years ago," I offer him.

"Don't contradict me."

I put my hands up in surrender even though I want to fucking kill this guy.

"Mona, why don't you tell Ryan why we're here?" He carelessly handles the gun.

Her face is full of pain—not just for this moment, but also for my entire life. Regret, I see it. Demons she couldn't quiet long enough to raise a son. Demons so loud that they kept her in dark rooms with unsavory people.

Ronan takes the gun and aims it directly at her. "Tell him, Mona. *Now!*"

She whimpers more, putting her shaking hands up to defend her face, something I'm sure she's had to do often.

"I-I took you to Dubbs's house. He-he was the only person I could think of." She wipes her nose with her sleeve. "I wanted to keep you safe, Ryan. I did."

"Maybe, if you had kept him with the people who gave him life, we wouldn't be in this predicament now, stupid bitch. Go on. Tell him."

"Dubbs isn't your father, Ryan. Ronan is."

"And can you believe the dismay I felt when I found out my own flesh and blood was a game warden? A fucking law enforcement officer. Can you believe what will happen when the guys start to find out who my fucking son is? It's over. It's over for me. I need to pledge my commitment to my people."

I fucking explode. "You're nothing but a fucking coward, Ronan. You've been running your entire life. Drugs. The law. It doesn't fucking matter. Hitting, beating on women to make yourself feel like you're some sort of god. Let's get one thing fucking straight. Killing me? That doesn't make you a man at all. You're just a coward, running from the truth. Go ahead and fucking shoot me."

I see the anger start in Ronan's face because he's turning a bright shade of red. His eyes are wide, and his lips are curved in a smile. It's an agreement he's made with himself that he'll always be on the other side of the law. He'll defend himself to his guys and do what he needs to show the right image. He was probably a kid who was never accepted by his peers. Spent his formative and high school years searching for acceptance. The bullied kid.

One thing Ronan and I have in common is, I searched for acceptance, too. But being raised with a man who beat my ass is the sole reason I'm in this position right now. I will always stand up for what is right.

"Shoot me, Ronan," I whisper. "Kill me."

A gun fires.

Smoke dances.

I feel my body give way.

I see Ronan.

I see blood.

I see black.

Thirty-Five

Ryan
Granite Harbor, Maine
Summer 1995

Merit, Eli, and I lie on the grass just past the harbor. It's been two weeks since Rebecca's passing.

The seagulls are a mess today. I swear, they get louder during the summer, begging the tourists for more food. Tourists feed them bread or whatever leftovers they have with them. I want to tell them not to do it, that it's bad for the birds, but I don't.

"Ryan?" Merit whispers.

I look at her. "Yeah?"

Her hands cradle her head, her blonde hair falling around her. "Who was that lady at your house today?"

"My mom."

Merit turns on her side to look at me. "It was?"

I nod.

"Why'd she look so sad? Wh-why'd she have a black eye?"

I shrug. "Dunno."

"Why'd she come back?"

It's quiet for a moment.

"Said she wanted to get help, so she could be the mom I needed."

"What's she gonna do?"

"I don't know."

"Has it happened before?"

"Once. I think I was five."

Merit rolls to her back, staring up at the same blue sky as me.

Eli's on the other side of me. He rolls on his side to face me and Merit. "What are you gonna do?"

I shrug. "Wait, I guess."

"Should you call the police? She looked real bad, Ryan. Skinny. And beaten up."

The difference between Merit and Eli and me is that I've seen her before like that. She always seems to survive. It's not that I don't worry; I do. But, when I ask her about it, she tells me not to worry and that she's okay. I want to believe her.

"No."

"Maybe we should talk to Pop about it?" Eli asks.

I shrug. "Maybe."

But all I want to do is let the sun soak into my face, allow its rays to warm my body. Lie in the grass like a kid without a care in the world. Not one who has to go back to the house of uncertainty and violence.

When I go back home, I'll smell—vanilla and cigarettes. It will waft through the house for a few days. It will make Dubbs angry. He'll leave on the boat for a week or two. It will be quiet again. I'll feel more at peace, knowing I don't have a fist coming at me for a week or so. That'll be nice. So, things are good. Things are real good for the moment.

Maybe my mom will come back, and she'll be wearing a blue dress, like Rebecca did on Sundays. Her face will be like a doll's. Her nails will be clean, and the white powder under her nose and on her fingers will be nonexistent. I think that's the stuff that makes her act the way she does.

"Worst-case scenario," Merit whispers, trying to take away my fear.

"She turns up dead."

Merit turns to her side again and faces me. She stares at the side of my face for a long minute. "That she's been abducted by the circus and forced to perform as a tightrope walker. She fought tigers and elephants and bears to come find you." A grin starts on either side of her mouth as she twists back onto her back.

A warm feeling starts in my stomach and moves to my heart.

Yeah, I like that, I want to say but don't.

"Sorry, not all worst-case scenario. I blame it on my optimism."

I love Merit for giving me her best, even when she doesn't feel it on the inside.

I wonder, too, if Merit is trying to bring back her own mom. Maybe the scenario she wants to believe is about her own mom. Because, truth be told, in my scenario, it's my best-case scenario.

I think it would be better if my mom was dead. It's hard for my brain to wrap around this thought that I have as it washes over me. What boy wants his own mother dead? I see the hurt and pain in my mom's eyes. Rebecca never had that. Not even as she was dying. Life wasn't a burden for Rebecca. Eli and Merit weren't her burden; they were why she fought until she couldn't fight anymore.

Rebecca had always tried to protect us, put an escape route on both our plates, an allowance of time and space to be kids. Even if it's just for a moment.

"She won't die, Ryan," Eli adds. "Worst-case scenario. That she comes back a few more times in a few more years, more tired. But she'll come back to check on you to make sure you're all right."

Worst-case scenario started as the three of us playing out the worst that could happen. But Eli and Merit always seem to bring in the positive in my scenarios.

Fools.

I smile and allow the clouds to soothe me, my two best friends on either side of me.

We walk home in silence. Dusk meeting the streets, the trees, of Granite Harbor as the sun slowly travels to a new part of the world. Streetlights pop on, as if on a timer. The peak of the day's heat is behind us. Somewhere between the harbor and Sand Street, the sun fades.

Worst-case scenario: I lose Eli and Merit. That we grow apart. That, one day, all that exists of us is a faded picture of our childhood.

"Hey, what are you kids doing out so late?" a man who doesn't fit as a Granite Harbor resident says to us.

He doesn't look familiar. He must be a passerby from Portland or Augusta.

"It's not late," Eli says to the man.

His eyes are blazing red, his demeanor calm, but there's something about the twist of his lips that I don't like when he speaks. His hair is a dark brown and pushed to one side, like he's covering up a bald patch. His words, the way he speaks, are as if he makes a living selling used cars at Mel's, outside of town. Something tells me there's nothing innocent about this guy.

"Come on, guys. Let's go home."

The three of us, Merit in the middle, walk fast, passing the man with bad hair.

"Hey," the man says.

I stop and flip my head around to show him that he doesn't scare me.

"What do you want?" I ask.

"I know you from somewhere." The man smiles and rubs his whiskers on his chin.

He eyes Merit. My blood boils.

"Get lost, asshole." It's not something I intentionally want to say, but it comes out in a tone I've used a handful of times in my life.

Don't look at her like that.

"Go back the way you came. We don't want you in our parts."

I don't ask how he knows my mother. I assume it's one of the guys she lives with. But I've never seen him with her before. I've never seen her with any man, so it's hard to say. I can't prove that they're traveling together, but when my mom comes to town, there's always a little bit of trouble.

Standing my ground, my fists balled at my sides, I feel Eli and Merit tugging at my arms.

"Come on, Ryan. It's not worth it. He looks crazy anyway. Let's go home. Come on," Eli says.

Merit hooks her arm in mine, and she and Eli pull me in the opposite direction.

Tears start to build in my eyes. He's the one who hurts my mom. He's the one who gives her the black eyes and the white powder I see under her nose.

Can I prove it? No, it's just a gut feeling.

He's the one who took my mom away.

Thirty-Six

Merit
Monterey, California
Present Day

"It's me, Bug." Eli's voice is broken.

Something's seriously wrong.

My heart hits my feet. "Is it Pop?"

"No." He coughs, trying to clear away his tone. "It's Ryan."

The silence on the line feels like lead. It's heavy, dark, and thick. I'm terrified to continue the conversation. My lips become too numb to speak. My fingers barely hang on to the phone, and my insides run hollow as my heart begins to hammer against my chest, banging for a way out. I don't ask what happened because that's not important right now.

From Eli's tone, I can tell that things aren't all right, so I ask him the most important question, "Is he all right?"

"I don't know. He's been shot." I hear the groan on the other end of the line. A groan of terror, one he's trying to hold back but can't.

"Where's Alex?"

"On her way."

"Where are you?"

"Ryan's house." He stops and chokes back a sob. "Merit," he whispers, "I should have gotten here sooner."

"Eli, listen to me right now. You can't protect everybody. Not everybody, all the time." My voice is strong, not full of fear even though it's vibrating in my bones. Even though, so badly, I wish Eli had been there earlier, too—whatever that means.

Get control, Mer. Get control.

"Alex just pulled up, Mer."

"Go to her. I'm catching a flight back home."

"Mer," Eli stops. "Come home for good."

"I will. Where's Ryan?"

"Taken by ambulance."

"Who shot him?"

"Ronan Fields."

"Why?"

"I don't fucking know, Mer."

"Is Ronan still there?"

"Yes."

"Is he in police custody?"

"The threat has been neutralized." His voice is robotic. As if he's repeated this statement time and time again.

"I don't speak game warden, Eli. What does that mean?"

"I killed him."

Oh, fuck.

It's quite amazing what the human brain can do. It shuts out distractions when you hear your loved one is in pain. It makes you jump into action, ask the right questions, and once your loved one is taken care of, that's when you fall apart.

As soon as Eli and I hang up, I slide down the wall of my bedroom and fall apart.

Get up, I tell myself. *Book a flight. Pack your shit. Move forward.*

But what is different now from the other times this has happened?

When tragedy looked me in the eyes and said, *I'm sorry, but …*

The difference is, I kept moving. And here I am, once again telling myself to move when maybe I shouldn't. I'm not sure, but I let whatever that looks like pour through my body all at once. I let it live in the dark caves, the big fractures of my body. I let it move and stretch and just be.

I allow this to happen until there's a calmness to me. Until there are no tears left. Until the fear is done pushing through my mind.

Worst-case scenarios:

Ryan's brain dead.

He's paralyzed.

He's dead.

I sit with this last thought. Ache fills my heart, my chest, with regrets. The things I never told him that I wish I had.

I'm in love with you, Ryan. I always have been.

I want to grow old with you.

I want to share my life with you.

I want to tell you my fears.

These past seventeen years was me living in hurt and pushing every goddamn person away because I didn't want to hurt again. I thought it was easier to live like that. Thought it was the right choice.

My mind shifts to my brother.

How is he?

How bad is he hurt?

I should go to him.

They both need me.

He's never killed anyone before. But Alex has. I'm glad she's there with him.

Alex took down Clay Mahoney. He'd messed with the wrong woman.

A piece of me feels relief when this thought sits in my brain. A shared experience between Eli and Alex. Unity. Joint feelings. Collective trauma. It's easier to experience it together than be in the dark, fumbling, running. Alone.

Timing in the world can run in perfect order if we let it. Things fall into place as they should if we get out of the way.

After the shock has worn off and the feelings that keep coming my way are felt, I pull myself from my bedroom floor and book a one-way ticket back to Granite Harbor.

It's Pop who picks me up from the airport.

When I see him waiting at the *Granite Harbor Welcomes You* sign where he usually picks me up, I turn into a little girl. First, I walk fast and then jog. Then, I flat-out run to my dad. When my head meets his chest, I wrap my arms around him as tight as I can. I take in the same scent I did as a little girl. The scent of safety. The scent that told me everything would be all right. After my mom passed, it was Pop's scent in the morning that put my feet into action for another day. I never told him that.

I guess that was hope that I buried away deep for so long. Maybe it was the same hope that kept me pushing one foot in front of the other, unrealized.

"Oh, Bug."

I feel his arms tighten around me and his breath in my hair. He doesn't ask what this is about. He doesn't need to. Sometimes, there aren't words to explain what touch feels like. It can just be experienced, but more importantly, it is understood. We stand here, holding on to one another, holding our experiences in our hands as if a sack of treasures in tow. We bring them to the table, unwrap them, and feel through them.

Gently, I finally pull away, and when I look into Pop's eyes, I see the tears.

I'm caught off guard. I'm not sure that I've ever seen my dad cry. Not once. At least, from what I remember.

"Pop, what's wrong?"

He holds his finger up, a silent gesture for me to give him a moment. He coughs to clear his throat. "Never once have you relied on me like that." His eyes fill with tears again. "Never once have you asked for help. Asked me to hold you up. Asked for love, Bug." His bottom lip quivers. "You've always been my tough girl. The one who gets me and Eli through. And never once did I think I needed a daughter who needed her father." He shakes his head. "Not till now." He gently pulls me in by my neck and kisses the top of my head. "Thank you."

My father, put together at all times, always knows what to do in situations, except when Mom died. He got lost. Though he always showed up even if it was just with his presence and not his mind.

I've never thought Pop needed me to rely on him. The same father who pulled children from lakes. An empty shell of who they had once been. He saved lives. Recovered bodies. The same father who lost his best friend, my mom. The same father who put his children first. The same father who never remarried—for us.

I think we're more alike than we think.

We pull apart and he opens the truck door for me.

I'm terrified to ask the question, one I wouldn't have asked a week ago, but the only way through is through.

I ask about Ryan as I hop in.

"Stable," he says with a sigh as he drives toward Granite Harbor. "He had his bulletproof vest on, Mer, or he wouldn't be. He took a direct shot to the chest."

I nod as my eyes trace the ocean line of the East Coast, trying to process the scene in short seconds of thought. Of what could have gone wrong. Of what went right. The magnitude of my gratitude for keeping all three of my men on solid ground doesn't begin with words; it begins with a feeling.

"Shit," I whisper, wiping my nose with my sleeve, knowing Pop doesn't carry tissues in his truck, knowing I used the last of my own tissues on the flight.

My dad reaches over and rubs my shoulder. "You okay?"

"Of all the things that have gone wrong and all the things that could have gone wrong, I'm so grateful I still have you, Eli, and Ryan." I untangle my fingers. "There's something I need to tell you about Ryan and me."

A slow smile spreads across Pop's face, one hand on the wheel.

I tell him the story about us. I tell him about Destiny and her passing. But I don't tell him about what Ryan said to me that day. It's not my story to tell. Sometimes, people say things and do things in the moment, solely out of fear, and I can understand that. I lived in fear for a long time. Too scared to get close to anybody, for fear that they'd break my heart. Besides, if I've forgiven, there isn't a part to tell.

"Pop, I've always loved Ryan. I always have."

"I know. I could tell when you guys were young, when you didn't know what love was." But his eyes fill with sadness, not tears. "But I'm sorry you felt you had to go through losing Destiny alone. That you didn't tell anyone. Why not, Bug?"

"I didn't want to burden anyone, I guess. Just thought I could do it on my own."

He watches the road, a road he's driven a thousand times in his line of work. "I asked myself where I'd gone wrong. What would keep you all the way out in California, away from your family. I questioned myself as a father. Where I'd messed up along the way."

"It wasn't you, Pop; it was me. I was in the way of my own self."

Pop lets a big breath out. "I don't tell you this out of pity, Bug. I tell you this out of the realization that every father wants his daughter to be happy. To rely on him for everything—until, of course, she gets married. Hell, even then, Dads still want to be the heroes for their daughters."

"I know this now, Pop."

We weave next to the coastline, around trees, big bodies of water. We knit the road home.

It dawns on me. Maybe, if Eli had died instead of Mom, he wouldn't have been there to save Ryan.

Thirty-Seven

Ryan
Granite Harbor, Maine
Present Day

Wasn't I just here two months ago? Fuck, my chest hurts.
     "You'll be sore for a few weeks, Ryan," Dr. Phillips says, holding the bullet that was stuck between the many layers of protection in my bulletproof vest.

My body feels heavy as I try to push myself up to a sitting position. "How long will I be in here, Doc?" I ask.

"We'll get you out of here today. You're just going to be real sore, so light duty, just for a week or so."

"Hell, I don't think I'm off the light duty from the last time I was in here."

"More light duty for a while. At least. I'll have the nurse come in and start the discharge paperwork," Dr. Phillips sighs. "This was lodged in your vest, Ryan." He holds the bullet between two fingers, mesmerized by the chunk of lead.

"How close did it come?"

He drops it in my hand. "Within an inch of your heart."

There's a knock on the door.

"I'll be back later," Dr. Phillips says.

"Thanks, Doc."

Lieutenant Shreeves comes around the curtain that separates the door from the room. "How's he doing, Dr. Phillips?" Shreeves asks.

"I'll let him tell you." Dr. Phillips nods to both of us and leaves.

"Lieutenant."

"Sergeant. Seems like you've had a rough couple of months." He laughs and casually pulls up a chair, a file in his hand.

"I'll survive." I hold the bullet in my hand.

"Listen, Hallowell PD has been interviewing Fields's people. A lot of interesting information has come to light." Shreeves reaches up and grabs the back of his neck, his lack of sleep written on his face. "First, this needs to come from me," he sighs. "Dubbs's body was discovered on the train just south of Connecticut."

Both relief and peace of mind run through me. As if my childhood can no longer be remembered because the only piece of evidence that the trauma existed is dead. But a piece of me is sad for him—not for myself, but for him. Glimpses of regret I'd see in his eyes on mornings when it was too quiet. I'd see him sitting at the dining room table, cigarette in hand. He never apologized for the beatings, but there was a look in his eye that screamed he was sorry.

I guess, maybe, some behaviors are learned.

"I'm sorry to deliver that news, Sergeant."

"Expected," is all I say.

It'd been too long. The feeling that he was still alive faded as time passed.

"Anything else? What about Fields?"

"At the morgue."

"What?"

"Eli got him right as he fired the gun at you."

"Eli?"

"Yeah." He laughs and smiles. "I knew you two were tight, but for the timing to work out just that perfectly … I don't know. That's a pretty close connection."

Silence fills the air.

Lieutenant Shreeves leans forward and pulls a folded piece of paper from the file. "Thought you'd want to see this. The PD found it when they searched Dubbs's place." Shreeves looks out the window of my hospital room. "This guy, Pauly, said that he saw Dubbs give Ronan five thousand dollars in cash. Said, when Dubbs heard there was a payable job for the hit on you, Dubbs tried to talk him out of it. Seems they worked out a deal because, the next day, Dubbs gave him the cash, and the hit was no longer talked about." Shreeves stares long and hard at me. Picks at a callous on his hand. "Look, I don't know much about your upbringing, but I think I can safely assume Dubbs wasn't the best role model, but I want you to take this. Read it." Shreeves hands me the piece of paper and pauses again.

I shake my head, taking the piece of paper from Shreeves.

"Letter from Dubbs. Doesn't say who it's addressed to, but I think it was written for you."

We use small talk to fill the rest of the time he's here with me. Sports. Weather. Fishing. The moose lottery. Then, he leaves.

Carefully, without anyone around, I open it.

My name is Sal Dubbs Taylor. When Ronan finally gets to me, because he will, tell Ryan the situation in person. Don't do it over the phone. He doesn't deserve that. He deserves a man-to-man conversation. I've raised him like that, so he'll expect it. Give him this letter, too.

I guess I just assumed he was mine. Mona and I had slept together a few times. Nine months later, she came back and left this little fucking baby for me to deal with. I know I messed up with him. Real bad. I wasn't sure how to be a dad. I wanted to make him tough. Raised on the streets myself, I knew what it took to survive. The mental toughness that was needed. I'd put myself in vulnerable spots when I was a kid. Not because I didn't know, but because it was the only choice I had. Things had happened, and I didn't want that to happen to Ryan. I tried to create mental toughness. Stamina. Somewhere along the line, I know I'd failed.

I'm just a drunk. A fisherman who raised a boy the way I had been raised. Taught him how to survive when shit got real bad.

I didn't know that Ronan was Ryan's father until I found Mona's journal with a birth certificate in all that shit of hers she'd left when Ryan was about three or so. I got real drunk and real mad. The thing I was fucking pissed about was the fact that I wasn't his dad. Because I'd grown attached to his stupid questions. He would ask why and how all the time.

Why do you have to bait the hook to catch fish?

Why don't you use spears to catch fish anymore?

Why does the boat go so fast?

How do boats float?

Why don't you take me to school?

Why do I have to walk?

All the other mommies take their kids.

Where is my mommy?

And then he asked the question that still gets to me.

Why don't you love me?

I did. I do.

I thought, if I prepared Ryan for the world of disappointment—equipped him with shit, life tools he needed—he'd never have to be let down.

The truth is, I loved him, and I failed him.

So, tell Ryan in person when they recover my body.

I tried to protect him.

Tell Ryan I'm proud of him and that I'm sorry.

--Dubbs

My hand eases down to the hard mattress. My childhood flies by me like moving pictures. The doubt I felt as a child. The lack of love shown. But he did the best he could with what he had. He didn't have a choice to raise me.

Now, I know, somewhere down the morbid line he walked, he began to love me.

Whenever he was asked for a birth certificate, he'd always say he couldn't find it. When I asked to see it, he would lie. Maybe because he knew I'd see Ronan's name. Maybe he didn't want to confuse me. Maybe he was trying to protect me.

I hear footsteps coming down the hallway, but they're not heavy; they're light and they stop. I look up, but there's the curtain of separation. I don't ask who it is because it's probably just another nurse to take my vitals. Maybe it's the nurse with the discharge paperwork.

"Suppose this is the worst-case scenario, huh?"

That voice.

That fucking voice.

The only voice I wait to hear when I wake up in the morning and go to bed at night.

The voice that's the only one trapped in my head when I can't sleep.

Her.

Merit.

"Merit." My voice is hoarse.

She's still behind the curtain.

"You walk in this room, and there's no way you're going back to California again."

"I know," she says as she walks into view.

In life, we take moments for granted. We allow our memory to wash them away and change our perception. I pray to God that these moments will never go away.

The way her blonde hair, always tied back, is now down and around her shoulders. The light dusting of freckles that lay over her nose. The ones I used to kiss when we made love. Her green eyes that push the limit with my heart.

Every flashing moment from ages eight until now appear in my mind.

Age eight: relief—when we met.

Age nine: sadness—when she stood on my doorstep and told me about Rebecca's diagnosis.

Age eleven: anger—the day Rebecca died.

Age thirteen: fear—when Dubbs took a swing at me in front of her.

Age sixteen: pride—the day I told her that I stood up to Dubbs.

Age seventeen: happiness—the day she got accepted to University of San Diego.

Age seventeen: anguish—the day I lied to her about another woman.

Age thirty-four: heartbreak—when she told me about Destiny.

Age thirty-four: heartache—the last time we made love.

I touch the mattress next to me, needing to smell her, take her in, wanting to touch her. She takes the spot next to me. I reach up and grab her neck and the side of her jaw in the palm of my hand, wanting so badly to kiss her, but it dawns on me that I don't remember the last time I brushed my teeth, and I don't want our first meaningful kiss to be botched on my accord, so instead, I stare into her eyes, the only place I've wanted to see my reflection. I take my thumb and slide it across her jaw—slowly, not softly. I want her to know I will be the last man to touch her in ways she deserves to be touched. To love her unconditionally.

"There's no way in hell I'm letting you leave again, Merit. Do you understand me?"

"Yes."

Her lips barely part, and I move my thumb over her bottom lip. I feel this in my dick, knowing full well it will be really tough for Merit to explain—because that's what she does—to the nurse whose boyfriend has a hard-on.

"That was too close, Ryan. I came too close to losing you." She takes my hand from her face and slides it down her body, my hand now resting between her thighs.

"All right, Mr. Taylor, let's get the discharge paperwork started. Oh. Merit. I'm sorry. I didn't mean to interrupt."

Merit doesn't move. She stays put, next to me. A bold move she's never done before. Our relationship has always been hidden.

"It's okay, Fran. I'm here to take him home."

"Will you be in Granite Harbor for a while?" she asks.

Merit to me. "Indefinitely. If he'll keep me."

Thirty-Eight

Merit
Granite Harbor, Maine
Present Day

The Harbor Inn is where I booked the room.

Ryan doesn't need any help getting out of Pop's truck, which Pop let me borrow to get Ryan and me where we needed to go for the time being.

"You don't look or act like you just took a bullet to the chest," I say, my nerves getting the best of me. The good nerves. I grab the room key from my purse.

"You don't look like you just spent the night flying across the country." He grabs my hand and kisses it. "And thanks for stopping by Granite Harbor Grocery."

He said he needed to stop and grab a few things. Came out with a toothbrush, toothpaste, and deodorant.

There is no way we're ever going back to his house in Hallowell—unless it's to pack it up.

"You're sure Hero is okay with Brand?"

"Ryan, you know my dad. I think he needs his own dog."

I use my hip to push open the door, and when it opens, Ryan places his hand there.

My heart begins to race.

I've imagined this moment, fantasized about it. And there's no way in hell I'll let it go by without making a memory that we both will remember. A fucking amazing memory.

Ryan shuts the door behind us but quickly takes my hips in his hands. He pulls my body to his, and anticipation that's been building since the hospital is almost unbearable.

I drop my head to his shoulder.

He whispers, "I'm going to go brush my teeth. Shower. Then, I'm taking you to dinner. But, shit, I don't have clothes."

I shake my head. "Eli packed you a bag."

"What'd you tell him?"

"The truth."

Ryan stares at me and drops his chin. "Like … everything?"

"Most of it. Yes. I'm sorry I made you keep us from your best friend, Ryan. I'm so sorry."

"I'd have kept it from him forever if that meant saving you."

"You don't need to protect me, Ryan. I've got to learn to protect myself."

Ryan takes me by the hand and sits me down on the bed. "I'm going to go brush my teeth. I'll be right back."

While he brushes his teeth, I take off my clothes. There's something about allowing a man to see you naked in a room with awful lighting, in a room that isn't dark, and doing something that doesn't involve sex.

It's vulnerable.

It's open.

I'm giving Ryan all the pieces of me.

He walks out of the bathroom, looking down, as if in thought, but when his eyes meet my body, it's as if everything in the world around us disappears. He walks to me, his jaw in a tight line. He takes in my eyes, my shoulders, my breasts, my stomach, my hips, my thighs.

"I want this body to be the last body you touch, Ryan." I take his hands and place them around my breasts.

He closes his eyes, smiles, and moves closer, allowing his hands to have minds of their own. His eyes stay closed as he cups them. He takes my nipples between his fingers and squeezes.

"I want to give you everything I couldn't when we were young. I want to make your body cry my name. I want to show you the way a man makes love to a woman, not an inexperienced boy who doesn't know where to put his hands. So, I'm going to do this slow and right this time, Mer. And, if you say no, I'll have to accept it. I will. I won't like it, I won't agree with it, but I'll go with it because that's how you feel."

I don't fight this. I won't ever fight against my feelings for Ryan Taylor again. I've learned my lesson.

He takes my hand and leads me to the bathroom, shutting the door behind us. He leaves me to turn on the water. He undresses, and I cannot remember a time when I've felt so open to love. Open to a man who knows my secrets. My past. My future. A man who holds me up when I'm broken. That man is standing in front of me, naked, exposing his own worn truths. Open to me. To us.

He reaches out to me—not because he doesn't want to see us like this, but because there's a need for our skin to be touching again. When he does this, I feel his hardness against my stomach, and my body grows with ache.

"I can't look at you like this and not get hard, Mer. I've never been able to do that. That takes power that just isn't in me." He smiles as he nuzzles my ear.

I want him inside me.

I want his best side.

His worst side.

I want all of it. I've seen all of it.

He leads me to the now-hot shower, and we step in. The beats on my back feel like divine purpose, as if we've lived these tragedies, these experiences, to be right where we're at today.

When my mother died, I remember how angry I was that Dubbs, a cruel man, was still walking this earth. But, if Dubbs had died instead of Rebecca, maybe Ryan would be dead. Dubbs wouldn't have been able to save him.

Eli told me what had happened with Ronan and Mona and Ryan. I had gone to Eli first when I came home just because I knew the situation with Ryan would take a lot longer. We have a lot of lost time to make up for.

Ryan puts his mouth to one breast. The mouth that I've longed for. He probes, the heat of his tongue when he teases me. He takes his mouth and moves to the next one. The urgency grows with each flick of my nipple, telling me he doesn't just want me; he needs me.

The shower pushes its wall of hot against my back while Ryan takes care of my front. He comes up to meet my lips, his hard chest against me. With both of his hands, he cups my jaw and stares down at me, looking at me with need.

Needing my lips.

Needing my body.

Needing my whole heart.

I want to feel him between my legs as my middle grows with weakness.

"If I can't have all of you, Merit, I'll take small pieces instead."

Then, his lips crash against mine. It's not soft. It's hard. It's not the kiss he wants to give; it's the kiss he needs to give.

My mouth is open, my body, too. Passion builds between my legs, inside my stomach, and straight to my heart as if I'm hearing it for the first time. Like I've been awakened by the last guard I had up, and I watch as it comes tumbling down.

My fingernails trail down his back.

My mouth takes him and we collide like it's our first kiss and our last kiss and a lifetime full of memories.

I can't miss this.

My body is fire, and Ryan is fuel.

Our mouths push and pull.

My hands slide down to his hips, and I hold him there, spreading my fingers apart to get a better grip. His hardness only reaffirms that we're exactly where we need to be in life.

I want to spread my legs, so he can do what he needs to in the shower. What we both need. Because this isn't about promises.

It's about love and being wholly connected.

Ryan looks down at me—not adoringly, but with dedication, with love. "I'm going to wash your hair, Merit." He reaches for the inn's small bottle of shampoo. He lathers it in his hand and washes my hair from the front.

My breasts are against his chest, his erection against my stomach, and my hands are the only things holding us together.

My folds pulsate.

He rinses my hair and then takes the world's smallest bar of soap and begins to wash my body. I reluctantly release him from me.

His hands reach my thighs, and he pushes the bar of soap between them. Then, when I least think he'll do it, he takes his fingertips and gently opens me up.

I whimper, and my head drops to his chest.

"Eyes on me. I need to watch you, Merit." His tone is sweet and direct, all at the same time.

I pull back and spread my legs a little bit, wanting to feel more of him.

His fingers push inside me.

I stare at Ryan and watch him as he watches me. I bite my lower lip as I feel his fingers move between my pink folds. My legs grow weak. He reaches the notch and lightly moves his fingers over it, and my entire body screams out in anticipation.

"Ryan," I cry out. "Please don't make me come yet."

Slowly, he slides his fingers inside me. He stretches me. "I will be the last man to touch you like this. Do you understand, Merit?"

"Yes," I hiss.

I call out.

Once.

Twice.

Pause.

"I will be the last man to make you cry out like this," he says.

"I need you, Ryan, inside me." My voice quivers as I grab for his shoulders.

"I know."

His mouth meets mine again, and our tongues push and move. We can't get enough of each other through this kiss.

I pull away, and his lips trail down my cheek, down my neck, as he moves his hand over my breast again.

"Come on," I say, turning off the water, pulling him by the hand.

We step out, and I grab a stark white hotel towel. I pull it around both of us, knowing it won't quite dry us off, but at least it will get some wetness off.

I turn Ryan around to dry his back and once again see the cigarette burns. They used to make me furious. But, right now, I can look at them and know that Ryan is the man he is today because of what he's been through. Still, I kiss each one. I kiss each one to remind him that he is loved, that he is so important, and that he matters.

When we were kids, when Dubbs added a burn to the collection of burns, Ryan said he'd go to a place where he didn't matter to overcome the pain. This broke me apart. We were around twelve or thirteen.

"You matter, Ryan," I tell him as he turns toward me.

We walk to the bed I know we'll share for the next few days. Come up for air. For water. Food maybe.

This will take time.

Our love will take its time.

We'll fix where we went wrong.

He sits on the edge of the bed where I climb on top of him.

When I move down, he slides inside me.

I feel him again.

It first takes adjusting, but I'm ready.

He groans as he puts my breast in his mouth. I remember the red drips in my panties after the first time we made love. One thing Ryan isn't is small.

Ryan calls out as I reach the end of his length, "Oh my God, baby." He closes his eyes first and then opens them to stare down at where we're connected.

I move up and down, stretching and growing and moving.

Quickly, he grabs my hips. "Baby, you need to stop. I'm going to come, and I'm not ready to yet."

With ease, he lifts me up off him and holds me against him as I wrap my legs around his waist. He switches our positions. Putting my head at the headboard, he gently lays me down and pulls my legs apart.

I blush as he stares at my body. "What?" I cover my face and smile before letting my hands then fall to my sides.

Ryan smiles. My world lights up. For the first time in a long time, my world ignites when I see him smile.

"You're more beautiful than a moose in the early morning sunshine to a hunter with a moose tag."

I laugh.

"You're more beautiful than the love you give, Mer. You're more beautiful than the kisses you give on my back. You're more beautiful than when a sun rises and sets. You're more. So much more."

Ryan starts with his lips on my mouth and slowly trails them down my neck and my chest, paying close attention to each breast.

Down my stomach, down to the hair that protects my spot. Using his fingers, he pulls back my lips and pushes his tongue into my folds.

He plays with my notch, and I cry out, "Ryan."

He watches me as I watch him.

My breathing picks up pace with each flick of his tongue.

My legs, like jelly, whimper in need, just as I do.

Ryan pushes two fingers inside me.

Oh, fuck.

"No."

He freezes. "No?"

"I mean, no, you can't do that," I say breathlessly as I sit up and take him in my hands. I bend down and put his tip in my mouth. "Not yet," I say between licks.

Ryan closes his eyes and eases back on his haunches as I take him in my mouth completely. I hear him breathing, his breaths getting louder with each motion of my mouth.

He pulls me up to him, and our mouths crash together, our bodies moving with necessity. The necessity of each other. The necessity of love and desire.

Ryan flips me around, and I grab the headboard.

"Are you ready?" he asks.

"Yes."

He slides in me from behind, and it takes everything in me not to scream. Lovemaking is done behind closed doors. But, when he reaches around and touches my middle with his fingers, I cry out.

We both come together. Hard.

Thirty-Nine

Ryan
Granite Harbor, Maine
Present Day

Her still-damp hair is against my bicep while her head is against my shoulder.

Please, if I've gone to heaven, let me stay here.

Merit's hand on my chest, she strokes my chest hair, and I feel her sigh against me, our bodies tired from telling each other just how much we need each other.

"So, Dubbs isn't your biological father." Merit looks up at me.

I shrug. "That's what Ronan said. Guess Mona pretty much confirmed it when she didn't say anything."

"How do you feel about all this?" she asks as she runs her hand over my chest.

"Some people have mattered in my life, Mer. Some people have made an impact. Some people have come and gone. My parents are two I can think of. But nothing like you, Eli, Brand, and Rebecca. At this point in my life, I guess it doesn't really matter who my parents are." I'm quiet for a minute. "It might give my past some validity, I guess, just knowing where I came from, but it won't make a difference. Might give me more insight, but I'm raised, Mer." My arms tighten around her. "I don't want to waste any more time. I spent a good chunk of my adult life looking for forever in all the wrong spots. But it was you I knew deep down that I needed."

Merit looks up at me, her green eyes wandering from my face to my chest and back to my face. "I've realized something." I can tell she's choosing her words carefully. "I blamed you, Ryan. I blamed you for my hurt. I blamed you for my mom and Destiny by pushing all my anger toward you. It wasn't fair. I wasn't sure how to process grief, so I didn't. I just stuffed it deeper."

"Hey." I try to pull her to me, but she stops by putting her hand on my chest.

"Wait. I promise that, no matter what in this life, I won't leave you."

"Mer, stop. It's okay."

She shakes her head. "No, Ryan, it's not okay. It's not okay that others treated you like that. It's not okay that I treated you the way I did. You deserve better."

I take a deep breath and rest my head back down against the mahogany headboard that has somehow survived the last hour of us making up for lost time. "Mer, there are no guarantees in life."

Merit's face changes. Her eyes grow big, and her mouth opens. "What? Are you all right?"

"Oh my God," she whispers.

"What?"

She sits up and pulls the sheet to cover her breasts. "There was no other girl when I left. Was there?" Shock colors her face. "You didn't want me to get an abortion. You just said it. There are no guarantees in life. You said this to me seventeen years ago. You couldn't guarantee we'd make it, but you sure as hell knew my dream was not in Granite Harbor, that it was always in California. You weren't going to let *us* hold me back. Oh my God. How come I didn't see this before?" Merit's head is in her hands, and then she stares back at me, waiting for an answer.

Fuck. What should I say? I won't lie to her. So, instead, I turn on my side and lightly touch her face. "What, Mer? What could we have done differently?"

"I don't know."

I can deal with my regret. The way I hurt her. I will take that on so fucking willingly, but I can't stand the fact that Merit might have regret. The way she had to deal with Destiny and her death on her own, that's another story.

"You did it all for me." She stares up at me as her eyes fill with tears.

"I'm sorry you were alone when Destiny died." My voice breaks because, now, I feel the wave of emotion. I catch the tears that fall from her eyes.

She shakes her head. "I chose to have her on my own, Ryan. Don't you see that? You can't take responsibility for that. You didn't know."

Her blonde hair gets lost among the white sheets, and it's her stark green eyes that stand out the most.

"I'll spend every day making sure you know how much I love you, Ryan Taylor."

She takes my hand from her face, wet with her tears, and places it over her breast. Instantly, I feel it everywhere. Our bodies, which were once tired, are now on fire again as I harden against her opening.

I drop my mouth to her breast again.

"Again," she says as I feel her legs widen for me.

I sit up but not before giving her what she asked for. I take the other breast in my mouth, and then I see her splayed out in front of me, naked and vulnerable and beautiful. I slip two fingers inside her.

"God, baby, you're so wet again."

I watch her as she closes her eyes, and a small whimper escapes from her lips. My dick hardens for her, only for her. I push her folds back, so I can see how beautiful and pink she is. Sliding my fingers out, I put my mouth down on her to alleviate the itch that she so desperately needs scratched.

"Ryan!" she calls out as her body tenses. "Stop."

She pushes back on my shoulders. She flips around, reaches for my hands from behind, and puts them on her. She takes my shaft in her hand and puts it inside her. She drops to her elbows, and I fucking groan. With her ass in front of me, I grab her hips and pull her closer to get as deep as I can.

"Fuck," I hiss as she moans.

I reach around, take her notch in my hand, and apply pressure.

She sits up and grabs the headboard with me still inside her, and I push again. I take her hand and put it down there with mine.

Her hand guiding ours, she pushes on herself, and I fucking can't handle it.

"Turn your head. I need to watch you come," I say.

She does as she was told, and when she does, I put my tongue in her mouth as she moves her fingers. I grab her breasts from behind while pushing myself inside her.

She comes loudly in my ear, and I do the same.

We make good use of our time. Against the bathroom counter. In the shower. On the floor. Making up for lost time.

It isn't until six at night when we become hungry, and a text comes in from Eli.

Eli: Meet us at Angler's for dinner at six thirty?

All Merit seems to do when she gets ready is jump in the shower, which we've done a few times today, blow-dry her hair, and put that shiny stuff on her lips—lip gloss or whatever it's called.

I really haven't talked to Eli since the whole thing happened. I've been trying to find the right words to thank my best friend for saving my life.

When we get to Angler's, Merit moves to our table in her little red summer dress. Merit is talking with her hands, which means she's excited. I think she's missed Alex and maybe she's excited about us, too.

Felix is working the bar. "Heard about what happened. These are on the house." Felix passes Eli and me two beers.

"Can't. Gotta pay for them," I say. "But thank you, Felix." I throw two twenties down. "Can we also get two house reds?" I look at Eli. "These are on me."

"Sure thing." Felix goes to retrieve the wine.

I look at Eli. "Thank you. For everything."

"You would have done it for me." He tries to be casual. Takes a drink of his beer.

There's no doubt about that. I would have.

Felix comes back with the wine and takes the cash on the counter to the register.

"Do me a favor?" Eli asks after he takes a drink of his beer.

"What's that?"

"Stay out of hospitals for at least six months. Please."

Aaron and Ethan Casey, twins, friends and fellow wardens, walk into Angler's just as Lydia does.

It isn't awkward with Lydia at all. First of all, my fucking ego said to learn her name. There are Merits to other men and should be treated as such. I think Merit is secure enough with me to know that she's my only forever.

"Something's different about you, Taylor." Shannon, the cocktail waitress who hates me, approaches the bar to get her drink order from Felix. "The cocky bastard you once were doesn't seem to be the same guy you are tonight. So, thank you, on behalf of women all over Maine. Thank you for not being a total cock." She goes about her business.

Eli looks at me and laughs. "I'm glad you and Merit are a thing." He shakes his head. "I haven't seen her this happy since before Mom died."

What he says hits me in the gut. Wasted years. But maybe they weren't wasted. Maybe that's how she and I got here today, where it all started back then, building the foundation for us. Maybe we were both at the right place and at the right time. For each other.

"I'd like to ask Merit to marry me, Eli. If that's okay with you?"

Eli's smile starts at the corners of his mouth. The same grin he gave Alex on their wedding day. This way, I know it's genuine.

"You as a brother-in-law? Oh, fuck. Pain in my ass."

We both smile. Take a pull from our beers.

"Yeah, brother, absolutely." He sets his beer down. "Did you talk to Pop yet?"

"I'll do that tomorrow. Merit mentioned something about a barbecue at Brand's tomorrow."

Eli nods as Felix hands us the wine.

We take our seat next to our ladies. They're deep in conversation.

I look around the table at our friends. Eli, Alex, Ethan, Aaron, Lydia. Some old, some new. This is right where I wanted to be my entire life. Not just with my friends, but where my insides matched my outsides. Not searching for the next challenge of a woman's body—except one woman, now and forever. I watch her as she talks excitedly about Emily, and I know that there's nothing between us now. Nothing that separates us. No wall.

Eli talks with the twins, and Merit talks with both Alex and Lydia.

I quietly take a swig of my beer. Merit in this dress is killing me. I'll wait until she finishes her wine before I take her to the restroom.

I lean over to Merit and make sure my lips are against her ear. "Do you need another glass of wine?"

"Yes." She smiles. "We're going to go get another glass of wine. Does anyone need anything?"

Alex shakes her head. "There's no way in hell I'm getting drunk. The last time I got drunk in here"—Alex eyes Eli—"I ended up married and pregnant."

Eli laughs. "Bring her one more. I'm driving."

"He's just trying to get lucky tonight," Alex whispers loudly.

"Lydia? You want anything?" Merit asks.

"I'm going to nurse this puppy until nine. But thank you."

Merit stands, and I stand behind her, placing my hand on the small of her back.

"I need to go to the restroom. Come with me real quick," I say.

I feel her dress against my jeans, and I know it's short but not too short. I think of all the things I can do to her while leaving her dress on.

We make it around the corner, and I guide her into a stall in the women's restroom, knowing they can be cleaner than the men's—from personal experience.

Her mouth is already on mine as my hands slide up her legs, and I get a good grip on her ass.

"Oh my God, are you not wearing panties?" My heart begins to pick up pace as I grow against her.

"You said you needed easy access," she whispers as she kisses my lips.

I pull up her dress and hold her sex against me.

She spreads her legs in her heels, and I slide my fingers to her front and meet her soft pink space. The space that only belongs to me.

I open her up, and she's glad I'm here because I feel her wetness against my fingers. I push back her folds as she groans in my fucking ear.

"More, Ryan," she sighs as I push into her.

"Like this?"

"Yeah," she sighs again.

But, as I push once more, the restroom door opens, and I see the disappointment on her face.

The other stall door shuts as the woman goes about her business, and I take my time with her and make her crazy.

"Shh," I whisper into her ear.

The woman flushes. I push on her favorite spot, and she whimpers in my ear, her grip tightening around my shoulders.

The woman washes her hands.

Merit's lips collide with my mouth, and I devour her. Quickly, I move my mouth to her soft spot between her legs and pull up her dress, so I have full access to her. I open her up with my tongue. But I don't allow her to come just yet.

I pull away, stand up, and watch her almost wither beneath me. I take her mouth with my own. "Your taste is the only taste I want in my mouth."

Her body shakes in an almost satisfied way, a permanent smile on her face. "You're going to need to take care of this situation when we get back to our room."

I grab her by the hand and let her dress fall back to its position. "Don't worry; I fully intend on doing that."

Forty

Merit
Granite Harbor, Maine
Present Day

Ryan takes me by the hand, the blindfold still tight around my eyes, and he walks me from our room to a destination he's keeping a secret.

Passing cars.

A few honks.

"Hello, Ryan, Merit."

"What are you guys doing?"

"Good luck."

"Hey, Merit! Glad you're home!"

"It's a surprise," Ryan says. "Just a few more minutes."

A loud door opens, and a familiar smell fills my nose.

"I've smelled this scent before." I try to think about where the hell this could be.

We're inside, and now, there's an echo, like we're in some sort of hallway or something. He gently pulls me left.

"A few more steps."

I trust Ryan, and because I do, I pull his hand to my mouth and kiss it.

He stops. "Okay. I'm going to ease you down to this chair." He does and takes off the blindfold.

I look around as my eyes adjust.

"Granite Harbor Elementary?" I say, a little stunned but smiling. I catch his eye.

"This is where I first laid eyes on you." Ryan moves back to a desk in about the middle of the room. "Do you remember? This is where I knew I wanted to love you forever, Merit Young. When life got hard, I'd go to my happy place, which was always you and me, counting our forevers. Because there are second chances, Mer. We're a second chance. And I swear to God, I will never get this wrong again."

He moves back to where I'm sitting. First row, second desk from the left. "I want to be the last thing you think about when you go to bed at night because there's no worry about us. Know that our love will get us through anything, no matter the tests life puts us through. Because there will never be anything we can't handle together."

He sits in front of me, takes my hands in his, and stares down at them. "These hands, Violet, are the only hands that can reach me. Your eyes are the only eyes that have ever been able to teach me how to love. The only eyes that hold my past, my truth. But you hold everything in your hands, our future. A future that was lived only on a day-to-day basis, but you give me hope. Our future is bright and full of hope, Violet."

Ryan pulls something from his pocket. He looks at me and grins. "Worst-case scenario?"

I drop my head back, laughing. "That this is all a dream." I shake my head.

Ryan drops to one knee. "Merit, we've been through big tests in our lives. Losing your mother and losing a daughter, but that's not what defines us. We define us. And I'd love it if you made me the luckiest man on this earth and became my wife."

And, just like that, time freezes.

The air is quiet.

A beautifully pieced-together man is down on one knee.

The sun shines brightly.

Our hearts heal.

Our broken past has led us to this exact moment.

Call it God, a divine spirit, our path. Whatever you call it, this is our story.

If we hadn't lost my mom, we wouldn't know how to cope with grief.

If we hadn't lost Destiny, we wouldn't have been able to see our own truths.

If Eli hadn't shown up when he did, Ryan wouldn't be here.

We are supposed to be here.

We are supposed to live this story.

I take the sides of his face in my hands. "Today, I hold the most precious thing I have. It's always been you. I can't wait to be Mrs. Ryan Taylor. On one condition." I grin.

He smirks. "Anything."

"That this will be the story we tell our children, our grandchildren. That love fought for us. That truth fought for us, but most importantly, that we listened."

Ryan puts his lips to mine and slowly pulls me up onto my feet. This kiss is the kiss I want forever. It's not hard or soft. It's a memory he's giving me that will remain in my heart forever. Even when all that's left of us are plaques in the ground or ashes on a mantel, I want the feeling of this kiss in a deep memory that I'll draw on for eternity.

I am whole.

Ryan pulls away and slips the ring on my finger.

We're all born whole. As life moves, pieces of our whole being are chipped away. Some pieces are added back, not exactly fitting into the right specifications, but we take them anyway. Some pieces though don't come back, leaving holes. Some pieces come back broken. Some pieces we don't want back. Some, we do. But this is who we are. It's what we do with the missing pieces, the broken pieces. It's how we define who we are and not just to see truth, but seek truth and build a whole new picture.

Our two broken pieces were meant to fit together after all.

.

Epilogue

Merit
Granite Harbor, Maine
One Year Later

"Is that the last box?" I ask, wiping my forehead with the back of my hand.

"Last box," Eli says, setting it down in the living room.

"Here, I'll take it, E," I say.

"And have your husband rip my face off for allowing you to? Don't think so, Bug. Where do you want it?"

My husband.

"Our bedroom." It still sounds so surreal and beautiful at the same time.

We got married not long after I came back to Granite Harbor from California for the last time. Neither Ryan nor I is big on lots of people, but Ruthie insisted on helping to plan the wedding. In front of two hundred seventy-five people, Ryan and I were married. In true Granite Harbor fashion, the entire town shut down for the day.

I wore my mom's wedding dress and her veil. Emily, too young to be a flower girl at the time, still wore a flower girl dress, and Alex carried her in. Hero and Rookie were our ring bearers.

Though we didn't allow Hero to carry the rings. He was still a puppy at the time and extremely inquisitive of anything that moved, which was everything mostly. We gave that responsibility to Rookie and did so with pride. I thought Rookie, too, was happy for Ryan. He'd always had a soft spot for him. Abbey and Alex stood with me while Eli and Pop stood with Ryan as we tearfully made our words count when we exchanged our own written vows.

Eddie married us in the same board shorts he still walks the aquarium with. Though rumor has it, he's retiring soon and giving Abbey the reins, who married Ruben not long ago. I think Eddie and Abbey have worked out their differences, too. She might be late, but she's a damn good leader.

A hit in the ribs makes me yelp. I look down at my extra-large belly and run a hand over it. "You can come out anytime, you know." I'm a week overdue, and I feel it in my hips and legs.

I go to shut the front door, but before I can, our Chinese food shows up. I pull cash from my expandable mom jeans, the ones with no butt.

"Thanks, Eddie." I exchange money for food.

"No problem, Merit. Dig the new house, by the way."

It's an older house that we renovated. Ryan is really crafty with his hands, and with the help of Eli, Ethan, Aaron, and Pop, they were able to get it done. The house is open from the living room to the dining room to the kitchen where there are granite slab countertops. There are four bedrooms. Our bedroom is downstairs, and there are three upstairs. A heated hardwood floor is in every room.

I feel Ryan's arms slide around me, stealing the Chinese food.

"Hey! I will carry that."

"Nope. Sorry. Doctor's orders." Ryan walks to the kitchen and places the two bags of Chinese food on the counter. He grabs paper plates and utensils, which we purchased earlier from Granite Harbor Grocery. No need to dig through the boxes to find plates.

Our friends, our family, are gathered out on the back deck. Hero and Rookie keep close tabs on each other and little Emily, who's fully walking now. She looks just like Alex. Dark brown hair, brown eyes, and the longest eyelashes I've ever seen, and she's got my brother wrapped right around her little finger. She's got all of us wrapped around her tiny finger.

The house sits on an acre, just above the Atlantic, next to the harbor where Ryan and I spent many days and nights.

Ryan walks to me as I watch our friends from the other side of the French doors. Eli, Alex, Emily, Pop, Meredith, Ethan, Aaron, Lydia, and Bryce—who made a surprise visit back to Granite Harbor because Alex, too, is due any day now with baby number two. They're laughing. Loving. And enjoying what the last of summer brings.

Ryan reaches around and touches my stomach. "I can't wait to meet her."

We decided to find out what we were having. I know our Destiny is with my mom, watching us in close proximity. Keeping tabs on the family. I know my mom would be happy for Pop that he finally found a woman who pales in comparison to her.

Meredith and Pop said they'd never get married again, but they have promise rings. It's really cute. A promise to each other that they'll love one another until their days come to an end.

"Dinner's ready!" Ryan calls, opening the French doors to our backyard. He sets the food down on the table along with the plates, utensils, and napkins.

I feel a gush of water come from between my legs. "Oh, God."

Alex says, "Her water just broke."

Hope Rebecca Taylor was born two hours later. A beautiful little girl with ten toes, ten little fingers, and a mess of hair. I guess that explains the heartburn.

I watch as Ryan sits with her in the chair, her on his chest, his arms securely holding her.

Some children are raised in extreme conditions. Some children don't overcome. But some do. Ryan was terrified that he wasn't going to be a good dad. Worried about not being able to bond with our daughter, love her like he should.

I repeated it over and over. *"You're going to be a natural, Ryan."*

The only reason I knew that was because of the way he treated me. The way he treated the people around him. The way he treated the clientele he came across in the field.

Sometimes, we live through traumas to show others how to do it. I believe we each have a walk of life, and sometimes, human decisions are made that affect us. But it's how we come out of it, hopefully as better people.

I watch my life rock back and forth in the chair.

"I love you," I whisper to Ryan.

But he's fast asleep, holding the world in his hands.

The End

Acknowledgments

A writer always has a team behind her. My team is unbelievable, and I'm so lucky to have these women behind me, pushing me and rooting for me.

Hang Le, thank you for creating the most beautiful book covers. Not only are you an incredible graphic designer, but you're also a fantastic human.

Jovana Shirley, my editor and formatter, you always blow me away. Your attention to detail and all your hard work on my manuscripts never cease to amaze me.

Julie Deaton and Kaitlyn Moodie, my proofreader experts, thank you for your time. Thank you for the hard work. Thank you for adding the best finishing touches on *Violet Ugly*.

Nazarea at InkSlinger PR, thank you for the marking and time you put into each of my books.

To my ARC team—You're mothers, wives, professionals, and you still make the time to read and write reviews for my books. I adore each of you.

To Brandon, Teyler, and Kate—Not a day goes by that I don't thank God for giving me the three biggest blessings in my life.

Lastly, to the wonderful readers and amazing bloggers who support my work—THANK YOU! I'm so incredibly grateful for each of you.

A Note to the Reader

THANK YOU FOR READING *VIOLET UGLY*.

If you enjoyed *Violet Ugly*, please leave an honest review on Amazon and Goodreads. By leaving a review, it makes the book more visible to more readers. The more reviews, the better promotional opportunities for the author.

Get the latest information on book releases, sales, and more.

Sign up for J. Lynn Bailey's newsletter at
http://eepurl.com/db34Iv.

Don't miss out on the next book in the Granite Harbor Series, titled *Magnolia Road*, due out January 29, 2019.

Connect with J. Lynn online:

www.facebook.com/AuthorJLynnBailey

www.instagram.com/jlynnbaileybooks

https://twitter.com/authorJLynn

www.jlynnbaileybooks.com

About the Author

J. Lynn is an award-winning author and the mother of two beautiful children and a wife to an adorably supportive (and super-tall) husband. He's her high school sweetheart. She's also a mother of two fur children (cats) who are extremely needy, Leo and Vinni.

OTHER BOOKS WRITTEN BY
J. LYNN BAILEY

Black Five
Standing Sideways

THE GRANITE HARBOR SERIES

Peony Red

www.ingramcontent.com/pod-product-compliance
Lightning Source LLC
Chambersburg PA
CBHW021106110726
47900CB00007B/2056

* 9 7 8 1 7 3 2 4 8 5 5 1 8 *